SUZANNE ELLISON

Harlequin Books

TORONTO • NEW YORK • LONDON
AMSTERDAM • PARIS • SYDNEY • HAMBURG
STOCKHOLM • ATHENS • TOKYO • MILAN

Published November 1990

ISBN 0-373-70427-5

Printed in U.S.A.

"I didn't want you to know," Clay said gruffly.

"I didn't want you to know I was a coward."

She sat down close beside him. Very, *very* close beside him.

"You're not a coward, Clay. It takes a lot of courage for a man with your fear of public speaking to do what you just did."

He did not move away from her, but he did not draw her nearer. At last he looked her in the eye. "Almost as much courage as it would take you to ride a camel," he suggested softly. "Or even a horse."

Roberta didn't answer the challenge. She had her mind on other things. "Life requires all kinds of courage," she admitted a bit tremulously. "For me it would be very hard to risk falling in love with you...."

ABOUT THE AUTHOR

An extremely prolific author, Suzanne Ellison is hard at work on future Superromances as well as historical and mainstream books. How does she do it? Suzanne gives a good deal of the credit to "the world's most liberated husband." Suzanne, her husband, Scott, and their daughter, Tara, make their home in California.

Books by Suzanne Ellison

HARLEQUIN SUPERROMANCE

165–WINGS OF GOLD
258–PINECONES AND ORCHIDS
283–FOR ALL THE RIGHT REASONS
308–WORDS UNSPOKEN
315–FAIR PLAY
369–CANDLE IN THE WINDOW
393–WITH OPEN ARMS
420–HEART OF THE WEST
423–SOUL OF THE WEST

HARLEQUIN INTRIGUE

46–NOWHERE TO RUN

For Pat Ellison,
living proof that
the spirit of Susan B. Anthony
lives on

CHAPTER ONE

"CHECKMATE, VIOLET!" Clay Gann declared with a smug sense of victory as he lightly slapped his worthy opponent's shaggy hump. Violet was a tall, honey-blond camel whose greatest virtue was her skill as a long-distance spitter, but he'd just beaten her at her own game. He'd actually succeeded in saddling the obstreperous beast without being on the receiving end of a single kick, bite or well-aimed wad of camel cud. "Don't take it so hard, sweetheart," he crooned as she glared at him malevolently. "I'm sure you'll get me next time."

Clad in spit-stained buckskin jacket, pointed boots and jaunty Stetson, Clay looked like the quintessential Colorado cowboy, an image he did his best to promote. After all, nobody was likely to go on a trail ride—with camels, no less—unless the ramrod knew his way around the big outdoors. And Clay knew every inch of the west. He'd been born on a ranch and had traveled extensively right from birth. And anywhere he hadn't been in person, he'd visited in a book.

The young cowboy beside him had not been so lucky. Ozzie Edwards was a tall, gangly nineteen-year-old who went about his work with quiet efficiency unless an outsider forced him into conversation. Even with Clay, who had taken him under his wing a year ago and still served as his most staunch defender, Ozzie was uncomfortable speaking and stammered acutely under stress.

"Are you g-g-going to race Luscious Laura this w-w-weekend?" he asked, gesturing toward the mother camel next to Violet. At her side swayed her infant, Baby Bev, an eight-week-old with all the wide-eyed wonder of a leggy foal. Although Clay often let a baby camel run with its mother during races, he'd been a bit protective of little Bev, who had been seriously underweight at birth. She was still remarkably tiny, which made her wondrously long-lashed eyes seem even bigger.

He knelt down to meet the baby eye to eye, smiling as she licked his cheek. "What do you say, sweetheart?" Are you up to chasing your mama through the dust today?"

As Clay reached out to scratch her ears, he heard the high-pitched warble of the steam engine coming in from Redpoint.

"Slow Joe's comin'! Slow Joe's comin'!" hollered little Sally Henderson as she scampered toward the train.

Clay grinned at Ozzie, and Ozzie grinned back. According to Brady Trent, who ran this refurbished ghost town— Patchwork, the original miners had named it—this little gal's daddy owned the Slow Joe and she'd spent most of her life on board. But nothing in her vibrant young face or the bounce of her pigtails even hinted that she thought of the steam locomotive as old hat.

To Clay, the Slow Joe was like any other restored train in the west—part of the background, part of the show. Trains were all right; mules were better yet.

But camels were really something special.

In the first place, they were unique. You couldn't just roll into any dude ranch west of the Mississippi and expect to saddle one up for an afternoon's romp. In the second place, even if you *did* happen to stumble upon one, chances were better than average that you couldn't stay on for more than half a second unless you found a critter who'd been specially trained. And even if you did stay on, you never got to be complacent. A camel was, at best, a worthy opponent—at worse, a determined foe. Even Violet, who was Clay's favorite of the herd, could never be called a *pet*. He'd owned her—or vice versa—for over seven years, and she'd never yet so much as *hinted* that she thought of him as the boss. She deigned to let him ride her when and if the spirit moved her. And when the spirit grew still, she cheerfully tossed him off.

Clay had yet to meet a woman like Violet—headstrong, determined, impossible to subdue. He liked fire in the people and animals that were part of his life, and the animals rarely let him down. But when it came to people, he was often disappointed. People were so . . . well, so tame. So commonplace. So predictable.

Brady and Tess Trent were exceptions to the rule. They had abandoned the rules of modern life and had deliberately time-traveled back to the old west, earning a great deal of Clay's admiration. Clay had some other friends in the ranching business who had, one way or another, done the same. They understood what drove him to live the life of a modern-day nomad, ushering his camels to spring celebrations and autumn fairs when he wasn't shepherding courageous tourists on the trail near his northern Colorado ranch. They even understood the loneliness inherent in such a life, a brand of loneliness that had less to do with the time he spent on the road than with the fact that he was forty-two years old and had never met a woman who cherished the things that mattered to him. He had loved one or two, tried to love some others who had hoped to change him and failed; sooner or later, they had all disappointed him. And he knew he'd disappointed them, too.

Of course, he'd disappointed nobody more than he'd disappointed his own mother, who had once had such plans for him: Harvard, law, politics...maybe even the presidency. She'd valued all the "finer" things in life—or at least the symbols of such finery—and had browbeaten Clay since childhood with the need for academic distinction and public acclaim in order to reach her goals. She had never considered the possibility that he might have had different aspirations...or the probability that he was simply incapable of achieving the ones she'd chosen for him. As a child, he had failed miserably to please her, and it had broken his heart. As a man, he had planned a career that required pleasing nobody but himself.

And it pleased him to help the Trents make a success of launching Patchwork on this opening celebration weekend. For two long years they'd been breathing life into the old ghost town—refurbishing the buildings, planning the recreation, and rehabilitating the original narrow gauge railroad track that connected Patchwork to Redpoint, the nearest small town.

Of course, it wasn't as though no tourist had ever visited Patchwork, which was attached to the Double Bar T ranch. Ever since last summer, shortly after the Trents' baby had arrived, Brady had been running wagon-train treks on the new ranch he'd named for his wife. Tess was a historical preservationist and had worked for a nonprofit organization before she'd married Brady. The establishment of Patchwork as a restored ghost town had allowed the two to unite their hearts and careers. As far as Clay could tell, the whole venture was a rousing success.

Although wagon-train guests and Slow Joe tourists who had viewed the ghost town from a distance had been encouraged to spread the word about its official opening, until now none of them had been allowed to walk the wooden sidewalks, visit the gift shops, or spend the night. Brady had also hoped to open the opera house this weekend, but that undertaking, he'd explained to Clay, had been postponed until the local sesquicentennial celebration scheduled in the fall. Instead the highlight of the opening weekend would be the Ute Bear Dance, arranged by Harry Painted Hat, a good friend of his.

The camel races had also received top billing.

Clay grinned at the thought. Few things amused him more than watching his camels run. During a race, they were likely to charge forward, backward, straight up or hunker down and refuse to budge. Their riders—experienced folks who followed the camel race circuit as well as greenhorns—were always surprised at how things turned out, but Clay never was. The rules to the game were really very simple. *Expect the unexpected, and always remember that the camels are in charge.*

The Slow Joe whistle sang out a second greeting, and Clay gave the train another glance, making sure to step beyond the range of Violet's unerring front hoof as he did so. By now there were maybe twenty people gathered around the small station, which was draped with red, white and blue banners. A half dozen brass-band musicians fumbled spiritedly through a patriotic number. Vaguely Clay recalled that Brady had hired somebody to be a visiting politician—William Jennings Bryan or some other famous orator of the day—who would make a whistle stop speech on the back of the train's platform before it moved on. In reality, Brady had told him, the Slow Joe would crawl up into the mountains and circle around, coming back through the town half an hour later. Normally it only took this route twice a day, but during this special weekend, Joe Henderson, the train's owner, had promised to keep it running from dawn till dark.

It had been Clay's intention to give Violet a chance to get used to working in Brady's arena this afternoon before he did his rope tricks with her tomorrow in front of a crowd. This evening he was joining the Trents for dinner at the Broken Wheel Saloon and Grill—their pride and joy—and once the races began in the morning, he wouldn't have a second to spare.

But before he could mount his intrepid steed—who was glaring at him from beneath her inch-long lashes—the excitement at the back of the train drew his attention.

"We will not hold ourselves bound to obey laws in which we have no voice or representation!" boomed a vigorous female speaker. "Woman's degraded, helpless position is the weak point in our institutions today!"

Clay double-checked the halter rope still tying Violet to the corral fence, told Ozzie he'd be back in a second, then edged a bit closer to the crowd. He couldn't see the young woman who was so eloquently quoting Susan B. Anthony, but she sounded like a brave and determined soul. And a natural born orator as well.

Old Mr. Carey would have loved having her in his class, he thought wryly, remembering the high-school speech coach who'd shredded his young ego so totally that he'd once feared he'd never get even a scrap of it back. *A natural born talker. I'll bet she never went blank in front of a panel of judges.*

Of course, if blanking out had been Clay's only problem as an adolescent speaker, his heart scars never would have run so deep. And his mother, of course, would have not been so horrendously embarrassed by him.

"Woman has not been a heedless spectator of the events of this century, nor a dull listener to the grand arguments for the equal rights of humanity!" cried the speaker with sterling conviction. "From the earliest history of our country, woman has shown equal devotion with man to the cause of freedom, and has stood firmly by his side in its defense."

By now Clay was close enough to see her, and in an instant he knew that he liked what he saw.

She was tall—even tall enough for him. At six feet four, he had no patience with puny females! She was solidly built—properly husky, but not at all fat—and she had a no-nonsense face that sported a strong jaw, firm nose and wide-set hazel eyes that revealed the depth of her passion. *Her passion for the cause,* he corrected himself ruefully. Then again, she was only acting out her part. Still, Clay knew, on the basis of his own experience—he had often taken on the role of the cavalry officer who had supervised the U.S. Camel Corps in 1860—that certain roles were natural ones. He found it hard to believe that a woman who could deliver a feminist oration like this one was really a doormat in everyday life.

It was hard to imagine what she looked like in everyday life. At the moment she was wearing a floor-length wine-colored velvet dress with a matching, fitted jacket. A small, flat hat, adorned with one discreet black plume, cupped her fine head. Although it was obvious that her dark hair had been plastered under the hat to imitate the long, pinned up style of the late nineteenth century, the brace of incorrigible curls peeping out at her temples gave the lie to Susan B.'s stern image.

"We ask of our rulers, at this hour, no special privileges, no special legislation," she insisted, her powerful voice ringing with conviction and integrity. "We ask justice, we ask equality, we ask that all the civil and political rights that belong to citizens of the United States be guaranteed to us and to our daughters forever!"

As she finished, everybody clapped, but otherwise the group remained largely silent. The speechmaker, whatever her real name was, was peering out at the crowd almost belligerently, despite the applause. Suddenly Clay realized what was lacking: opposition. He knew that during the early days of the traveling chautauqua speakers, heckling from the crowd had been an integral part of the show, and a speaker's mettle was often judged by the way he or she responded to it.

Clay took a few more steps until he was firmly wedged into the heart of the crowd. Then he called out, "Why don't you go back to your pots and pans! Here in Colorado our women know their place!"

A nearby chauvinist called, "You tell 'em, brother! We don't need no outsiders gettin' 'em all riled up none, neither!"

Clay stroked his full mustache, trying to cover his grin. He'd recognized the voice of one of Brady's men, an old geezer named Ragweed Willie, who surely knew how to play this game; between the two of them, maybe they could get the ball rolling.

"I heard that in Kansas, the women got the vote and threw out all the men!" Clay yelled at nobody in particular. "Is that what y'all want here in Patchwork?"

A few other men chimed in before Susan B. archly replied, "It is a sad demonstration of your masculine inadequacy that you fear the ascendancy of women, sir. And your information on our sister state is woefully inaccurate."

Her head was held high, like that of a wild mustang sniffing the wind. *My, but this one's full of fire,* Clay found himself thinking with ripe admiration. He almost forgot to call back, "This here's a man's country. Indians and gold! Why don't ya hustle yer li'l bustle back wh're ya come from?"

This time two bright spots of color flagged her cheeks, and Clay was amazed to realize that she didn't understand what he was doing. She actually thought he was some local redneck baiting her just for fun! No matter. He'd gotten the crowd stirred up for her, and she was lecturing them again. Every set of eyes was focused on her face.

Including Clay's. As he watched her preach her gospel with fierce passion and articulate skill, he realized that he'd never met a woman who seemed so sturdy, so confident, so sure of herself. He'd studied Susan B. Anthony, the real one, enough to know that she had been a gifted person who clearly understood the role that real women had played in settling the west. No wimpy, eyelash-batting females in French lace had defended their babies and raised their crops and actually pulled the yokes of plows to cut the flint-hard prairie soil. Solid, honest, enduring, strong . . . these were the traits of pioneer stock, the traits of the woman Clay had been looking for all of his life... the traits of the compelling woman who stood before him now.

He only hoped it wasn't just an act.

BY LATE AFTERNOON, Roberta Wheeler was tired. Playing Susan B. Anthony was always exhilarating—especially on the road—but once a performance was over, she always had to take a deep breath and sit down.

Today, sitting down had been out of the question until dinner time, when she was scheduled to meet Tess, her best friend from college. Two years ago, Roberta had persuaded Tess to join her on a summer wagon-train trek in this part of the country as a change-of-pace summer vacation. A few months later Tess had married the wagon master and started refurbishing this old mining town, her place of business and her home.

Although Roberta lived several hundred miles away in Arizona, she had been in on a good deal of the planning, especially that involving atmosphere and entertainment roughly appropriate to the time. Tess's specialty was historic preservation, so her focus was on buildings and artifacts. Roberta, on the other hand, was a professor who specialized in the social history of the west; her expertise lay in the fascinating everyday lives of these people. As she strolled through the old mining town—keeping in character, with Susan B. Anthony's proud head held high—she congratulated herself, and the Trents, for achieving such a charming replica of mid-nineteenth century Colorado.

The main street of Patchwork was narrow, dusty, and lined with wooden sidewalks and wood-plank fronted stores. The railroad depot—freshly painted but otherwise unchanged for over a hundred years—stood at one end; the livery stable at the other. In the center, opposite each other, stood the Last Stop Hotel and the Broken Wheel Saloon and Grill. Tess had painstakingly refurbished both to accommodate guests. A few doors down, right in the middle of all the hoopla, the old jail stood nestled between the haberdashery and the blacksmith's. Restored and redecorated from top to bottom, the quaint building now served as the Trents' year-round home.

As Roberta reached the former jail, she marveled that Tess had adapted so well to her unorthodox surroundings. Until last month, she and Brady had lived in total isolation except for the daily comings and goings of the Slow Joe and the sporadic arrival of assorted work crews. Now, for half of each year, the family would live in the heart of the tourist hubbub; the other half, they'd be alone. But Roberta had no doubt, as she knocked on the private side entrance reserved for family and close friends, that Tess was thriving in her new life with Brady.

"Roberta!" Tess burst out as she spotted Roberta and gave her a hug. "I didn't hear the train come in."

"It came in three hours ago, Tess. In fact, it's come and gone twice since I've been walking the streets, so to speak."

Tess grinned sheepishly as she tossed her waist-length braid back over her shoulder, then straightened her broad-brimmed turkey-red bonnet. Like Roberta, she wore a dress that covered her ankles, but Tess's was a yellow-and-red gingham.

"Sorry. I've just been so busy I can't think straight! The phone has been ringing off the hook all afternoon and I've had umpteen visitors in the office."

"And nobody to help you, I suppose."

"Well, Joe loaned me Karen—Mandy's niece—and his oldest daughter has been keeping an eye on J.J. most of the afternoon. But Brady's been down at the corral all day watching his precious rental horses. We've got so many more people than we expected that he's afraid the boys will send the horses out too often without a break, even with Ragweed Willie there to ride herd on them."

Roberta took in this uncharacteristic rush of words with a grin. It was good to see Tess so happy. She had taken a terrific gamble when she'd married Brady—an educated man who'd chosen the life of a cowboy—and had largely allied her future to that of his best friends, Joe and Mandy Henderson, who ran the railroad and had loaned Brady money when he'd desperately needed it in the past. Nowadays the Trents and Hendersons were partners in a thriving business that embraced the ghost town, the wagon train and the Slow Joe, the Hendersons' restored steam locomotive. Mandy also worked as a schoolteacher in town.

The Hendersons lived on the Slow Joe property in a little red station house, which was, in Roberta's opinion, as cute as a bug's ear. The Trents' remodeled house was considerably more rustic—it still had unfinished wood plank walls—but was equally charming. In one corner of the small living room, a hand-carved child's rocking horse, complete with a pint-sized saddle, sat on an exquisitely woven walnut and rust Navajo rug. The furniture was authentic—wooden and spare—but brightened by soft quilted pillows. On one wall hung a dozen family portraits in period-style frames, including one of Brady's favorite buckskin horse in front of the little cabin he'd built on his first ranch. He'd loved the Rocking T with all his heart but had given it up to make a new life with Tess after they'd gotten married.

No man is likely to give up anything like that for me, Roberta thought with a twinge of regret. There had been a time when that discovery had wounded her deeply. But now, when forty loomed on the not-so-distant horizon, she was trying to accept the possibility that marriage might not be on her personal agenda. Oh, she suspected that she could still snag a man if she were willing to put on an act, but the one thing of which she was absolutely certain was that she had no desire to spend her life living with anybody who didn't love her for herself.

It was a lesson she'd learned the hard way.

"So, how did your performance go?" Tess asked as she turned back toward the nursery, where the sound of a squalling toddler could be heard. "Were you as dashing as ever?"

Roberta grimaced, unaccountably recalling the mustachioed yahoo in the buckskin jacket who'd made such a fuss. Ragweed Willie was an old friend, and she knew he'd just been helping her out by getting folks riled. But the other redneck—as good-looking as he was close-minded—was the real thing. She knew the type. She'd grown up on a Texas ranch and spent half of her life trying to distance herself from subliterate, Neanderthal cowboys. Being an intellectual—especially an intellectual in a small rural town—would have been painful for any big-boned female. And Roberta, an outspoken woman who valued honesty over finesse, had the added disadvantage of being raised as "one of the boys" along with her three brothers. She had never learned how to act "female" in the way that potential boyfriends seemed to expect, and her interest in academia had further set her apart from other girls as well as boys. The only way she seemed to fit in was as a crack rider, an option that had ceased to exist when she was seventeen.

"I was great," she declared with a wry grin as she followed Tess into the nursery, "though you couldn't tell it by the local rednecks. One particularly vocal fellow actually told me to 'hustle my bustle' back to Kansas. Or something like that." She didn't mention the cowboy's rugged appeal, because it was irrelevant; she'd rather remain celibate for life than get tangled up with a chauvinist like him. Mulling over his exact words—and the delighted expression on his handsome face—Roberta wondered, in hindsight, if he might have been putting on a act.

Apparently Tess thought so. She laughed as she said "I love it when everybody gets into the spirit of the thing."

It was obvious that Tess loved her fifteen-month-old baby, too. At that moment, J.J.—named Jacob Joseph for his grandpa and his dad's best friend—woke up red-faced and squalling. As he reached out for his mother with both pudgy arms, she tucked him snugly against her chest and kissed the top of his head. In an instant he was silent.

"That's my baby," Tess whispered, more to herself than to J.J. or Roberta.

Roberta said nothing as the little boy fiercely wrapped his arms around his mother while she rocked him for a moment or two. Although she enjoyed children, Roberta had never felt great maternal longing. Still, at moments like this, she always asked herself whether she had decided that she didn't want to be a mother because she really didn't want the burden of kids or had simply acknowledged, somewhere deep within her heart, that she would probably never have a husband to complete the family circle.

Granted, men were more acceptant of intellectual women nowadays than they had been when she'd first dated, but so far this societal change had had no effect on her social life, only on her career. The men in her department—and the professors she had met from other schools—admired her as a colleague and respected her as a peer. But none of them had ever treated her as an appealing, beguiling female.

Certainly not the department head, Charles Trumbull. While it would hardly be proper for a man in his position to go about sniffing the skirts of the women under his supervision, with prudence, a relationship with one would not be out of the question.

Charles was everything Roberta had ever wanted in a man. Well, almost everything. He was bright, urbane, witty and well educated. He lived for history, cared about his students, and truly believed that women were his intellectual peers. And best of all, he'd never even *been* to Texas.

But he had never shown the slightest romantic interest in Roberta. And, in all honesty, Roberta couldn't say that her feeling for him was exactly passionate. But he was a good companion and would make a good lifemate, if...well, if the thought ever occurred to him. Roberta had never hinted to Charles of her personal interest. In the first place, she didn't know any subtle way to do it. If she just followed her instincts and said, "Hey, Charles, you want to start dating?" she knew she'd only succeed in embarrassing both of them.

"I told Brady we'd meet the Hendersons and him at the Broken Wheel at six," Tess informed her friend as she dressed J.J. in a darling tiny cowboy outfit including handmade bandanna, vest and little boots. "I sent Lynne—" that was Joe's oldest daughter, who was now sixteen "—to find the other two kids." She grinned. "Ira'd kill me if he heard me call him a 'kid.' Out here he works like any of the men, but he's still just a senior in high school."

"He graduates in June?" said Roberta, who'd first met Ira on the wagon train and had gotten well acquainted with him since then. "It's hard to think he's really that old."

"Old enough that Mandy wants him to go away to school this fall."

Roberta studied Tess. "*Mandy* wants him to go? I didn't think the Hendersons had any stepmother problems."

"They don't. But Mandy's concerned that if Ira stays in Redpoint—or worse yet, comes to work on the Double Bar T full-time—he'll never go to college. And he's a great student. She thinks it would be a terrible waste."

Robert, who believed that every person on the face of the earth should have an education, had to agree. "What does Ira think? Should I take him aside and have a professor-to-student chat?"

Tess pondered that a moment. "You might. But be gentle. I think right now he could jump either way. He says he wants to go to college, just not yet. He says he can go to school anytime, but getting Patchwork off the ground is a once-in-a-lifetime experience. He's been with Brady right from the start, you know, and I'm afraid it's in his blood." She didn't need to add that Ira felt a keen obligation to support his "uncle" Brady in everything he did. The two couldn't have been closer if they'd been blood kin.

"What do you think?" Roberta asked, sensing that there was more to the subject than she'd heard so far.

Tess was quiet a moment before she said, "Frankly, I'm not sure. I think Ira feels that he owes it to Brady to stay on here because Brady gave him a chance to prove himself when he was so young and also because standing by Brady has always been so important to Joe."

"Has anybody asked Ira what *he* thinks?" Roberta asked sagely.

Tess grinned ruefully as she walked to the bedroom. "Everybody's asked. Maybe nobody's listened. Or maybe not listened hard enough."

Roberta nodded. She'd dealt with confused adolescent students for years and usually felt good about the advice she offered them. Ira was a good kid, and she had no doubt that if the grownups in his life had enough sense not to crowd him, eventually he'd make the right choice.

Tess placed J.J. at Roberta's feet as she started to change her earrings. Roberta grinned at the child as he tugged on the buttons of her ankle-high boots, then gently picked him up when he tried to eat them.

"Clay Gann's going to be joining us, too," Tess commented almost absently as she pinned on an ancient brooch. "Have you met him before?"

Roberta pondered the name. "No, I don't think so."

"He's an old friend of Brady's who owns a stable north of Fort Collins. He runs a camel trail ride up there whenever he isn't doing the racing circuit. Sometimes he does cameo appearances on the wagon train, too."

"Racing circuit?" Roberta repeated, gently removing the string of her bonnet from J.J.'s mouth before she set him down. The rest of Tess's sentence seemed to echo belatedly in her ears. "He's the fellow with the traveling camel herd?" Having helped Tess plan the activities for the weekend, she knew that a camel herd was coming to Patchwork, but she'd forgotten the name of the owner.

Tess nodded. "I think you'll really like Clay. He's a lot like you."

Roberta scowled. "What does that mean?"

"It means he's got an off-the-wall sense of humor and doesn't give a damn what anybody else thinks about the way he acts."

"Spoken like a true friend," Roberta observed good-naturedly, exchanging a smile with Tess. Tess frequently told her she was too bold, too abrupt, too pushy. But Roberta knew that Tess loved her anyway. And once, after a man who'd stopped dating her had listed the same litany of complaints, Tess had consoled her by saying, "You just wouldn't be you if you tried to be somebody else, Roberta. I love you just the way you are, and someday, the right man will love you, too."

Roberta didn't believe it, but she'd appreciated the sentiment. However she didn't appreciate Tess's obvious attempt to arrange a blind date for her. She'd had other friends over time who'd done her the same "favor"—which had always been embarrassing—but she'd credited Tess with more sense.

"This fellow—"

"Clay."

"This Clay fellow—how, exactly, did he get invited to this shindig tonight at the Broken Wheel?"

Tess met Roberta's eyes directly. "The same way you and the Hendersons did. He's a good friend in town for the evening to help us get the season launched."

"That's all?"

Tess nodded. Her eyes were sincere. "That's all. Brady would have invited him even if you hadn't been here."

Roberta took a step back, shrugging apologetically. "Okay, then. Let's eat."

They crossed the noisy street in tandem, J.J. holding on to Roberta's watchful hand. Once they stopped to allow a carriage to cross their path, and soon thereafter a buckboard wagon pulled into town. Honky-tonk music blared out of a saloon up the street, and fake gunfire blasted from the vicinity of the train station. It felt, all in all, like any ordinary Friday night in 1860, and Roberta loved it with all her heart.

She loved the inside of the restaurant, too. The rough wooden walls were adorned only with a few kerosene lamps at appropriate junctures, and each table was covered with a hand-embroidered tablecloth, courtesy, she knew, of the ladies of the Pioneer Community Church in Redpoint. Near the back was one long table full of people she already knew—Joe and Mandy Henderson, Joe's three kids, and bowlegged Brady, standing up to take his baby and kiss his wife—and one she didn't. It was the redneck who had insulted her that afternoon.

Roberta greeted her friends, then studied the intriguing camel man with a bit more care. At once she realized that if he, too, was one of the clan, so to speak, then he might have been baiting her in the same spirit as Ragweed Willie. It put his comments in an entirely different light. Still, in Roberta's experience, a cowboy was a cowboy—and he definitely was one—and if she'd wanted to spend her life with cowboys, she never would have fought so hard to escape from her daddy's Texas ranch.

Slowly, the cowboy stood, nodded to Tess, then pulled off his battered Stetson, revealing thick brown hair that should have been cut a month ago. But as his sparkling gray eyes found Roberta's, she found herself surprisingly uncritical of his appearance. He looked rugged, natural, exceptionally tall. There was a quiet virility about him that made her swallow hard.

"Howdy, Miz Anthony," he told her in a fake Texas drawl. It was a good imitation, but Roberta could tell it wasn't the real thing. "Hope you don't mind me an' the boys joshin' you none. Was a right fine talk you gived, ma'am."

It was red-haired, freckle-faced Mandy Henderson who rolled her eyes. "Honestly, Clay, you set my schoolteacher's hackles on edge when you talk like that. I'll be correcting Ira's grammar for a week." She grinned affectionately at her blond stepson before she turned back to Clay and teased, "Can't we all take some time off from western role-playing while we eat?"

Brady, warming the room with his gracious smile, quickly interjected, "I don't think you've met Clay, Roberta. He's sharing his camels with us this weekend." He turned to Clay as he laid a hand on Roberta's arm. "This is Roberta. Well, Roberta Jean Wheeler, if we're going to be formal. We couldn't have put Patchwork together without her."

Roberta was taking in the praise—and the welcome sight before her—when Clay drawled, "A pleasure indeed, Miz Bobbie Jean. My friends call me Clayton Gann, the Camel Man."

Roberta couldn't suppress a smile. He was pushing it— God, how she hated her childhood nickname!—but he was acting precisely the way she usually did, so she couldn't really fault his chutzpah. Nor could she break character when he refused to. What fun to find a man who broke the rules as willfully as she did! It felt utterly natural to curtsy deeply and take on the Texas belle role he'd apparently chosen for her to play. Nobody had called her "Bobbie Jean" in twenty years, and the Bobbie Jean of her youth had never been a Texas belle. Still, she'd spent enough years rubbing elbows with the type that she thought she could muster a fair imitation.

"A camel man!" she gushed, batting her eyelashes with all the melodrama she could muster. "My goodness, Mr. Gann, I am *so* impressed. I can't say that I know very much about camels."

They were the magic words. His beguiling grin tripled in a flash. "Well, Bobbie Jean, you have come t' th' right place, 'cuz Ah can tell you everythin' your pretty li'l heart ever wanted to know about them fine humped beasts."

"And a great deal that she did *not* want to know," Joe chimed in dryly. Dressed in an engineer's outfit, he looked even more authentically dressed than the other men. He leaned back in his chair, draped one friendly arm around his wife's shoulder and predicted, "Before dinner's done, Roberta, you're likely to learn everything there is to know about the U.S. Camel Corps."

Roberta grinned. "Why, Mr. Henderson," she swooned in her sauciest Texas drawl, "I am certain that Mr. Gann is too much of a gentleman to bend my ear about his *own* interests. Surely he wants to know about the suffrage movement and will volunteer to help the ladies of America in every way he can."

To his credit, Clay kept a straight face. "Oh, yes, sweet thing, Ah have a great interest in the ladies."

And then the most amazing thing happened. Clay Gann smiled again. And this time he wasn't smiling like a man who was impressed with a colleague's dissertation or who had just read a fine professional paper by Roberta Jean Wheeler, Ph.D. He wasn't smiling like a man who was playing a role or flirting just to kill time. He was smiling, jaw to jaw, as though he were a miner who'd been looking for gold all of his life and had suddenly found a streak of color in a played-out mine.

And he was looking straight at *her*.

CHAPTER TWO

DINNER TURNED OUT to be a mixture of time periods and tastes. Clay knew that buffalo meat was nearly impossible to get by the time Susan B. Anthony was touring the country, but it represented the old west and he enjoyed the tangy flavor immensely. The spoon bread spoke of an even earlier era, but it was tasty, too. As far as he could tell, everything on the regular menu was genuinely connected to the frontier. There was a separate menu, called "Greenhorn's Gourmet," which offered hamburgers, omelets and salads, but Brady privately confided that his waiters, dressed as turn-of-the-century bartenders, were instructed to produce it only when a guest looked desperate.

Little J.J., as it turned out, was the only one of the group who required such pandering. He was also the only one who had to be assured that there was nothing to fear in the weekend's entertainment: when Harry Painted Hat trotted into the the Broken Wheel dressed in skins and feathers to confer with Brady, the toddler's eyes grew huge.

"Mama!" he cried out, tugging on Tess's long sleeve as his beautiful big eyes flared with fear. "Injun!"

Joe's two daughters, eleven-year-old Sally and sixteen-year-old Lynne, exchanged patronizing glances.

"Honesty, J.J.," scoffed Sally. "It's only Harry. He's not going to scalp you or anything."

Clay grinned as Harry squatted beside the little boy and said kindly, "Take it easy, J.J. It's just me all dressed up."

J.J. blinked twice, then relaxed. Clearly he recognized his father's Ute friend. With an embarrassed grin, he reached out to tug on the tiny shells—rows and rows of them—that adorned Harry's elk-skin-shirted chest.

Harry winked. "More fun than mommy's necklace, huh?" he told the child, patting him gently on the back. "I'm supposed to be reminding people that we're going to put on a big show tomorrow night, J.J. We're going to dance for everybody, just like my family used to dance a long time ago." He tousled the child's blond hair. "It's called the Bear Dance. Maybe I'll teach you how to do it someday."

Although J.J. couldn't follow the words, it was obvious by the glow in his young eyes that he appreciated Harry's friendly explanation. As Harry's face grew more sober, Clay wondered if he was thinking of how things had changed for his people. Harry was the quintessential modern-day Native American—a man who was a successful plumber in the white man's world but still kept close ties to his friends and elderly family members on the reservation. Clay suspected that he had mixed feelings about "selling" his heritage to the tourists. He knew it was a special favor that Harry did for Brady, and his reservation friends were well paid for their participation.

While Brady and Harry discussed some last-minute details of the evening's performance, Clay focused on the fetching female across the table. During the course of the meal, she had dropped the Texas belle act and begun to speak like a typical twentieth century female.

Yet he still doubted that there was anything typical about Roberta.

In less than half an hour, she'd expounded on pollution in the Grand Canyon caused by a local plant providing power to L.A., lambasted the current federal administration and analyzed the shortcomings of several Central American governments. While Clay hadn't agreed with all of her comments, he couldn't find fault with her logic, though he'd engaged her in some lively debate. At the moment he was looking forward to learning her beliefs about the role of the U.S. Cavalry in Indian country during the Civil War, when frontier Army policy was whopperjawed by the mass defection of southerners who abandoned their western posts to join the Confederate Army.

Before he got a chance to bring up the subject, however, Joe's youngest daughter piped up, "Is Harry going to kill Uncle Brady again?"

Roberta shook her head. "Nope. Different show this time." She turned to Clay to explain, "When Tess and I first took Brady's wagon-train ride years ago, his Ute buddies pretended to attack us. I almost beaned Harry with a cast-iron skillet before he stabbed Brady with a Bowie knife, and poor Tess went berserk." She giggled in a delightfully girlish way. "Brady made quite a splash as a dying hero."

"And Roberta made quite a splash as a pioneer suffragist," commented Brady as he waved goodbye to his Ute friend. "Everybody thought I'd hired her for color."

"And well you should have," she upbraided him with a grin. "Not only did I liven things up for your guests, but I also served as your marriage broker."

Brady grinned so joyfully that, for just a minute, Clay felt a bit jealous of him. Brady Trent was a man who had everything Clay had ever wanted in life—the chance to live out his western dream with a woman who was his partner in every way. Most of the modern cowboys Clay knew were either single or married to women who constantly badgered them to find a more practical form of endeavor. The former were lonely, the latter as defeated as his poor father had been. Clay was determined never to end up like him.

"So are you having any luck with your idea for a circuit?" Brady asked Clay just as the waitress handed him a salad. "Last time I saw the lieutenant, he was working out a plan."

Realizing that Roberta was listening, Clay turned to her courteously to explain, "Lieutenant Edward Beale was the man in charge of the U.S. Camel Corps in 1860. Sometimes when I do cameo appearances for Brady's wagon-train guests, I take on his role."

"I don't think he 'takes on' the role any more than you 'pretend' to be Susan B. Anthony," Brady corrected his friend with a grin. "I think he was Beale in another life."

Roberta smiled at him. "I'll take that as a compliment, Brady." She turned to Clay. "What kind of a man was Beale?"

He shrugged, not sure how to answer briefly. "An honest man, an Army lifer...a fellow who was frustrated because he couldn't get anybody to listen to his dreams."

Brady glanced down at the table at his wife and son, then back at Clay, as if to underscore the point that he had finally achieved his greatest dream. "Clay's dream is to start a professional camel racing circuit, like the

Grand Prix," Brady told Roberta. "He's a man who takes his camels seriously."

Clay shot a quick glance at Roberta, not wanting to continue this particular discussion if it was going to bore her, but he read intense interest in her hazel eyes. He wasn't sure which intrigued her: the camels or the man who loved them, but either way he was warmed by her vivacious smile.

He was about to explain his long-range goal of organizing numerous camel racing events during the summer season, building up to a grand finale in Virginia City, Nevada, where modern-day camel racing got its start, when Joe's youngest interrupted again.

"I heard you talk on the back of the train today, Roberta," Sally gushed. "You didn't sound like you at all!"

Ira asked cheerfully, "Who are you this weekend, Roberta?"

Roberta gave him a winning grin. "My favorite. Susan B."

"You do other people?" Clay asked, intrigued by the whole process of character interpretation . . . especially any character that interested Roberta. In fact, he was beginning to think that anything that involved Roberta could turn out to be downright fascinating.

"Oh, yes. It depends on the situation." She started to glow. "I've got a whole collection of costumes and a file of speeches. Most of them are memorized."

"Memorized?" Clay asked, images of painstakingly rendered high-school oratories under Mr. Carey's stern tutelage filling his mind. "You mean you reproduce these people word-for-word? You don't just create the characters spontaneously?"

Roberta looked taken aback, almost insulted. "When the situation warrants it, I improvise. And certainly when I was on the college debate team, I didn't walk into a round with a memorized presentation. I gathered up those awards from thinking on my feet."

Clay knew she was still speaking, but suddenly he went deaf. From the moment she said "awards" right on the heels of "college debate team," he knew he'd made a terrible mistake. He could have tolerated her attendance at college if she'd hated it; he could have commiserated with her debate team experience if she'd also been through hell. But she was practically *bragging* about her success in the kind of program that had destroyed his adolescent years. The very tone of her voice—not western and folksy now but growing more academic and supercilious by the second—was making his ears twitch.

"...but historical oratory is different," she was saying, her eyes sparkling as she warmed to her latest topic. "Technical accuracy is a vital component of any legitimate historical represen—"

"Roberta will be giving living history presentations all summer, Clay," Tess cut off her friend, pointedly smiling at Clay as she did so. She might as well have said out loud, *Forgive my friend. When she gets on her high horse, she gets carried away.* "She's going to be riding pretty much the same circuit you are, giving chautauquas to centennials and western days celebrations."

"She is?" Clay tried to look intrigued, but it was a challenge at the moment. An hour ago—ten seconds ago!—he would have been delighted to know that he'd have a natural opportunity to see Roberta again. Earlier he'd assumed that her interest in chautauquas reflected his own fascination with living history. But now he had the definite feeling that her presentations were more than just a hobby. Her approach to the whole process was so polished and formal that he almost had the feeling they had something to do with her job. *And what is her job?* he asked himself a bit belatedly. He'd assumed it was something ordinary, or maybe off-the-wall, but nothing that placed her out of his social milieu . . . beyond his reach.

But now he wondered.

Fortunately, nobody seemed to notice that Clay had all but dropped out of the conversation; nobody noticed that he failed to turn to Roberta to eagerly ascertain when their paths might be crossing again. In fact, nobody seemed to be paying much attention to him. Not only was the waitress trying to lower hot, heavy plates of roast buffalo to the table, but now chatty Sally was asking, "What's a cha-ta-ka?"

"Chau-tau-qua, honey," her stepmother Mandy corrected her gently. "It's what the folks in the olden days did before television. People went place to place on trains giving speeches on important subjects or making music. It was sort of a traveling church service, news program and variety show."

Sally's eyes widened. "All on a train?"

"There wasn't any other way to do it," Roberta explained. "Stagecoaches were just too slow and uncomfortable, and nobody had invented airplanes yet."

"But we've got airplanes now," the child pointed out reasonably. "So why are you going to be riding around on a train all summer? Do you just love trains like my daddy does?"

Clay had to grin. From what he knew of Joe Henderson, the man's personal view of hell would be anyplace where no steam engine ran. To Clay, hell was anywhere without horses or camels. And, of course, the Devil himself would likely turn out to be his high-school speech coach, Mr. Carey.

"Well, I *am* fond of trains," Roberta answered diplomatically, "but I actually won't be traveling on them to get to the places where I'll be speaking this summer. The really important thing about a chautauqua is what you say and how you look when you say it. The idea is to try to teach people about how it was a hundred years ago...how some things have changed and some things never do."

Clay couldn't help but meet her eyes as she said the last line with conviction. There *was* a magic in the past, a magic that warmed his life as much as it obviously warmed hers. *Maybe,* he told himself, *the college debate thing was just a tiny episode in her life. Maybe it's not that big a deal. If I just think about the woman as she is here and now, maybe I can forget that a small part of her background reminds me of Mr. Carey.*

Lynne asked, "What hasn't changed? I thought everything was different now."

Clay could guess what was coming, and he relished the expectation of another round of Roberta on the podium. The fire was already lighting up her hazel eyes.

He had the sudden sensation of being trapped on a roller coaster this evening. One minute he was soaring, swept along by the charisma of this unusual female...the next he was crashing down as he saw her hoity-toity side. But the roller coaster was swooping upward once again with Clay strapped to the very first seat, and at the moment all he could do was welcome the feel of the night's tangy wind pummeling his face.

"In those days, women started fighting for their rights as human beings," Roberta informed the teenage girl, her eyes flashing with indignation. "They did finally get the right to vote, but in many ways, women are still subjugated by men."

In the house where I grew up it was the other way around. The thought popped into Clay's mind unbidden, and he knew that it was beside the point. His mother hadn't trampled his feelings, or his father's because of her gender or theirs. If she'd had only daughters, or lived with a sister or a maiden aunt, she still would have ruled the roost with an iron hand and an upturned nose.

"What does subja-subja...whatever it is...mean?" Sally asked.

"It means that men believe that they're better than women. It means that boys think they can do better in school than girls. It means that it's harder for girls to get jobs and scholarships and—"

"*Some* girls," Joe Henderson suddenly broke in, using a sterner tone than Clay had ever heard him use before. "*My* daughters give their best to school and everything else they do, and they'll have no trouble becoming successful in whatever career they choose, *will they*, Roberta?" he asked pointedly.

Roberta's lips tightened at the subtle rebuke, but she seemed to get Joe's point. Backing off slightly, she explained to the girls, "I wasn't talking about either of you, of course. You're lucky enough to have a daddy who understands how terrific his daughters are. But he's not exactly your typical, run-of-the-mill father, you know."

"Joe's not your typical, run-of-the-mill man," said Mandy, with quiet but unmistakable pride.

It occurred to Clay that those two girls—and Ira—weren't lucky just because their father wasn't a chauvinist. They were lucky because they were growing up with adults who loved and respected each other. Sarah, Joe's first wife, and her new husband Bill were wonderful role models, as were Joe and Mandy. And Joe and Sarah, long since divorced, built each other up instead of tearing each other down. And together they soldered the egos of their children.

He wondered, for a moment, what kind of childhood Roberta must have had to make her such a determined woman. She didn't seem to have any weaknesses, and he doubted that she tolerated them in others. When she leaned toward him, he felt breathless, tangled up inside. It was only when he recalled that highbrow tone she'd used earlier that he wondered if he'd misjudged her. He knew she had enough fire for him, but he wasn't sure if she had enough heart.

"Roberta's doing a full chautauqua tour this summer to see if she can start a program for graduate students next year," Tess suddenly announced, looking straight at Clay as she picked up her earlier conversational train. "Her department head, Charles Trumbull, has been very impressed with the students' comments on her classes since she started incorporating role-playing into her lectures. He even arranged for Roberta to write a paper about it for the university history review."

"He's the editor," chimed in Roberta, who was suddenly glowing like a hen that had just laid its first egg. "Dr. Trumbull really has an eye for style and always gets straight to the heart of the matter. I've never worked for anybody I admire more."

He got it then. He had pretended, for maybe half a day, that Roberta was an ordinary working girl who just happened to share his zest for history. But suddenly he knew he'd pegged her all wrong. She was one of *those*. An academic type. A blue blood. Just the sort of woman his mother would have picked out for him. Just the sort of woman his mother was.

In a quiet tone, which could not fully hide his apprehension, Clay asked, "You're a college history teacher?"

"A history *professor*, thank you," Roberta corrected him with blatant pride. "I was promoted from assistant professor less than a year after I earned my Ph.D. My specialty is social history...the day-to-day life of the common people—not just the famous ones—who settled the west."

Her eyes met his proudly, as though she were waiting for an awestruck—or at least complimentary—reply. But suddenly Clay wasn't sure that he wanted to encourage her. Suddenly he regretted that he'd ever encouraged her at all.

If she knew she was talking to a childhood stutterer who hadn't darkened a schoolhouse door since his high school graduation, he wondered, would she still sparkle whenever she looked in his direction?

Clearly she took great pride not only in her knowledge but in her academic achievements—and in the outer symbols of academia. Not only took pride but actually looked down a bit on those mere mortals who were self-educated, like Clay...or not educated at all.

Oh, she had fire. And yes— God, yes!—she tempted him. But Clay was nothing if not realistic about the choices that life offered him, and he could not avoid the reality staring at him now. Tug or no tug, a fact was a fact. And the fact was, plain and simple, that there was only one thing Clay Gann needed less than than a woman who actually *bragged* about her achievements in collegiate debate, and that was a woman who bragged about her Ph.D.

WHEN ROBERTA SAUNTERED down to the arena on Saturday morning in her tailored gray Susan B. suit—complete with bell-shaped skirt and a blouse bedecked with a fichu of white lawn—she told herself that she didn't really care whether she watched the camel races or not; she simply had nothing else to do until her speech at one. And when she perched gingerly at one end of the bleachers, as though she might leave again at any moment, she pretended that her eyes were drawn to the starting gates only because that was where the action was. The fact that Clay Gann was there, supervising his precious camels, had nothing to do with her rapt interest. After all, he'd made it perfectly clear the night before that *he* certainly lacked such an interest in *her*.

Somewhere between the main course and dessert, she had lost him. It was as simple as that.

Roberta didn't know what had happened. She did not know what to expect from men in general when they looked at her as a woman, not a pal, because it didn't happen very often, and she wasn't entirely sure it had happened the night before. Early in the evening there had been moments—lots of them—when she'd had the feeling that Clay Gann had liked her a lot. But by the time she'd left the Broken Wheel—alone—she was quite certain that she'd totally turned him off.

It was an odd feeling, an unexpected hurt. After all, she had barely had time to get to know the man, let alone get her heart broken. Roberta rarely played the dating game, and what skills she had in that department were rusty from disuse. This morning, when she'd joined Tess for breakfast, her friend had insisted that it didn't matter; Clay Gann was as unconventional as Roberta herself. But for all Tess's attempts to buck her up, nothing she could say could change the obvious fact.

Roberta had been charmed by Clay Gann. He had not been charmed back.

She told herself she didn't care; she told herself that she'd already put him out of her head. She even told herself that she wouldn't mind in the least if she didn't run into Clay before she left Patchwork Sunday evening; in fact, she probably would prefer to stay out of his way. That wouldn't be easy if she spent much time at the barn or the arena, and Roberta knew that despite her uneasiness in both locations, she couldn't stay away. She could no sooner turn her back on today's trick riding demonstration than turn down a brownie for dessert, and there was no way on earth she was going to leave for Arizona without spending a few minutes with that darling baby camel she'd spotted at the barn.

For over an hour she watched the scheduled camel races, and she had to admit that she had never seen anything quite so comical in her life. Each rider, sponsored by a store or company eager to publicize its name, was assigned to a given camel by the luck of the draw. The animals came equipped with a halter, reins, and a wooden frame around the hump that served as a saddle. The rider sat directly behind the double-pronged "horn" in the front, which kept him or her from sliding off the hump onto the camel's neck. It did not prevent the camel jockey from rolling from one side to the other—or even rolling off.

The camels, of course, had not been polled as to whether or not they were interested in participating, and some made it all too clear that they preferred other sources of amusement. While Roberta watched, several lumbered along from the starting end of the arena to the opposite fence as they were supposed to do, but two spiraled off toward the sides and circled around, one refused to budge an inch, and one took off with three heroic leaps; the instant its rider threw in the towel and jumped off, it folded up its knees and rolled around in the dust.

Roberta grew tense when the rider hit the ground, but he was shortly on his feet and in control of his balance, so she wasn't too afraid. Still, the scene made her nervous, and she was grateful when Clay came out to check the camel a few moments later and declared that it was time for a break.

She took advantage of the moment to go buy a cold drink and stretch her legs. From a distance, she could hear a comedian doing a cornball country routine on the mike. And then, after she'd been gone maybe half an hour, she heard the crowd give a communal *ooh* and *ah* that all but shouted their admiration. By the rattle of the bleachers, Roberta knew that some of the tourists were on their feet.

The crowd was positively roaring when she returned to the arena. There were two men performing on one horse—the one dressed in red hanging upside down beneath the specially-made trick riding saddle, the blue-clad one doing a handstand on the pommel. Roberta caught her breath, fighting a sudden urge to look away. It was obvious that they knew what they were doing—neither the men nor the horse demonstrated the slightest hesitation—but she knew how dangerous trick riding could be. The top of her spine began to throb, and unconsciously she rubbed the vertebrae at the base of her neck. Forcing herself to be calm, she climbed back up in the bleachers and took a seat just as the rider on top suddenly started a Cossack Pass beneath the still-cantering horse, and the one underneath surfaced for a One Hand Layover the Saddle. Both were waving Colorado flags from a free hand.

By this time the folks were stomping their feet in approbation, but Roberta wondered how many of them truly realized that they were witnessing consummate riding skill. All trick riding looked flashy, but some of it was elementary for any good rider. She'd once performed any number of basic tricks herself. In fact—the memory both warmed and wounded her—she hadn't been half bad.

A moment later, the two riders vaulted off the horse—one on each side—and took their bows. It wasn't until they faced Roberta, holding still, that she could see their faces. The one dressed in red was a short, bowlegged man who sported a daredevil smile with a single gold tooth. The one in blue was Clay.

Her stomach lurched in sudden panic. Why hadn't Tess mentioned that Clay did riding like this?

Because she knew it would upset me, came her own reply. *She knew it would be hard enough to watch if I didn't care about the rider.*

Roberta *had* heard that Clay did fancy roping—an impressive skill that rarely required one to risk one's safety. But the Cossack stunts were always death-defying, even done by one rider at a time.

Mercifully, Clay seemed to be done for the moment. As he picked up his hat—the same old dusty Stetson he'd been wearing the night before—a voice over the microphone called out, "Hey Clay, is it true what they say?"

Clay stuck the hat on his head, squinted at the microphone, and shrugged his shoulders as though perplexed.

"Ain't no horse that can't be rode, ain't no rider can't be throwed," taunted the amplified voice. "Ain't that right, folks?"

The crowd roared as Clay called back from the arena, "Ain't nothin' on four legs I can't ride, George."

The other voice laughed. "You want to bet on that?"

Clay made a great show of digging into his pocket and producing a foot-long piece of paper resembling a hundred-dollar bill. Roberta wasn't surprised to see him take on the role of a rodeo clown. In fact, she wasn't even surprised to see the four-legged creature that an egg-bald cowboy led out for him to ride a moment later—the most hostile-looking camel that Roberta had ever seen.

The audience hooted but Roberta shivered as she watched the camel stab its tail straight out in disdain, salivating heavily as it pulled against its halter. When the bald cowboy handed its lead to Clay, it let loose a hilarious string of wild chirping sounds.

Clay made quite a show of insisting that the bizarre looking creature was not a horse, but George, on the loudspeaker, pointed out that Clay had claimed he could ride *anything* with four feet, a point he reluctantly conceded. After a series of catcalls and comic accusations from the other cowboys who flanked the arena, Clay began the arduous task of "taming" the wild beast. Of course he had no post in the center of the arena, so he had to ground-tie the camel—who refused to stay tied. It took Clay five funny minutes to put on the wooden frame "saddle"; another two to get both reins attached to the bit in its slobbering mouth. By the time Clay got up on board—virtually dragging himself up the camel's side inch by shaggy inch—the Patchwork celebrants were in stitches.

Roberta knew it was funny. She knew he was good. But she also knew that the paramedics waited at the far end of the arena as they did during every other horse- or camelback ride. And every once in a while, she glanced back at them.

By the time Clay began to shake out a long lariat to prove he could make his camel do anything a pony could do, the crowd was all but bellowing encouragement. After several minutes of fancy rope spins, a young cowboy trotted in to retrieve Clay's hat just as Clay's camel galloped—or rather, lurched at high speed—down the center of the arena. The ocean-wave rope spin that Clay was executing got away from him—or so it seemed—and the next thing Roberta knew, the lariat had snaked out behind Clay and the camel to rope the young man's chest. As the crowd shouted a warning, Clay dragged the staggering camel to a stop at the last possible instant before the boy would have fallen in the dust.

Despite the young man's great show of relief, Roberta was certain that he was never in the slightest bit of danger. The boy had been roped by a champion in the saddle. Anybody who could rope a target backward while riding a lumbering camel would look as sleek as lightning roping from a well-trained saddle horse.

The tourists were on their feet, hollering their pleasure, by the time Clay dismounted, took his bows, and led the salivating camel away. Clearly they were awed by his skill. Roberta was impressed, too, but another emotion was crippling her delight. It wasn't until Clay was safely on the ground that she realized that she was gripping her skirt so tightly that her nails were cutting into her palms.

Twenty years, and the panic had never quite left her. She wondered if it ever would.

"HEY, OZ, you wanna get something to eat?"

Ozzie Edwards glanced up from his task—brushing the baby camel—to give a wan smile to Ira Henderson, a sunny-haired boy a year his junior who worked part-time on the Double Bar T ranch. All he really knew about Ira was that he was sort of related to Clay's friend, Brady Trent. And though neither Brady nor his wife had ever made fun of Ozzie, he wasn't positive that he could expect the same treatment from a young shirt-tail relation. The only people he was sure were safe were the men Clay hired, because courtesy to Ozzie was one of the requirements that went with the job. Between his own intellectual interests and the fact that he was raising camels as well as horses, Clay was a choosy employer anyway. But during Ozzie's first month on the ranch, a young cowhand had cruelly mimicked his speech, and Clay had fired him on the spot. While Ozzie didn't feel particularly close to the three older men who usually traveled with the racing camels—or the half dozen others who worked on Clay's Fort Collins spread—he now lived in perfect confidence that he'd never be mocked by anybody who depended on Clay for a living.

"I d-d-don't think so, Ira," he stammered, cursing his inept tongue. "I've got t-t-too much work to do."

He'd spoken to Ira several times before, but there had always been so many other people around that he'd counted on the noise to cover his stutter. That was one of the great things about ranch work—everybody was always too busy, too tired or too far away to listen to him closely. And the animals seemed to love the sound of his voice.

"Well, you gotta eat sometime," Ira pointed out. "We've got buffalo burgers at the Broken Wheel."

It had been a long, long time since Ozzie had chowed down a burger with a friend his own age. Then again, he wasn't sure he'd really *had* a friend since his family had moved to Denver when he was fourteen. The kids he'd grown up with had accepted his verbal difficulty, and he'd almost accepted it himself. But the new teen-age group had never tried to get acquainted with the real Ozzie Edwards. All they saw was a cartoon character to lampoon. His parents had been loving and supportive. Even his big sister had always been exceptionally kind. But the new school had been pure hell and his first part-time job selling ice cream had been a disaster. The family vacation the summer he'd graduated from high school had taken the Edwards to Clay's camel trail ride, and by a miraculous fluke, Clay had mentioned during the course of the day that he had an opening if any-body was looking for a job. As soon as Ozzie had fig-ured out that he'd get to work with animals and wouldn't have to talk much to the tourists—who were more likely to be courteous adults and oblivious chil-dren than taunting teens—he'd asked Clay to take him on. And by September he'd decided that nowhere on earth was he likely to be any happier than under Clay Gann's protective wing, and he'd absolutely refused to carry out his parents' college plans for him that fall. Now, a good eight months later, he sometimes regret-ted that decision, but his fear of rejection was even stronger than his great love of books, not to mention his longing for adolescent friends.

"M-m-maybe I'll go over there later," he told Ira, hoping the other boy wouldn't press him.

But Ira climbed up on the fence and offered, "I could wait a few minutes if you want. Gosh, Ozzie, I love working out here, but sometimes I just really wish I could talk to somebody my own age, you know? My friends in town don't understand why I want to be here, and in the summer, I hardly see anybody under thirty-five." He made it sound as though thirty-five was just short of senile. Doddering, at the very least.

"Aren't there g-g-girls on the wagon trains?" Ozzie asked. "G-g-girls always like horses. At least my sister d-d-did when she was eighteen."

Ira laughed. "Oh, yeah, there are girls. And sometimes, I mean there are *girls*."

Ozzie found himself grinning. There were some girls, well, that *were* worth a second look. And some of them even looked back, as long as he kept his mouth shut.

"But Uncle Brady says no messing around with girls on the wagon train. Of course, he married Aunt Tess when she was a tourist on the Rocking T, but whenever I rag on him about that he says there were 'extenuating circumstances.' What do you think that means?"

Ozzie wasn't sure whether Ira was asking what 'extenuating' meant—which Ozzie knew—or what Brady's circumstances had been—which he didn't. But he wasn't about to ask because he knew he'd never get through the words without making a fool of himself. And so far, Ira wasn't laughing at him. In fact, Ira seemed so eager for a friend his own age that he was actually acting as though he enjoyed Ozzie's company.

Ozzie wasn't going to put much stock in that possibility, but he did rather like the feeling.

"I don't know," he answered lamely. "I guess it m-m-means he married her."

Again Ira grinned. "I'm glad he did. My Uncle Brady was the loneliest fellow in the world until he met Aunt Tess. Now he's even got a baby! Wow. Anything can happen, you know."

On that bright note he said goodbye and bounced off toward the restaurant, leaving Ozzie to ponder both Ira's cheerful friendliness and his last optimistic comment.

Lately he'd been giving a lot of thought to his future, and he'd talked to Clay about it once or twice. He wanted to believe that anything could happen; he had a lot of dreams that he desperately wished could come true. And he knew that Clay would do everything to help him. So would his folks. But the fact of the matter was that none of them had a magic wand that would make his stutter disappear.

He hid a smile as he heard Clay sweet-talking Violet while he led her toward the barn. The other men were right behind him, bringing in the rest of the camels after the afternoon races.

"Good work today, Warner," Clay told the gold-toothed cowboy who had performed the Cossack stunts with him. "You up for another show tomorrow?"

"Why wouldn't I be?" asked the bowlegged man. "I been ridin' since you were in diapers, Clay. I'll still be ridin' when they put you in the ground."

Clay grunted noncommittally as Warner sidled off with several camels and George and Roscoe, the other cowboys who supervised the camel herd on the road. Ozzie was never quite certain if he should join the other men, stay with Clay, or just get out of everybody's way. Today he opted to hang around, at least until Clay finished rubbing down Violet. Besides, he had a question to ask his boss, though it took him a good ten minutes of small talk to lead up to it.

"Clay?" he finally muttered.

"Mmm?"

"D-d-do you think I could t-t-take some classes by mail or something?"

Clay shrugged, his eyes on Violet's feet as he scratched her sweat-slick belly. "Sure thing, Oz. If you want to. But it's sort of the coward's way out, don't you think?"

It wasn't quite the answer Ozzie was looking for. Actually he wasn't looking for an answer so much as a solution. Somehow he wanted Clay to make it happen, to whisk away his fear and his stutter, to make him into the man Clay himself had become. Clay was his hero, his idol, his mentor. Clay had licked his boyhood problems and gone from a wimp to a blue-ribbon winner. Ozzie wanted to do the same.

Ozzie tried again. "Even if I c-c-can't be a vet, I c-c-could learn a little bit more about how to t-t-take care of the stock."

Now he had Clay's full attention. "The University of Colorado is only fifteen minutes away from the ranch, Oz, and there's no finer vet school anywhere. And there's half a dozen choices for undergrad work in Denver if you'd rather live with your folks."

Ozzie didn't answer. Convenience had nothing to do with his rocky plans for college.

Before he could press the issue further, he spotted Tess Trent and her friend, the tall one who gave speeches, heading his way. Briefly Ozzie watched the two exchange some quick words, and it was obvious from the look on the tall one's face that it had been Tess's idea to come talk to Clay.

He tried to clear his throat to tell his boss they had company, but Clay spotted them by himself.

"Howdy, Tess," he murmured. "Howdy, Bobbie Jean."

There was an edge to Clay's voice that Ozzie had not heard before, a tightening that could have signaled pleasure or distress. The only thing Ozzie was sure of was that Clay's feigned casualness might fool a stranger, but it would never fool a close friend.

Clay turned to Ozzie and said, "Have you met Tess's friend? This is Roberta Wheeler, aka Susan B. Anthony." His eyes flitted back toward Roberta but did not linger. "This is Ozzie Edwards, my right-hand man."

Ozzie tried not to visibly swell with pride, but he always felt a little light-headed when Clay praised him that way.

"Nice to see you, Ozzie," said Tess after he and Roberta had exchanged hellos. Roberta, he noticed, didn't seem too interested in anybody but Baby Bev, who was snuggling up to Violet at the time. But while she patted the baby camel, she seemed to be eyeing Violet's saddle on the fence. Then again, considering that Clay was standing near the fence himself, she might have been eyeing Clay.

"Clay, I've got a message from my hubby," Tess continued brightly. "He said the Utes looked good wandering the streets last night but he overheard somebody ask why there were Indians and no soldiers. He wants to know if you can be Lieutenant Beale this evening."

For some reason, Clay glanced at Roberta before he answered.

"What do you mean 'be' Lieutenant Beale? You just want me to dress up and walk around?"

Tess shrugged. "Sure. What else?"

"He could lead a charge on camelback," suggested Roberta. She was a tall woman—a lot taller than Ozzie—but he noticed that she only came to the bottom of Clay's thick mustache. "Or I could share the platform with you this afternoon if you want to enlighten the crowd about camels."

This time when Clay's lips tightened, Ozzie didn't have to wonder why. On a scale of one to ten, he knew that giving a public speech—even about camels—rated about a minus three with Clay. Just the mention of it was making his boss's fists clench into tight balls at his side. But the chautauqua woman, he was certain, had no way of knowing she'd just stabbed Clay in his Achilles' heel.

"I'm too busy here to waste time speechifying," Clay snapped.

Roberta's eyes opened a shade too wide, and Ozzie could see her edge ever so slightly back. It was a subtle motion, one he would never have noticed if he weren't so sensitive to the slightest rebuff. But Clay spotted it, bit his lower lip, and then apologized.

"I didn't mean to cast aspersions on your own duties here this weekend, Roberta," he said a bit stiffly. "I only meant that *my* schedule is pretty full with the races and riding. Besides, I don't have anything... uh... prepared."

Roberta stared at him, but said nothing.

"You gave a fine speech yesterday. You're very good at public speaking." His tone was low, cautious.

"Thank you," said Roberta. Her tone was clipped.

"I mean it." He sounded almost angry now. "You're great behind a podium. You're a natural."

She nodded, just once, as though to acknowledge his praise. "I've been trained to speak effectively. It's part of my job."

"Of course."

Ozzie sensed the anger there, the anger he knew had been triggered by her suggestion that Clay speak. But there was something else in his boss's voice that was new to him, something Ozzie suspected had nothing to do with public speaking.

"Uh, Clay, can you dress the part?" Tess asked, studying Clay and Roberta with a look on her face that revealed much the same confusion Ozzie himself was feeling. "All you have to do is stroll around."

Clay nodded, but he kept his eyes on Roberta. "I can stroll." There was a long silence until he added softly, "But I'll look pretty silly strolling alone. An officer wouldn't come into town on a Saturday night without a bunch of fellow cavalrymen unless he had a date with a young lady."

Roberta's spine seemed to straighten. The tiniest flush lit her cheeks.

"Maybe Roberta could stay in costume and walk with you," Tess suggested, since nobody else seemed to be saying anything.

"That's a g-g-good idea," seconded Ozzie. Normally he didn't volunteer comments that might force him to reveal his stutter to a stranger, but he was sure that Roberta had long since forgotten he was standing there. Besides, the awkward pauses were getting eerie.

"I could do that if Clay wants me to." Roberta was speaking to Tess but looking at Clay, who was still facing her stiffly. Ozzie couldn't tell if he was trying to keep himself from moving closer or trying to get away.

For what seemed like an endless moment, punctuated only by a camel's groan, nobody said anything. At least not with words. Ozzie could tell that Clay and Roberta were having some kind of urgent conversation with their eyes, but it was in secret code—lovers' code?—and he knew that no third party was ever going to translate their unspoken feelings.

At last Clay said, "Walk with me."

Roberta's shoulders lifted, and her chin edged up just a fraction of an inch. In a husky tone which wasn't quite a whisper but wasn't the same tone she'd have used to talk out loud, she answered stoutly, "I'll walk."

Ozzie had the strangest feeling that neither one of them remembered that all Brady had in mind was some background color during the Bear Dance of the Utes.

CHAPTER THREE

BY SEVEN O'CLOCK that evening, Roberta felt as though her whalebone corset had been laced up far too tightly...and she wasn't even wearing one. Her breathing was shaky by the time she spotted Clay heading up the wooden sidewalk to the Last Stop Hotel.

It was the first weekend that the place was in operation, and Tess had asked her to take a room to check everything out before a paying guest could encounter any problems. Roberta loved the room, but she'd had to tell Tess that there were a few rough edges yet. The bed was charmingly adorned with a homemade quilt, but it had been missing one sheet. The window had opened just fine to let in some cool air in the morning, but had refused to budge when Roberta had tried to keep out the heat of the afternoon. And when she'd tried to close the calico curtains to dress for the evening, the curtains—rod and all—had come right off the wall.

She'd chosen a different dress for the evening, appropriate for the period but frothy and dramatic enough for a young woman on a Saturday night. It was a blue-green silk taffeta with a multi-flounced long skirt, huge puffed sleeves and an airy petal-and-bow trim. She told herself that her job was to get into the character that Clay would need as a foil for Lieutenant Beale. She also told herself that the reason her palms were sweaty was that she was such a fine actress. She was feeling the "young woman's" tension.

And then she told herself, *Roberta Wheeler, you lie.*

She wasn't sure just how she felt about Clay, and she wasn't sure whether or not he'd read her hurt as anger that afternoon. She certainly had no idea why he'd asked her to spend the evening with him when he'd given her the brush off the night before. She wasn't even sure what she wanted him to do.

She only knew that she felt off kilter just thinking about him. And off kilter was a curiously unsettling and peculiarly joyful way to feel.

He knocked on the door at seven-oh-three, three minutes exactly past the time he was due. He was wearing a clean but faded cavalry uniform, brass-buttoned, gold-braided, in a beguiling shade of dark blue. Under one arm was a forage cap. In his free hand was a clump of wild columbines.

"For you, Bobbie Jean," he drawled almost sweetly. As he handed her the flowers their fingers touched, and Roberta felt a quiet shiver at the unexpected contact. She wasn't accustomed to feeling wobbly in the presence of men, and she wasn't sure that she liked the feeling now. There *was* a certain delicious dizziness to the way she felt when Clay touched her, but she felt insecure when she was out of control.

"Sorry I'm late," he told her with a rakish grin, "but my pony threw a shoe."

So that's how we're going to play it tonight, she realized, grateful that he'd laid the ground rules for both of them. *We keep safely to our roles and everything will be just fine.*

"Why, think nothin' of it, Lieutenant," she forced herself to drawl in reply, gingerly removing her fingers from the vicinity of his tempting hands. "When I see wildflowers as lovely as these, you know Ah just cain't stay mad with you."

She batted her eyelashes once or twice and pasted on a goofy grin. Clay grinned so widely that she knew she'd passed muster.

"Come along, sweet petunia," he ordered comically, offering her his arm. "Ah understand the natives will be puttin' on a wild show this evening on the main street of town. But not to worry. Ah won't let my buttercup come to any harm."

Roberta slipped her hand through the crook of his elbow, feeling at ease in her promenading pose. The artifice was comforting, somehow. If this had been a first date, she would have had to make small talk with Clay. Under the circumstances, Bobbie Jean only had to act silly with this talkative young officer.

She tried to think about what young lovers would have discussed one hundred and fifty years ago on such a pristine evening, when the pungent scent of ponderosa pine hung in the air. Off in the distance, a red and pink sunset beckoned, as though somebody had set up a romantic backdrop for their real-life stage. Nearby, the happy bustle of Saturday night filled the once-empty ghost town. The players were already in action.

Mentally getting into her own role, Roberta saucily asked her escort, "How long have you been in the Army, Lieutenant?"

He took her query in stride. "Makes two years now, Bobbie Jean. Never thought I'd end up a soldier, though. I grew up in the eastern part of this territory on a cattle ranch big as any they've got in Texas."

"So why'd you choose the Army for a career?"

"Oh, it wasn't the dust of the cattle ranch I wanted to shake, Miz Bobbie Jean, if that's what you're askin'," he replied. "I loved the land and I loved my daddy, but my mama was a city girl from Baltimore who couldn't be bothered with dirty little boys. She had plans for me that I couldn't abide. Politics, you know. Wanted to send me to her relations back east."

"So you headed west," Roberta observed sagely.

"Yes, ma'am. Counted the minutes till I turned eighteen, then lit out as fast as I could go."

Roberta smiled at him, because it was what her role called for her to do. But suddenly she realized that she couldn't ignore the hint of leftover pain in Clay's tone. Despite the joking, she was certain that he was telling her the truth, and suddenly it seemed imperative that she tell him the truth, too.

"I'm sorry things were so rough at home, Clay," she said softly.

He looked surprised at her willingness to break character, but he did not deny her observation. "My mother had no business marrying my dad," he told her in his own voice, lightly covering her hand with quiet intimacy as they crossed the busy street. Cheerful throngs filled the wooden sidewalks and leaned against the permanently parked stagecoach in front of the hotel. Honky-tonk music blared from an old saloon. "She wanted somebody else altogether. Just liked the raw material and decided to fashion him into the man she had in mind." His eyes met Roberta's with a hint of fire. "When she failed in that attempt, she thought she'd try to mold me in her image instead."

"And failed again, I take it," said Roberta.

He nodded. "I was a major disappointment to her. I failed at everything she tried to make me do. Every time my dad *invited* me to try something his way, I was a success. Not that my dad was perfect, you understand," he told her, "but he never tried to make me into somebody I wasn't. He always loved me for myself."

As Roberta listened to the lingering bitterness in his voice, she realized that Clay had really confessed a great deal about himself. And she realized that she had admitted very little.

But before she could speak, he continued with his tale. "You know, he did love her, in his own way. As much as she hurt him, he never wanted her to go away." He shook his head at some unfaded memory. "Once we were driving through Kansas on the way to visit my grandparents—her folks—and this good-looking fellow started flirting with Mom by a gas station vending machine while Dad was putting gas in the pickup. I guess the guy thought she was alone, because he made a pass at her, and he didn't take the hint when she told him to back off. I was watching all this from the front seat of our truck, you know, waiting to see what Dad would do." He cocked one eyebrow at Roberta, as if to ascertain her continued interest. "He waited, and watched, and never said a word until the guy put his arm around Mom's shoulders and she physically tried to push him away—you know, put both hands on his chest. She cried out, 'No!' just once, but pretty loud, and Dad bolted over the bumper and punched the guy out in a flash."

Clay's smile was twisted, more a grimace than a grin. "I thought it was great. I thought she'd be pleased. But after he got into a full-scale brawl and somebody called the cops, Mom called Dad a Neanderthal and claimed that he'd embarrassed her to tears. She didn't speak to him again until we reached Nebraska."

Roberta wasn't sure how to respond to this story; she wasn't sure just why Clay had shared it with her. Obviously it had some special meaning for him. Uncertainly she asked, "Do you think your dad did the right thing?"

He lifted his chin, considering the question for a minute, then replied, "Probably not. But he did it for the right *reason*, and she never understood that. When he died of a heart attack at fifty, she was downright resentful; said he'd worked himself to death. She insisted that if he'd given up the ranch and let her father set him up in business in Baltimore, he'd have lived forever."

This time Roberta didn't need to ask Clay's opinion. Softly she suggested, "But you know that if he'd gone to Baltimore, he would have died at twenty-nine."

Clay's smile of gratitude for her quick understanding warmed her. "I would have died, too, if I'd gone with her to Maryland. Fortunately I was seventeen at the time and she wanted me to finish my senior year while she got things in order. Then she went east with the cash from Dad's ranch and I went west with his lucky Stetson, and that's the end of the story."

Roberta stared at him, a bit surprised. "You haven't seen her since?"

He shrugged. "I saw her once or twice. I wrote her when I could. But she didn't last too much longer than Dad did. Had cancer of the pancreas. I got what was left from the sale of my Dad's ranch after she died."

And I've had no family since then, he might as well have added. Roberta didn't need to ask if he'd ever been married; Tess would surely have mentioned it by now.

They were strolling past the Trents' jailhouse for about the third time that evening, but this time the sight of it seemed to bring Clay up short. Abruptly he stopped and stared at Roberta, letting her hand slip from his arm. "Now how'd you get me to tell you all that, Bobbie Jean?" he asked in honest wonder, letting Lieutenant Beale's drawl reclaim his voice. "I've got no huge secrets, but I don't usually spill my guts the first time a pretty li'l lady gets me alone on a moonlit stroll."

Roberta smiled. She knew why he'd told her so much of his past. Despite his contradictory behavior, he wanted to get to know her better; he wanted her to get to know *him*.

"I take it you were an only child, Lieutenant," she suggested flirtatiously, trying to follow his lead without letting the intimate moment slip away. "I was the youngest of four."

He studied her for a moment, as though trying to decide if he wanted to keep the conversation personal or retreat once more into the character of Lieutenant Beale. Then he held out his elbow and made a show of helping Roberta cross the dusty street. Once they were on the other side and retracing the route they'd just taken, he asked jovially, "Boys or girls, sweet petunia?"

"All boys," she admitted, her affection for her brothers warming her sassy tone. She was thrilled that Clay seemed willing to continue the personal conversation, even though he'd retreated into the relative safety of his chosen role. "All bossy, rough, and passionately protective if any man so much as looked cross-eyed at me. I wrestled with all of them from the time I was born. They taught me how to handle menfolk, all right. They just didn't give me much training in how to be a girl."

Clay's deep gray eyes swept over her face, then down to the comparatively low neckline of her taffeta gown.

His appreciation for the view was unmistakable. "I reckon some things just come naturally, Bobbie Jean. Don't you worry none on that account."

Roberta felt a rush of pleasure that was new to her; she even felt her nipples tighten under his flattering gaze. Ever since she'd first met Clay she'd felt this curious sense of kinship...and this baffling sensual yearning that seemed mutual only about half of the time. She tried not to worry about his withdrawal the previous night, or his baffling anger in the morning. All that mattered was that he seemed to be drawn to her *now*.

Clay's eyes met hers, and his grip seemed to tighten on the feminine hand that lay on his arm. His long thigh, brushing hers despite the layers of fabric, seemed to grow taut and move ever so slightly in her direction. His free hand slowly edged toward her waist, and Roberta suppressed a shudder of anticipation as she waited for him to pull her closer.

But the tense, silent moment of hope was suddenly smashed when Clay was hailed by a trio of booted and spurred cowboys clanging along the wooden sidewalk. Two of them were strangers to Roberta, but she recognized the short one as Clay's partner in the trick-riding show.

"Clay, you old polecat, what the hell are you up to?" he asked, eyeing Roberta with interest. "We ain't been in town more than twenty-four hours and we spent halfa that time shoveling manure. But here you got—"

"Warner, this is Roberta Wheeler, a friend of Tess Trent's," Clay introduced her soberly, as though a bit embarrassed by his friend. He didn't release her, exactly, but he swiveled in such a manner that she felt as though he'd thrust her away. "Roberta, these are three of the best cowboys west of the Mississippi—Warner, George and Roscoe. They just happen to be lucky enough to work for me."

Warner nodded; Roscoe doffed his hat. George shuffled his feet and said, "Howdy, ma'am."

"Brady asked us to promenade in costume," Clay declared, as though Roberta's presence on his arm required an explanation.

"Prom-a-what?" asked baldheaded Roscoe.

"Don't ya go talkin' fancy on us again, Clay," joshed Warner. "Honest to God, why can't ya never talk like a regular fella?"

A muscle worked in Clay's jaw, and the darkness in his eyes confirmed Roberta's hunch that he might have been embarrassed by the arrival of his men. Listening to Clay, it was easy to assume that he, like Brady, was a solid rancher with an impressive education. Looking at him with his employees—his friends?—she wondered. Obviously he was better educated than his men, but a sudden vision of Charles Trumbull with this group made Roberta wish she could get away. Not from Clay, of course . . . but from the others.

"Man rides a horse like that thinks he don't need no manners," observed skinny George, looking apologetically at Roberta as he cocked his head disparagingly at Warner. "Don't pay him no need, miss. You just go ahead and look pretty, now."

Roberta tried not to sizzle; the middle-aged man was clearly trying to be kind. Still, she suddenly knew she didn't want to prolong this conversation with Clay's rustic cowboys. Deciding that it would be safer, under the circumstances, to take the role of Bobbie Jean than Dr. Wheeler, she batted her eyes and said, "Why,

Lieutenant, I believe I'm catchin' a chill. Could we go back to the hotel for my shawl?"

Warner chuckled. His gold tooth seemed to leap through his knowing grin. "Woman wants to take you up to her room, Clay. I'd get a move on if I were you."

"Shut up, Warner," Roscoe muttered, coloring slightly. He grabbed the other man's arm and tugged. "Nice to meet you, ma'am."

Roberta nodded. "A pleasure meeting all of you."

Clay said nothing, but pointedly led her in the general direction of the Last Stop Hotel. She tried to decide if she approved of the way he'd handled the situation. His men *had* been a little disrespectful—especially the trick rider, Warner—yet surely Clay ran a loose shop where humor was the byword, and they only seemed to be having fun. She thought about his father's reaction to the man who'd pressed his mother in Kansas, and decided that she'd rather handle any rowdy cowboys herself if anything ever needed to be done.

"They're decent fellows, Roberta," Clay apologized as they strolled on down the street much as they had before the interruption. "Warner's got a swelled head because he's so damn good on horseback, but he's not a bad guy at heart."

Roberta shivered as she remembered the daredevil feats Warner and Clay had performed that morning. Even now it was hard to think about it, hard to still the sudden rapid beating of her heart. Was it the mention of Clay's performance that so electrified and alarmed her, she wondered, or was it the memory of her own riding feats? Trying to focus on the present, she asked in a quiet voice, "How long have you two been riding together?"

"Oh, about six years. Warner's been a bulldogger, broncbuster, rodeo clown—you name it, he's done it. He even taught me a few things I didn't know."

There was no false pride in his tone. Clearly he took his excellence on horseback for granted.

"Did he teach you to rope?"

"Naw, my daddy taught me that." He acted as though his skill was commonplace, but Roberta knew better.

"Do the sponsors of these country fairs really book you for the camels," she asked him, "or is your trick riding the big draw?" She tried to control the quiet tremor in her voice triggered by the memory of the risks he'd taken with Warner, but Clay looked at her so closely that she wondered if he sensed her fear. "Some of those stunts," she heard herself saying, "look rather dangerous."

Clay shrugged off her concern. "We're not careless. We don't do anything in a show we haven't mastered months before. If your muscles are in good shape and you're always alert for the unexpected, you can bail out in time if anything goes wrong."

"Not always," Roberta countered before she had time to stop herself. Her eyes met his in suddenly remembered panic. "Sometimes things just happen too fast."

Clay studied her for a long moment, so long that she was certain he'd guessed her secret. Those quiet gray eyes seemed to know too much, probe too deeply. A moment ago she'd longed for this kind of silent understanding, but there were some things about her past she preferred that Clay not know.

Suddenly desperate to change the subject to something safer, she blurted out, "How did you get interested in camel racing? You have to admit that it is a rather, uh, unique sport."

Clay laughed, the prior moment's tension apparently forgotten. "That's what I like best about it. Makes me stand out in a crowd."

That's not the only thing, Roberta could have added. There was a lot she could have told him about the way he impressed an audience, and the impact he made on her when he wasn't even in a show. She could have told him that every time he touched her, she wanted to curl up against him; every time he smiled she wanted to toss away the artifice of roles. But he was on his soapbox again, preaching the gospel of camels, and Roberta could find no way to tell him she ached for some hint that she affected him, too.

Hadn't he been heading in that direction before Warner and the others had shown up? And once or twice before that? The feeling between them tonight was like a mighty ocean wave—swirling, frothy, powerful. Roberta's senses had been battered by Clay's provocative hands all evening. A steady undertow of desire for this man was tugging her into his open sea.

"Actually I stumbled on camels when I was reading a book about the west," Clay informed her cheerfully, as though he were oblivious to her rising need for some glimmer of his affection. "I was fascinated by Lieutenant Beale and all he went through trying to get the Camel Corps established. He was so frustrated by everything—the slow Joes in Washington, the terrified horses, the prejudice of the cowboys. But he insisted that camels were friendly, reliable and misunderstood. Since I'd always seen myself in the same light, I thought maybe I'd get along well with a camel." He grinned mischievously. "I bought Violet on a lark. Named her for my favorite aunt. After that my interest in camels grew by leaps and bounds, and I named each one for a relative. Fortunately the camel racing thing in Virginia City was just getting off the ground about the same time, so it all came together pretty—" He broke off suddenly as the sound of distant drums caused a dozen heads to turn toward the south end of town.

"Well, I'll be switched!" Clay drawled, suddenly back in his Army role. "Ah reckon that's Harry Painted Hat and his Injun pals. I've never seen them in action, sweet thing, but I've read a lot about the Ute Bear Dance. Ah understand it's quite a spectacle."

Roberta was at a bit of a loss. Aside from Clay's unpredictable mood swings this evening, she was startled by his expertise in areas where *she* should have been the expert. Although she was a specialist in western history, she'd never read a word about the Utes' version of the Bear Dance! She only knew that Tess and Brady had chosen it for Patchwork's opening weekend because Harry could provide dancers from the nearby reservation.

Letting her role conceal her ignorance, she batted her eyelashes again and said, "Why, Lieutenant, you know a li'l ol' country girl like me doesn't know much about Indians out here in the west. I'd love to hear all about the Bear Dance."

Clay studied her for just a moment, as though he wasn't quite sure whether or not she was teasing him. It was the moment of vulnerability that warmed her. It also made her wonder—as she had a dozen times all day—what she'd said at the corral in the morning to aggravate him. He'd blown hot and cold during the dinner at the Broken Wheel, but he'd never seemed downright angry. Last night she was fairly certain that he, like so many other men she knew, had been put off by her education. But she hadn't mentioned a word about school this morning. All they'd discussed was strolling around Patchwork and giving public speeches.

With a subtle wink, Clay started one now. "Well, you see there was this fine Ute hunter, Bobbie Jean, who came upon a monstrously shaggy bear dancing outside his cave after a long winter nap. And the bear told the hunter that he would become—distinguished, shall we say—with the lady Utes if he performed this dance each spring."

"Distinguished, Lieutenant?" she coaxed with mocking innocence.

Clay grinned at her almost rakishly. "He would impress them with his fine hunting skills," he clarified.

"Oh, I see." She smothered a laugh. "So ever since, the Ute men have done this dance in the spring so the ladies would be, uh, impressed?"

He chuckled and patted her hand, which was still in the crook of his uniformed arm. Her fingers unconsciously fondled the rough fabric. "Actually the way the dance is set up, all the Utes dance together, but the ladies do the asking. They all get in two lines—men on one side, women on the other—and dance until they're ready to collapse."

"Do they ever?"

"Collapse? Yes, sometimes. And then the men in charge of things poke them with raspy flutes to rev things up again. And in the mean time, the strongest ones break off in pairs. The man puts one arm around the woman's waist, like this—" he demonstrated with sure, warm hands "—and she puts one arm around him."

Roberta needed no urging to slide one arm around Clay's waist. Her only problem was figuring out what to do with her free arm. He seemed to be having the same problem.

"After that the dancing gets rather, uh, athletic, so the free arm is, uh, moving around."

Roberta lifted her free arm and moved a little closer, keenly aware that Clay was nearly close enough to brush her breast with his mustache. She thrust away a sudden fantasy of having him do just that, but her nipple tightened anyway. "Athletic, Lieutenant?" she managed to ask. "Whatever do you mean?"

He grinned again, and she wasn't sure whether the "Aw shucks, ma'am" look on his face belonged to Clay Gann or Lieutenant Beale. "They wriggle around a lot, Bobbie Jean. They do whatever the music tells them."

She felt his arm tighten around her waist; she felt him pull her ever so slightly forward. His glance dropped provocatively to her moist lips.

Suddenly the silk taffeta seemed to close in on Roberta; she couldn't quite breathe. She no longer cared what the Ute couples did *during* the Bear Dance; it was what they did afterward that she wondered about.

Bravely she raised her eyes to Clay's, and saw the strange, warm stirring there. His glance caressed her face, then centered lower, on her comparatively subtle cleavage. Her body quickened, and she instinctively leaned forward. Clay's free hand edged down to brace her waist, and she laid her hand on his arm.

He's going to kiss me, her instincts shouted. *And I'm not going to hold anything back.*

But an instant before his lips could find hers, a veritable thunder of drumbeats began to shake the old wooden sidewalk. As one body, she and Clay turned in the direction of the sound. The crowd seemed to part, to hush, and when the dancers made their appearance, a communal "Oooooh!" swept through the ghost town.

The sight was so glorious that it caused her to tremble.

The men were dressed much as Harry had been the night before—in leggings made out of elkskin or buffalo, beaded moccasins and layer upon layer of shells or beads around their necks. The women were similarly adorned, but they also wore brightly painted deerskin skirts. Most of the dancers had feathers in their hair.

The women stayed on one side of the street, the men on the other, in what Roberta assumed was a modification of the original dance around a Ute camp fire. Still, the all-male orchestra, brandishing flutelike instruments and ponderous skin drums, filled the air with such excitement that nobody was likely to worry about minor technical inaccuracies. Roberta was overwhelmed with the drama...and awed by this living moment of the past.

"Oh, Clay," she whispered, still half cradled in his arms...still aching to feel his lips claim hers. "Aren't they magnificent! Look at Harry! My God, he really *does* know how to dance!"

But the surge of tourists blocked her view almost at once, and this frustration was almost as great as the denial of Clay's kiss. For a moment his gray eyes warmed her hazel ones, and she felt a rocket of need shoot from his essence to hers. Was it the excitement brought on by the drums—or maybe the dancers—that made her feel so dizzy? Or the majestic feeling Clay brought to her own heart?

As though he could read her mind, Clay took her hand and ordered huskily, "Follow me!" as he threaded his way through the gawking throng of tourists. In a matter of moments, he reached the parked stagecoach in front of the Last Stop, hoisted her up to the driver's seat and clamored up beside her.

To brace himself, he stretched one long arm out behind Roberta and gripped the wooden seat behind her. His biceps brushed her back. Roberta wrapped both hands around her knees and leaned close enough to brush against his side. She tingled from head to toe as she watched the men beat the ground with their feet, conveying a traditional message of respect for their gods that had survived for several hundred years. And then, abruptly, the shiver turned to a different kind of chill as she realized that Clay's arm was now fully wrapped around her; his fingers, surprisingly warm and tempting, teased her bare arm. She glanced up at him—surprised, confused, hopeful—and found him quietly studying her instead of the dancers.

His gray eyes were full of longing, full of fire. There was no longer any question in her mind that he wanted her. It was miraculous; it made no sense, but it was undeniable.

For some reason, Roberta could no longer hear the tremendously loud drums. All she could hear was Clay's soft drawl as he pulled her closer.

"It wouldn't be fittin' for an officer to let his young lady get a chill, Bobbie Jean."

She leaned toward him, trying to think of the right thing to say at this critical juncture. Roberta Wheeler would say bluntly, "I'm not cold, Clay, but I want you to put your arm around me anyway." Susan B. Anthony would have said, "If I'm cold, sir, I'll get my own coat. I need no man to coddle me." And as for this

Texas belle, Bobbie Jean, she'd probably say, "Why, Lieutenant, aren't you the sweetest li'l thing?"

She tried to say it; she really did. But with the heat of Clay's body warming her womanly impulses and her long-lonely heart, Roberta suddenly wanted to be honest with Clay. She was frightened that she'd blow it and he'd think her a fool, but at least she'd know that she'd been true to herself.

It was a gamble, but once she made the decision, the words slipped out on their own. "I really like you, Clay," she confessed, her voice straightforward but full of feeling. She swallowed hard, wishing he'd say that he felt the same way, but afraid to wait for his answer. "I know we live pretty far apart, but if we work at it I'm sure we could find a way to get together again."

Clay's eyes grew wide; the virile arm around her tightened. Roberta felt him suck in a deep breath, felt his heat as he battled with some powerful desire. To pull her closer? To push her away?

His compelling gaze seemed to swallow her whole, seemed to pierce beyond all privacy into her deepest thoughts. *He knows how much I want him,* she suddenly realized, embarrassed that she'd been so terribly up-front. *I must be losing my mind. I've never come right out and told a man I wanted him before.*

Clay licked his lips. His heated knee seemed to press against Roberta's. The contact jump-started her female feelings, gave her a rush somewhere deep within that she felt helpless to control.

For just a moment, his glance once more dropped to her ready lips, as though he were going to claim her for sure this time. She had just started to lean toward him, her eyes closed, her heart hopeful, when she felt his body leave her. Her eyes flashed open—shocked, wounded—as she watched him gently pull away.

A long moment passed with nothing but silence between them; the wild rasps and drumbeats were only white noise. Miles were stretching between his chest and hers.

"You're a right fine filly, Bobbie Jean," Clay slowly drawled, his voice thick and husky, as though period speech were an effort now. "Why, if I didn't have orders to take the herd to Californy with the First Dragoons, ain't nothin' could keep me from beggin' you on bended knee. But I'm married to th' Calv'ry, don't you see, so there's no use in any young lady hopin' for what will never be."

Roberta wasn't sure which was worse—the belly-deep pain of his rejection or the red flush of embarrassment that branded her cheeks. All she knew was that a moment later, the dance ended, and she was deafened by the applause. Clay removed his arm from the wooden seat in order to clap, but it didn't seem to her that he was clapping very hard. A moment later he hopped off the stage, and though he reached up to help Roberta, he turned away the instant she was safely on the ground.

CHAPTER FOUR

CLAY WAS FILLING water buckets for the camels on Sunday afternoon when he saw Roberta approaching the far corral. She was wearing her wine-colored Susan B. outfit again, the one she'd been wearing when he'd first seen her speak on Friday. She looked good in it, but more distant, less vulnerable, than she had in that sexy taffeta thing she'd been wearing last night. Last night when she'd all but begged him to kiss her.

Last night when he'd had to force himself to walk away.

Clay wondered, for just a moment, if Roberta might be looking for him now. But after last night, he had a feeling that she would go out of her way to keep a safe distance. There had to be some other reason for her trip to the corral.

There was. While Clay watched from the shadows, she hitched up her skirts and crawled under the fence and—to his amazement—began whispering sweetly to the infant camel who watched her from its mother's side.

"You're not afraid of strangers, are you, sweetie?" she greeted the tiny, leggy creature. "If you are you just tell me, and I'll back off. I don't want to scare you. I just wanted to say goodbye."

Clay was shocked. In the first place, he would never have expected anyone—let alone a woman—to take the risk of walking into a corral full of half-tamed camels. In the second place, he would have staked his last bottom dollar on the certainty that tough Roberta Wheeler didn't know a single word of baby talk.

As she approached the baby camel—coming close enough to show her interest, but being careful not to startle the tiny beast—she glanced once at Luscious Laura, the mother, and greeted her nonchalantly as well. "Don't you glare at me, Mama. I won't hurt your baby. I won't hurt you, either. In fact, I would have brought you some sugar if I'd been able to clear it first. Once some idiot stuffed my Flame full of apples just before a show and he got colic and nearly died. So, sorry, sweetie, but no sugar until I get the word from Clay." She paused for a moment and then added stoically, "Assuming I ever see him again."

There was a wistful tone in her voice he hadn't heard before, and he wondered, for the first time, just how she'd reacted to the way he'd been treating her for the past two days. Most of their time together had been full of laughter, full of fun, but right from the start there had been undercurrents of something special between the two of them. And then, Clay had discovered her attitude toward higher education and the whole world of academic success—epitomized by her department head. Charles Trumbull. What a classic name! He couldn't imagine Roberta introducing a boss with a name like that to "Clayton Gann, the Camel Man."

Still, he was keenly drawn to the woman. He couldn't deny it. And he wondered if he'd really been fair to Roberta by hiding his cowardice under a mask of courtesy when she'd been so utterly straight with him the night before. It would have been more honest to do what he'd been dying to do all weekend—kiss her until she begged for more.

Luscious Laura, her sole focus on her hay, only glanced lazily at Roberta. Baby Bev, on the other hand, seemed interested in the newcomer and ambled over to nuzzle her hand.

"Ah, that's my sweetie," Roberta told the little camel. "Oh, my, you're soft. You feel just like a foal." Gently she stroked the neck and patted the tiny hump, while the camel pressed her cheek against Roberta's ribs. "You know when somebody likes you, don't you, precious? Everybody has something nasty to say about camels, but they don't know anything, do they? You guys are just misunderstood."

By this time Clay was beginning to feel like a Peeping Tom. Granted, Roberta had hardly said anything personal to Baby Bev, but he had a feeling that the tenderness she'd revealed to the infant camel was not a side of her she showed to many people. It was most certainly not a predictable streak of her strong-willed personality.

Making a great deal of noise with his pail of water, Clay marched into the barn as though he'd just arrived and was startled to see he had a visitor. With studied nonchalance, he said, "Well, hi, there, Bobbie Jean. I see you came to chat with our latest arrival."

Roberta stiffened a bit—as though she really hadn't been expecting to see him—but she kept on stroking the small hump. "Well, I've never met a juvenile camel before this weekend, Clay. I try to broaden my experiences whenever possible. There are some things you can't learn in a book."

Clay managed to chuckle. "Really? I had the impression that you thought book learning was all that mattered."

Roberta eyed him closely. "I'm an educator, Clay, and I do love books. I couldn't survive without reading. But that doesn't mean that I don't appreciate other aspects of life."

"Like camels?"

She favored him with a cautious smile. "I'm fond of animals," she admitted. "After all, I was raised on a ranch."

"Were you? I don't think you mentioned that before." In fact, he was certain that she hadn't mentioned it, even though she'd had plenty of logical opportunities.

She shrugged. "Well, it's hardly something I put on my résumé. All of us have something in our childhood we'd just as soon forget, don't you think?"

It wasn't the first time Clay had heard an educated person disparage a rural upbringing, but he didn't get the feeling that Roberta was bad-mouthing ranch life. There was a note of sorrow in her voice that hinted at regret, a sense of loss, rather than a rejection of her childhood home.

"Sure, but growing up on a ranch is at the top of my list of things I'm grateful for. You don't learn to be a cowboy sitting in some college class."

Roberta flinched. "You don't learn to do trick riding, either. My daddy's good with a rope, but he can't hold a candle to you."

He grinned. It was almost a compliment. "Oh, a lot of it's luck," he lied modestly. "And it helps if you know a few tricks. If you're nice to me I could teach you a few."

Come up and see my etchings, he might as well have said, surprised to realize that he was flirting with her once again. He was not a man who normally had much trouble distinguishing between right and wrong and sensible and stupid. Yet all of his mental circuits told him to keep his distance from this college professor, and all of his heartstrings started twanging whenever she came into view.

Guilt battled with desire as he saw the faintest glimmer of hope light Roberta's eyes. *Did I really hurt her last night?* he wondered. She hadn't given him a clue about her feelings after he'd lifted her off the stage coach. In fact she'd stuck doggedly to her Texas belle role for the rest of the evening, and they'd parted on a lighthearted note.

Now, almost shyly, she asked, "Could you really show me a trick or two? Like how you rope Ozzie backward? You wouldn't be violating any performers' code if you revealed your secrets, would you?"

How many secrets would I like to reveal to you, he longed to tell her. *Starting with the way I feel whenever I see your face.* He tried to remember why he'd decided that there was no future whatsoever between them, but at the moment, his mind was a complete blank.

"I'd be glad to show you what I know," he admitted almost gruffly as he set down the pail for his camels. "Would you like to take a ride with me? I don't think Laura and Violet would mind a nice stroll now that they're rested."

He knew it wasn't smart, but somehow he rationalized that it was the right thing to do. Riding with Roberta seemed like the most natural thing in the world to Clay. And maybe, in the peace of the mountains, he could tell her...well, he could tell her whatever he needed to so they could part on a high note. *I wish we could get closer, Roberta, but we're just too far apart. I regret it, but... I will remember you.*

To his surprise, Roberta's lips pursed as she turned away rather briskly. "Thanks for the offer, Clay, but I really can't."

He was surprised. The way things had gone the night before, he would have expected her to jump at the chance to spend some more time with him...or with the camels. Even a minute ago she'd seemed... well, interested. But now she was quite deliberately avoiding a chance to be alone with him, even if it meant sacrificing an activity that she surely would have enjoyed.

"Are you speaking again today?" he asked, hoping that she had some good reason for refusing him.

"No. I'm just... well, I'm not dressed for riding."

"You could change your clothes," he pointed out, unwilling to accept such a feeble excuse. It was one thing to tell Roberta he wasn't interested, he realized; another altogether to have *her* be the one to draw a line between them.

"I don't have any riding gear with me."

"Tess would loan you something."

"I don't fit in her clothes!" she snapped, suddenly abandoning the baby camel and marching toward the gate a fair distance away from Clay. "I said no! Just let it be, why don't you?"

For a moment Clay didn't know what to say. Maybe he had pushed it just a little—though it hardly seemed so in view of last night—but surely he hadn't said anything that justified discourtesy. But if that was the way she wanted to play it, maybe it was better that way. Deliberately he picked up his pail and headed back for the barn.

Instantly, Roberta stopped him.

"Clay, I'm sorry," she said in a hesitant voice unlike the Susan B. one he'd come to think of as her own. "It's just that...Tess is so petite and I'm so...bulky. And I'm just not in the mood for a ride."

He turned back to face her slowly, trying to understand what was really going on. Was it possible that Roberta had succumbed to that peculiar disease of modern American women, skinnyitis? Obsessed with looking like a toothpick that a strong man would be afraid he'd snap? He thought about last night on the stagecoach, when she'd so openly confessed her feelings, and he'd hidden his with a cowardly joke. Had he actually succeeded in convincing her that she didn't appeal to him? In his effort to keep himself from getting hurt, had he managed to wound Roberta?

Wanting to smooth things over but not quite certain how to go about it, Clay fell back into the role he'd played when the evening had been joyful...when she'd been Bobbie Jean and he'd been Lieutenant Beale. "Bulky?" he drawled. "Why, Bobbie Jean, don't you think for one little minute that there's anything wrong with the way you look. Miz Trent's a fine lookin' filly in her own right, but a big man like me wants a woman of substance he can hold on to. The first moment I clapped eyes on you, I said to myself 'Now there's a fine lookin' gal, a gal strong enough for me.'"

Clay had hoped that a light touch would dispel the tension, but he was wrong. To his surprise, Roberta's cheeks flamed, and even at a distance, he could see that her full lips were tight and trembling.

"I know how I look, Mr. Gann, and there's nothing I can do about it," she replied stiffly. "Fortunately my looks are what people expect of history professors and women who travel around giving speeches on women's rights, so—"

"Roberta." He said only the one word, his voice a soft command, and to his surprise she stopped in midsentence. Her eyes, big and hazel, met his uneasily, and he wondered how she'd ever become defensive about her looks. Didn't she realize she was a compelling, beautiful woman? Had she always judged herself lacking compared to those frothy, fragile women who did nothing for a man like him?

Clay dropped his pail and walked briskly toward the gate until he stood on one side of the log fence; Roberta still stood on the other. She was only two feet away from him, her eyes big and watchful, when he said softly, with no trace of humor, "The first time I saw you, Roberta, I said to myself, that woman has fire and she's strong enough to take on the world." He felt a tremor in his voice as he recognized the unvarnished truth of his words. "She looks like everything I'd ever hoped a woman could be."

There, he congratulated himself, feeling silly but somehow relieved. *I've been just as honest as I can be.*

To his surprise, Roberta still didn't believe him. Her lower jaw wobbled, and her eyes grew moist. "Don't make fun of me, Clay," she begged him. Her voice was hoarse. "I know who I am. I'm no ravishing rose or sweet petunia. Men respect me as a colleague and enjoy me as one of the boys, but unless I pretend to be gooey and stupid, they never take a shine to me."

He faced her squarely. "I can't imagine you acting gooey or stupid. I can't think why you'd want to pretend to be."

Unhappily she glanced away. "I only did it once. When I was twenty. It was an experiment. I wanted to see if I could get a boy to like me."

His eyebrows raised. "Did it work?"

She nodded sheepishly. "For a while. Long enough for me to see that it wasn't worth it. My grades dropped, my parents were disgusted, and even Tess was disappointed in me."

"So what happened?" he asked gently, remembering his own awkward adolescence, when so many things were painful.

She shrugged. "I tried another experiment. One day I decided to let him see the real me." She tried to smile, but even now, she could not completely hide the memory of the pain.

"And?"

"And it was over in less than a week. He decided I was pushy, unfeminine and too smart. Especially too smart. As I recall, he canceled a date with me when I got an A on a history test and he got a B." Her shoulders slumped. "I never heard from him again."

This time it was Clay who could not meet her eyes. He wanted to tell her that guy was a jerk—that she was an extremely appealing female who had every right to revel in her academic success. But then he remembered his own reaction to the news of her Ph.D. and her excellence in debate, and he knew he couldn't tell her honestly that he wasn't troubled by her academic brilliance. Somehow, he didn't think that his litany of reasons—no matter how reasonable they seemed—would cut much ice with Roberta.

"It was the same with you," she said suddenly, stunning him again with her bluntness. "Friday night you didn't think I was so bad until you found out I'm a professor. Then I could almost hear your chair scrape the floor as you struggled to get away."

Clay was ashamed. He floundered for an explanation, but nothing came to him. He had three choices—lie, dodge the subject like a coward, or tell her the truth.

He opted for the latter. "I only have a high-school diploma, Roberta," he confessed, suddenly awash in a surprising flood of shame. "The minute I realized how highly educated you were, I knew you wouldn't be interested in getting better acquainted with a man like me."

This time it was Roberta's turn to look chagrined. She took a deep breath, then met his gaze squarely. "You think I'm an intellectual snob?"

"Yes." The word just slipped out before he could stop it. When she jerked back as though he'd hit her, he rushed to explain, "I mean—in some ways. Dammit, Roberta, I didn't mean to say that. But you asked, and . . . hell, while you were rattling on about your department head, yes, you did sound like a snob. Like you'd never even deign to take an afternoon ride with an ordinary cowboy like me."

Suddenly she blinked very hard. "There's nothing ordinary about you, Clay," she whispered. "Your background has nothing to do with my decision about riding with you. I just can't ride...today. If you'd asked me to do anything else—"

"You could have suggested an alternative."

"No, I couldn't have. I mean, I didn't know if . . . I didn't know if you really wanted to see me, you know, or if you were just being polite. Especially after last night. Men don't . . . I mean, I—"

She stopped abruptly when Clay's hand came up to claim her face. He hadn't planned on touching her, let alone slipping his fingers under the straps of her velvet bonnet while his thumb gingerly stroked her fine jaw. He certainly hadn't counted on the sudden trembly feeling that gripped him as soon as his callused thumb skidded past her delicate throat. And he was stunned by his sudden desire to kick down the gate Brady had only finished building last month so he could get even closer to Roberta.

"I like you, Roberta," he heard himself say. His voice was low, crusty, as though he'd just been awakened in the night. "I like you a lot. You stir me in a way I haven't been stirred by a woman in a very long time."

Roberta stared at him, clearly dumbstruck. Her jaw seemed to go slack, but she didn't say a word. Nor did she look away.

"When we first met, I hoped you might feel the same way. I hoped we could do something about it, explore it, see where it led. But now that I know about your profession and your priorities, I know it can't happen. I know you'd never be happy with a man like me."

Her eyes grew larger yet, moist now, as though she were aching for what he'd just insisted he could never give.

"Don't mistake my common sense for any lack of passion, Bobbie Jean," he whispered, his voice ragged now. He tried to press against her and ran into the fence; he wanted to climb over it but forced himself to stop. He tried to force himself to release her face, but he seemed to have used up all of his willpower...and all of his common sense.

His thumb kissed her lips, sweeping over them once, twice, three times as he battled to keep his mouth from claiming hers. "You are one hell of a woman, Bobbie Jean," he swore softly, ashamed to realize that his hand was trembling, "so don't you ever let some jerk tell you otherwise. I don't wish you were smaller or sweeter or more helpless. I don't wish you'd boycotted higher education just so you'd be more like me." He swallowed hard, pressing his fingertips provocatively against her scalp as he fought the impulse to draw her closer. Then, with supreme force of will, he released her face and jammed both hands into his denim pockets. In a ragged undertone he confessed, "My God, Roberta, all I wish is that I could follow this trail wherever it leads."

CHAPTER FIVE

BY THE TIME Roberta arrived at Charles Trumbull's office on Monday morning, she had pretty much come to terms with the Clay Gann fiasco. She had, quite simply, blown her chances of developing a meaningful relationship with the first man who'd really appealed to her in years. Except, of course, for Charles.

Even though it was April in Tucson—with an average daily temperature of over eighty degrees—he was wearing a long-sleeved white shirt and a tie. The air conditioning was so intense that he may have been a bit chilly even in that formal garb, but somehow just the sight of that tie left Roberta feeling wilted.

I wonder how Charles would look in buckskin, she mused. *I wonder how he'd look with a mustache.* Studying him now—bent over his desk, methodically line-editing a submission for the *Tucson State Historical Review*—he looked positively regal. His pale blond hair almost glowed in the window's desert sun, and his blue eyes had just the right professional interest. He radiated professional competence. It was no match for the passion Clay Gann exuded doing rope tricks on camelback, of course, but it was certainly a more appropriate aura for the friend or lover of a college professor like herself.

Charles grinned—rather broadly for him—when he saw Roberta. He actually stood and closed the door, netting her in his small inner office. "So how did it go in Patchwork?" he asked, motioning for her to sit down in the padded bench by his desk while he lowered himself into his heavy swivel chair.

They were simple words, but the answer was not easy for Roberta. At once Clay's face filled her vision, all but shutting out the sight of Charles. She had not seen Clay again after that bewitching moment they'd shared at the corral. He had not, strictly speaking, actually kissed her, nor had he held her in his arms. And yet, twenty-four hours later, she could still feel his fingers in her hair and his palm on the edge of her jaw. His thumb's bold caress still riddled her senses.

"Was your oration well received?" Charles prodded her.

Roberta managed to nod as she belatedly sat down. "I was very pleased, Charles," she replied, automatically falling into the sophisticated tone that Charles's formality always coaxed out of her. Diligently she forced Clay from her mind. "The audience wasn't entirely certain what behavior was indicated when I commenced. They listened most attentively. But then two of Brady Trent's...colleagues...demonstrated the appropriate historical behavior and the crowd began to respond in kind."

Good God, I sound like a dry as dust textbook! she lambasted herself. *If Clay thought I came across as a snob at dinner, I wonder what he'd think of the way I sound now.*

"Splendid. So your venture was a success?"

"I think so. Yes."

Again Charles smiled, flashing that orthodontically perfect expression which so befitted a department head. "I'm glad to hear it. What's next on the agenda?"

"Little Horn, New Mexico." *Where camel races are listed as one of the weekend festivities.* "I'm considering giving a temperance speech this time because another orator will be doing a William Jennings Bryan presentation, which will probably deal with woman's suffrage as well as free silver. Despite his fundamentalist religious beliefs, Bryan was a supporter of Susan B.'s cause."

Charles nodded, then stroked his chin in a scholarly gesture. "Are you sure it's wise to try different personae? Might that not interfere with the data you're striving to collect?"

Roberta had always been grateful that her career had surrounded her with highly literate men, but at the moment she found herself wondering why Charles always talked as though he were dictating a legal brief. She wrote professional papers in this style, but outside of his office, her conversation was generally quite down-home. She wondered how Charles talked in the bedroom or on horseback. Or what he might have to say to a recalcitrant camel.

"I don't think this project can be analyzed from a purely quantitative perspective, Charles," she pointed out. "Each community and each celebration is unique. My presentations must be tailored to the given occasion and locale."

"I guess that's true, Roberta," he had to concede, "but don't forget that your purpose, during the trial run we've set up for the summer, is to ascertain the pluses and minuses of offering a traveling chautauqua graduate program next year. Despite the striking popularity of your approach during your own classes—" his smile was one of honest approval and heartwarming praise "—I still have some reservations about taking T.S.U.

students on the road. I'll be checking your sample circuit records very thoroughly and conferring with you often. Make sure not to deviate from the schedule and presentations to which we've agreed." He paused for emphasis, his robin's-egg-blue eyes holding hers. "I know that you can handle any untoward events that happen to come your way, but I don't have the same faith in the ability of our students to demonstrate such skill and flexibility."

Although there was a quiet warning in Charles's tone—a reminder that big brother would be watching— Roberta decided to take his final words as a compliment. She *did* have the ability to turn things around, to triumph over adversity. And she most certainly had the strength to forget the feel of Clay Gann's thumb on her lips.

Surely it was just a matter of time.

THE GIRL WAS LOOKING AT HIM. She'd been watching Ozzie ever since he'd helped her mount Luscious Laura ten minutes ago. But he wasn't sure *why* she was watching him; he couldn't remember if he'd said anything she could have overheard.

It seemed to him that she was staring at him the same way Tess Trent's friend had been staring at Clay in Patchwork. Roberta had been subtle about it, but Ozzie had seen. And he wondered if Roberta had anything to do with his boss's distracted mood the past few weeks.

It had been a hard month, a strange spring month of alternating blistering days and sporadic rain. The trail business had been unsteady as a result, and the camels weren't getting enough exercise. And Ozzie didn't have enough to do. Even the endless pile of books by his bed—most of them Clay's—weren't enough to keep him occupied.

The girl was pressing Luscious Laura forward, edging the clumsy creature to Ozzie's side. She was still smiling, albeit shyly, and he wasn't quite sure what to do.

"Hi," she said as she reached him. "Have you worked here long?"

He shrugged, wishing he didn't have to answer. "A year." Two words, and he'd gotten both of them out without stuttering.

"Part-time? Do you go to school?"

He shook his head. He always had extra trouble with *s*'s. He wasn't about to risk one with her.

"I'm a sophomore at Colorado State," she told him, eyes friendly now, but not exactly aglow. "I'm a math major. What's your specialty?"

It seemed like a long time since he'd thought of himself as being special in anything, but he did have a favorite subject. "I like animals," he said, certain that he'd never get through "biology" without three *b*'s, three *l*'s or three *g*'s. And he certainly wasn't going to risk explaining that he'd always longed to study veterinary medicine at her university.

"So do I," she told him. "I think I like everything about school. Except speech. That used to be hard for me. But not anymore. It's not easy, but it's okay."

Ozzie felt a little queazy. This was no longer a conversation he wanted to have. He *knew*, with every ounce of his being, that this pretty stranger was going to talk about his stuttering.

Before he could escape, she said gently, "I used to stutter, Ozzie. Much worse than you. I finally licked it.

I just wanted you to know that. I mean, you *can* beat the thing. It's hard, but . . . it can be done."

His eyes flashed up at her. He felt half embarrassed, half grateful. Suddenly all the effort he'd put into choosing stutter-free sentences was too much for him, and he fell apart on a single word.

"H-h-how?"

"I went to a special program in San Francisco that combined speech techniques with attitude therapy. It changed the way I talked and the way I thought about myself. It was just wonderful, Ozzie." She stopped a moment and graced him with a shy smile. "I can send you some information on the program if you want. Would you like that?"

Slowly Ozzie nodded. For years he'd been afraid of tackling yet another round of speech therapy, but he was growing tired of spending his life in hiding. Maybe it was time to give it another try. The program in San Francisco just might be worth looking into, even though it was so far away.

He decided to try to look at the girl's information with an open mind—if and when she sent it. But before he did anything about it, he'd have to talk to Clay.

IT WAS NOT UNTIL the first weekend in May that Clay found himself hauling his humped crew to New Mexico for another small-town founder's day celebration. And it was not until the first night he unloaded the camels in Little Horn, nestled high in the magnificent Sangre de Cristo Mountains, that he heard the sounds of celebration: a tiny open-air plane giving ten-minute rides to tourists, a monkey grinder providing archaic music, and the rumble of a steam-driven locomotive accompanied by the pomp of a political orator and a small brass band.

The speaker, a stately William Jennings Bryan, was booming out free silver theories and expounding on the need for women to have the right to vote. Clay, concentrating on the shaggy humps in front of him, wished he could have taken the time to go listen and heckle the fellow appropriately, but the camels always came first.

As he unloaded Baby Bev, whose slender legs were getting longer every day, he couldn't help but recall the last time he'd heard one of these chautauquas . . . from a speaker who'd sounded as tough as leather on the platform but was madonna-sweet when she'd cooed to his baby camel. He stifled the quiet swell of regret that always gripped him when he thought of Roberta. For a few brief hours, he had hoped—foolishly—that he had stumbled across somebody truly special. Even now, it bothered him that he'd left things between them so uncertain, so strained. He'd all but kissed her, then sent her away. But he hadn't managed to forget her yet. Not by a long shot.

"So it's goodbye to the demon rum, I say!" called a strident voice from the platform ten minutes later. A woman's voice. A woman's voice that was full of fire. "Wrecker of marriage, wrecker of homes. Until this evil is trapped and subdued, there will be no peace in America!"

Clay grinned. Against all logic, he suddenly felt terrific. The historical identity of the orator was new to him. Some temperance female—maybe the one who broke up saloons with a hatchet? But he knew that woman's voice, and it stirred embers not yet dead in him.

"Ozzie! George!" he called as he backed the last camel out of the trailer, grateful that sharp-tongued Warner had already taken a pair of camels over to the corral. "Get these guys settled and stay with them until I get back." He grinned as he plunked on his dad's lucky hat. "I've got business to attend to."

Without a moment's hesitation he headed toward the train, thinking up antiprohibitionist arguments as he strolled. It was a good thing he did, because the moment he reached the crowd and spotted that familiar, strong-willed face, he couldn't remember much of anything he'd ever read about the era before.

All he knew was that he felt better than he had in weeks. Better than he had since he'd last seen Bobbie Jean in Patchwork and had fought back the need to hold her in his arms.

ROBERTA WAS HALFWAY THROUGH her speech when she spotted the buckskin jacket and squashed Stetson, and she had to take a moment to swallow hard. She had realized that there was a good chance she'd meet up with Clay here—or at some future stop on the circuit—but she hadn't expected him to join the crowd around the platform. And she hadn't expected to find him grinning a welcome that only a fool could have missed.

"Knock it off, lady!" he called out, baiting her just as he had in Patchwork. "It's a free country! A man can have a drink whenever he feels like it!"

She remembered the first time he'd heckled her, when she'd thought he really *was* trying to make a point. Now she watched the smile in his eyes and she knew that he was on her side.

"The demon rum is the devil's own curse!" she called back to him. "Whiskey bespeaks not freedom! It is the chains of hellfire which pin a man down!"

"Forget the sermon, lady! We're celebratin' here! There's a party goin' on!"

He looked as though he was headed to a party. His hair was a little longer than it had been when she'd seen him last, and his eyes were full of laughter. His long legs looked relaxed and somehow sensual, smoothly encased in rough and well-worn jeans.

He couldn't have looked less like Charles Trumbull. In fact, he looked as though he'd just ridden in off some dusty range. But Roberta realized, despite the ongoing hubbub, that she didn't care about how he looked to anybody else. All that mattered was how Clay Gann looked to her.

And he looked... magnificent. There was something in his smile that always pulled her, something in his eyes that warmed her heart. She wanted to jump off the platform into his arms and let him swing her around so badly that it was a real effort to remember to play her part.

"'Tis an evil larger than life which brings me here today!" she shouted, raising one dramatic fist. "The bottle will be the demise of American marriage, American family—even American motherhood itself!"

"Ah, knock it off, wouldja?" another man chimed in, his voice somewhat slurred and lacking Clay's teasing tone. "No dogface dame gonna tell me whatta do!" He belched. "Get goddamned good 'n' drunk if I want to!"

By then a few other men took up the cry, until, to Roberta's amazement, another woman wearing a modern pink pantsuit called out, "She's right! My ex-husband was an alcoholic! Prohibition might have made all the difference to what happened between him and me!"

The crowd shouted her down, though not in a hostile way. Roberta knew they sensed, as she did, that the other woman had a personal problem that required professional therapy, not group joshing. Deftly Roberta recaptured the focus of the group and lectured for another ten minutes, while Clay grinned from the sidelines and shouted out something mildly offensive whenever the group's interest seemed to pale.

In spite of her keen involvement in her presentation, Roberta found her thoughts wandering as she gazed at Clay. She remembered the last calm moment they'd shared together...that tight, sure moment when he'd confessed his feelings before he'd pushed her away.

He didn't seem to be pushing her away right now. In fact, if he got any closer, she noticed joyfully, he'd be climbing right up on the stage.

CLAY HAD JUST FINISHED eating lunch at the Cheyenne Soire Saloon and was about to take a stroll through town when he spotted "Carry Nation" coming toward him on the rough plank sidewalk. Wearing the same sober gray suit he'd once seen her wear in Patchwork, she was marching along with a tiny hatchet in her hand—still playing the part—as she bore down on the saloon with a determined look in her eye.

Clay grinned. It wasn't a deliberate effort to sabotage her stern role, but the instant she saw him, Roberta smiled back. She even lowered her small weapon.

"Hello, Clay," she greeted him, her eyes just as richly happy as they'd been when he'd joined the crowd around her podium that morning. They hadn't had a chance to talk, and yet—after their creative interplay during her speech—he felt as though they'd had a conversation. It just didn't seem like a month had passed since they'd last said goodbye.

"Howdy, Bobbie Jean," he drawled with deliberate nonchalance. A tangle of feelings tripped him as her grin consumed her face. He remembered the last few moments she'd spent with him in Patchwork; remembered the pain in her eyes and the feel of her lips against his hand. He felt a sudden swell of longing, a swell of desire that took him off guard. It was an effort to keep from hugging her hello as he told her with tightly reined calm, "Caught your act this morning."

"So I noticed. I ought to hire you to follow me around and rev up the audience." Her tongue slipped out to moisten her lower lip. Her hazel eyes danced with pleasure. "I think the folks in this crowd are even more disturbed about temperance than they are about women's rights."

"Well, some folks don't like to have their liberties threatened."

"Temperance has nothing to do with liberty. It has to do with human health and happiness. Did you know that alcoholism is one of the major causes of death among Americans today?"

Clay reached out and gently took the hatchet from her hand, surprised that she offered no resistance. "No, I didn't, but I'm not surprised. I know it's a terrific problem. But before you forget that it's *nine*teen-ninety and you're off duty, let me inform you that Clayton Gann the Camel Man is not a drinking man, so you don't need to rehearse your arguments with me."

To his surprise, Roberta glanced down as though he'd rebuked her sharply. "I'm sorry. I know I tend to come on too strong."

Clay gave her back the hatchet, letting his fingers linger on her wrist. It had been a long time since he'd touched her—way too long—and he liked the soft and supple feel of her arm. "That's what I like best about you," he said truthfully. "The world is full of lily-livered women. I don't have much use for them."

Her eyes flashed up at him, big and wounded. He could almost hear her thinking, *And you don't have much use for me, either.*

With a jolt he realized that she was thinking of the last time they'd been alone. He'd never been happy about their final parting. And yet, if he had it to do over again, he wasn't sure just what he could have done differently.

Now he found his hand closing over hers warmly, savoring her feminine magic. In spite of himself, he took a step closer. His eyes lingered on her face.

He knew there was some good reason why he wasn't supposed to spend time with Roberta, but at the moment it escaped him entirely.

"I...uh...was going to do a little window-shopping before Warner and I do our thing at two o'clock," he heard himself admit in a low, almost husky tone. "Would you care to stroll with me?"

A curious blend of hope and confusion flitted over Roberta's strong face, a blend Clay knew was echoed in his own. He tried to remind himself that she was a highbrow who could never have a place in his life; he tried to remember what had happened the last time she'd encountered his men.

But all he could recall was the way he felt when she smiled at him, so he squeezed her hand and tugged her toward him ever so slightly.

"I was planning to hack up a few more saloons," she confessed with a chuckle, her tone too gentle to support her erstwhile Carry Nation role. "But I suppose I could always do that later."

He grinned and slipped her arm up to his elbow in what was now a familiar motion. "I imagine you could, Bobbie Jean."

Together they turned and floated along the bustling sidewalk, moving by mutual consent into the old museum sandwiched between a dozen refurbished shops. It was not unique, as small-town museums go, but that made it no less fascinating to Clay. Each tiny nugget of history drew him, warmed him, made him feel bonded, somehow, to the pioneers.

"Look at this uniform," he told her, pointing to a blood-stained butternut jacket. "Somebody must have died in it."

"Near the end of the war," said Roberta.

"Has to be, or it'd be gray."

Roberta's eyes flashed up at him, and he knew he'd surprised her again. Clearly she hadn't expected a man with his limited education to know that the Confederate Army had run out of funds for uniforms near the end and homespun butternut clothing had replaced the official gray. He felt an overpowering need to impress her with his knowledge, a need to prove that he knew something that her department head might not know.

"I studied Civil War uniforms in great detail before I bought my own," he confessed. "Every rank and unit had a different one. Sometimes they changed year to year. It took some doing to be sure that I'd gotten Lieutenant Beale in 1860."

Roberta's eyebrows raised. "You mean that's not just a generic Cavalry uniform?"

"Absolutely not. And there's nothing generic about what my Lieutenant Beale has to say about camels. I've studied every word he ever wrote and even accidentally memorized some of it."

"You know, Clay, the Camel Corps is not widely studied, especially outside of Arizona," Roberta observed. "I've run into it as a footnote here and there, but I've never seen more than a paragraph on it anywhere. It would be an interesting book or professional paper."

He chuckled uncomfortably. It had occurred to him, more than once, that he was just the man to write such a document. He knew he had the verbal facility to put it together, but then he'd have to submit it—somewhere—while the ghost of his mother cackled, "I *knew* my son would be published someday!" If it was rejected, he'd feel incredibly stupid and naive, and if it was accepted, he'd feel that his mother had gotten the last laugh. Either way he'd lose.

"Maybe someday *you* can write it," he told Roberta. "That sort of thing must be your cup of tea."

Before his eyes, he saw Roberta change just slightly. She straightened just a little; she almost preened. "Well, I have published a number of professional papers, Clay, in our own historical review and several other publications. In fact, I'm working on a chautauqua paper right now."

As she started to tell him the highlights of her project, he felt himself instinctively pulling away. A moment ago he'd forgotten how far apart they really were;

he'd been thinking about the 1850s ball set up in Little Horn that night, wondering if he should take the plunge and ask her to join him. But now, as he listened to her very proud and eloquent explanation of her research techniques, he knew that going with her anywhere would be a mistake.

"But you know there's no requirement that a submitting author have academic credentials if his background gives him special expertise," she concluded, her eyes alight as she warmly studied his face, "and you're certainly an expert on the Camel Corps. How did you get to be so well-informed, anyway? You know more about some subjects than people with master's degrees."

He tried not to bristle; after all, she had surely meant that ill-chosen line as a compliment. "I love the west," he explained, eager to talk about anything but schooling. "I travel to all these old towns and pick up old journals and diaries whenever I come across them. It sort of gives me a hobby... a way to keep busy during the long nights when we're on the road."

"I had the impression that most of the people who travel this circuit spend their nights doing the town," she replied. "I can't see your cowboys curled up before the fire with a good book."

He felt himself stiffen. He could not refute her observation. Ozzie was the only one who worked for him who had any idea why he loved to read. He had other academically oriented friends in Fort Collins—and a few in the towns he visited during his summer tour—but he often felt that he was surrounded by Neanderthals.

It was not something he intended to explain to highbrow Roberta.

Again he shrugged. "I'm not 'most' people, Roberta. I'm just myself. That's all I've ever wanted to be."

She stared at him oddly. "You make it sound like a goal that took a lot of effort to attain."

He pondered her observation for a moment, then admitted softly, "Yes, I guess you could say that. I spent the first half of my life trying to play a part that had been assigned to me. Once I was old enough to leave home, I took off like a shot and started learning how to be me."

"Is that why you didn't go to college?" Her hazel eyes studied him thoughtfully, resting for a moment on his father's hat. "I mean, from what you said, I gather your mother would have been thrilled to pay for your education."

"On *her* terms, certainly."

"On *any* terms, I'll wager," pressed Roberta, like a bulldog shaking a bone. "If you were not a school person, your lack of education would make sense, Clay, considering your profession. But you collect journals and read extensively, and you clearly demonstrate expertise in your field. With the right education, you could be a history professor yourself! I've never seen your writing, but when you get off on a subject, it's almost as if you've prepared a speech. Why, any student who listened to your lectures would—"

"I've made my choice," he cut her off, suddenly acknowledging the deep wellspring of anger within him that he'd been trying to ignore since the conversation had taken an academic turn. "About the last thing I need at this point in my life is some woman with a Ph.D. telling me how much better off I'd be getting a great education and honing my public speaking!"

Roberta stepped back as though he'd hit her, and he realized belatedly that the tone of his voice had probably been a blow. But he was angry—angry and regretful—that she'd spoiled what had started out to be such a pleasant afternoon. Every time he saw this woman he tried to forget why there could never be anything but friendship between them. And every time he found himself wanting her anyway... until she reminded him that the Clay Gann he'd chosen to become wasn't the kind of man she wanted. A camel-loving cowboy would never be good enough for her.

"Clay," she said gently, laying one hand on his bare wrist, "I'm sorry if I...well, if I spoke out of turn. But you said you liked me to be blunt, and the truth is that I'm perplexed by—"

"I don't give a damn if you're perplexed," he snapped, battling with a sudden image of his mother, which seemed to be superimposed over Roberta's face. "I am who I am, and you're somebody else. Stop trying to figure me out and make me over." He glared at her, watched the heat rise to her cheeks, quivered as his hand reached out to touch the red spot. *Don't do it, Clay,* he ordered himself, knowing he was headed straight for trouble. *Don't forget how it ended up with your folks.*

He stroked her cheek just once, then somehow reclaimed his own fingers. "Bobbie Jean," he said with a gentle, firm conviction, "I don't want to holler at you. I just want you to accept the fact that you and I can't ever be more than friends."

"DID YOU HAVE FUN with your fr-fr-friend?" asked Ozzie as he stood on the steps to the trailer after lunch. Although Clay was always friendly and willing to talk, Ozzie tried not to impose himself on his boss too much.

The men who traveled with the camels shared a cozy trailer of their own. Clay's was smaller, but on the road, it was his private home.

"Sure," Clay answered sharply, his face a bit tense as he glared at the can of soda in his hand. He didn't look as though he'd had a good time. "You know I always run into somebody I know in every town."

Ozzie knew this was true, but he could have pointed out that Clay was not in the habit of simply wandering off to spend time with miscellaneous acquaintances the moment he arrived in a town, leaving Ozzie to settle the camels. Especially when Ozzie was trying so hard to talk to him about something really important.

"Clay?"

"Hmmm."

"You know that letter I got just before we left?"

"Uh-huh."

"It was from this g-g-girl I met a few weeks ago. A girl who used to st-st-stutter."

Clay's eyes met his intently for just a moment before he glanced away. He looked all strung up inside. Confused and distant. Ozzie often felt the same way, but he wasn't used to seeing Clay look like that. He was a man who always radiated confidence. A man Ozzie desperately wanted to emulate.

"She's a friend of yours?" Clay asked, but it sounded like a question posed solely for courtesy.

Still, Ozzie persevered. "She . . . t-t-told me how she licked it before. About this program. In San Francisco. She sent me some st-st-stuff to look at."

Clay did not reply. In fact he didn't even look at Ozzie.

"I wondered if you c-c-could take a minute to look at it, Clay, and tell me what you think of it."

Slowly Clay's eyes met his again; he finally had the boss's attention. But Ozzie felt the tension in him. It was always this way when they discussed his stutter. Clay wanted him to just ignore it, to plow ahead and make it go away. Ozzie, on the other hand, wanted some magical solution.

"I've told you before, Ozzie, any program's worth a shot, but no program is a miracle. Until you decide to say to hell with everybody who laughs at you, nothing's going to work." He gestured at the envelope Ozzie held in his hand. "There's no magical cure for the panic that's inside of you."

Ozzie winced at the sharp tone. He had expected a lot more compassion. It wasn't like Clay to speak to him so harshly.

"S-s-sorry I b-b-bothered y-y-you," he managed to say, the hurt of the rebuff destroying his composure. Gripping the envelope tightly, he turned away.

"Oz!" Now Clay's voice was frustrated, almost angry. But Ozzie knew the tone. Clay was mad at himself.

"I didn't mean to bark at you. All I meant was—oh, hell, Oz, I wish you had more faith in yourself. You know that *I* believe in you."

Ozzie swallowed hard, but he didn't push the envelope at Clay.

"Look, Oz, I'm just... I'm not on top of things today. I've got a lot on my mind. If you'll leave me the information, I'll read it when I can concentrate. After my show this afternoon, or maybe tonight. Is that okay?"

When Clay reached out, Ozzie handed him the envelope. He didn't move when Clay gripped his shoulder with a firm hand.

"You can lick this thing, Oz. I swear it. I wasn't half the man you are when I was your age, and somehow I worked through it. I know you can do it, too."

Ozzie didn't answer. He admired Clay more than any other man in the world, even though he knew something that Clay had never admitted to anyone else. The last time he'd been asked to make a speech about camels at a local school, he'd made up three dozen excuses before he'd told Ozzie the truth. When it came to public speaking, he was no longer afraid he'd stutter—he'd long since licked the speech impediment that had planted the first seed of public speaking terror within him—but he had never quite killed the fear.

AT TWO O'CLOCK, Roberta found a spot near the south side of the arena and tried to look casual as Clay and Warner came barreling out on two horses, doing parallel tricks that she could hardly bear to watch. They slipped beneath their saddles for paired possum belly rides; they vaulted over the rear ends of their mounts and did handstands at the same time. They did twin somersaults and One Hand Hornspins while Roberta held her breath; they did Crupper Splits to a Hip Roll while she slowly died inside.

It was the same routine Roberta had watched them do in Patchwork, and she found her palms no less sweaty watching them now. She had watched literally hundreds of riding exhibitions and competitions in her life, and very few of them had ended in disaster. But her own disaster—lodged unforgettably in her heart and even in the weak joints of her upper vertebrae—made it impossible to watch a daring ride without passion. Not when the daring rider was Clay.

Their last parting had been harsh, but it made no difference to Roberta. Clay was fighting her, fighting himself, and she knew that she hadn't helped any by making reference to his education. Whether she put him down or built him up, the very mention of the difference in their academic backgrounds seemed to wound him. She vowed that—if she ever got another chance—she would keep from mentioning any aspect of schooling.

It's only my life, she reminded herself morosely. *It ought to be easy to keep the subject out of the conversation.*

The crowd was delirious by the time Warner and Clay started doing Cossack passes on the same horse, but Roberta was passionately relieved when their exotic routine ended.

Of course, Clay still had to do his comedic roping demonstration on Violet's humped back, but Roberta didn't find that spectacle nearly so frightening. The camel looked funny, not dangerous, and all Clay had to do was stay on some part of her anatomy while he did snazzy rope tricks. Roberta reminded herself that he did it all the time.

The audience cheered as he climbed on board the feisty camel. Violet was making hostile chirping noises and salivating profusely. Her tail stuck straight out in back, like a flag of danger. But even though Clay pointed out all of these signs of trouble to George on the loudspeaker—comically feigning terror—he showed no hesitation when he ultimately clambered aboard.

The fans roared as Clay knelt on Violet's back, his pointy-toed boots hooked into the wooden saddle frame around Violet's hump. He shook out a huge loop that embraced the bobbing camel, then twirled it dramatically on each side. He spun the rope in a dozen creative configurations, just as he'd done in Patchwork, with the crowd's noise growing louder all the time. And then, just as he began to whirl it above his head while Violet streaked toward Ozzie in preparation for the grand finale, the tiny plane giving rides down at the midway suddenly buzzed the arena, its high-pitched motor serrating Roberta's nerves. It seemed to have the same effect on the startled camel, who instantaneously bucked straight up and twisted sharply to one side.

Clay flew off just as quickly, first shooting high in the air and then plunging downward like a sack of grain. Roberta's view was blocked by the mountainous, bucking hump, but she heard Clay hit the ground with the force of a boulder caught in an avalanche. In the sudden plume of dust, all she could spot was one sprawled arm and his lucky hat floating away.

Her pulse clattered with such vehemence that she thought she would explode. The long-healed vertebrae at the top of her spine suddenly throbbed. Panic roped her heart. Without a moment's rational thought, she screamed one word—one desperate, incoherent word—with such force that it ricocheted off the bleachers.

"Claaaaaayyyyyyyy!"

It was a sob. It was a groan. It was a public confession of her all-consuming terror...and the depth of her feeling for the man who'd just plunged into the dirt.

Oblivious to anything but the panic within her, Roberta clattered down the bleachers and battled her way to the fence. Wildly she tried to scale it, succeeding only in getting her long skirts tangled on the jagged edges. Shaking uncontrollably, she tugged at the cotton fabric, listened to it rip. A moment later she was charging toward the center of the arena...where Clay, on both feet, was now gently patting the camel's heaving side with one hand and waving to the crowd with the other.

By this time Ozzie was tugging on her arm, whispering, "H-h-he's okay. He's always ready t-t-to jump and r-r-roll." His dark eyes met hers earnestly. "You can't g-g-go running out there, miss. It'll r-r-ruin the show."

Roberta found herself sucking in huge, dusty breaths. She was surprised to realize that Clay was on his feet and so was she. Even the camel was now steadily planted on all fours. It was little Bobbie Jean, the Bobbie Jean of her memory, who was lying eerily still upon the ground.

CHAPTER SIX

HE FOUND HER SITTING cross-legged under a tree, far back from the cheerful crowd, nursing a cup of tepid lemonade while she twiddled the end strings of the gray bonnet that lay on top of her torn skirt. Her eyes had that haunted, nightmarish look he'd seen in the eyes of veterans when they're jarred back to some keen memory of war. He knew that Ozzie's perception had been entirely correct. The boy had insisted that Roberta hadn't just been frightened for *Clay*. He was certain the scene in the arena had triggered some terrifying memory deep within her. Clay recalled the look in her eyes when he'd asked her to go riding with him in Patchwork, and he suddenly understood the panicked expression he'd glimpsed when she'd turned him down. It was the same look that grayed her face now.

"Howdy," Clay greeted her casually as he squatted beside her, hoping that a light touch would be the best way to handle the situation. "I appreciated your enthusiasm for my performance."

She glared at him, but he could tell that the anger was only a mask for the fear. "Your show was fine. You're a gifted rider."

He sat down beside her in the sparse grass, though she made no move to welcome him. "Ozzie said you were . . . a little upset."

"I wouldn't put much credence in what Ozzie says," Roberta growled. "I don't even know how you can understand him."

Every muscle of Clay's body clenched. He'd come here to support Roberta, but no matter what condition she was in, he couldn't let her bad-mouth Ozzie. "Ozzie's a terrific kid," he told her tightly, "and *I* don't have the slightest difficulty understanding what he says with his mouth or with his *heart*."

Shame filled Roberta's eyes, and then, to his astonishment, a glimmer of tears. "I'm sorry," she said at once. "I didn't mean to...cast aspersions...I mean—"

"I know what 'cast aspersions' means," he corrected her sharply. "Just because I didn't go to college doesn't mean I'm a dunce."

To his amazement, Roberta wrapped her arms around her legs and dropped her head on her knees. Incredibly his feisty filly seemed to be coming apart.

"Would you please go away?" she begged him, her tone almost desperate. "Go find somebody else to fight with. I just can't handle it right now."

Stymied, Clay wondered what he should do next. As a general rule, he did not argue with a woman who told him to leave her alone. But this one was special to him, and the one thing he was certain of was that at the moment, she needed a friend.

For a moment he said nothing. Then he reached out gently and laid his hand on the top of her head. Her curls felt soft beneath his fingers. "If you want to talk, I want to listen," he promised, doing his best to keep his voice level and kind. "If you don't, then maybe I can just sit here with you for a while. I'm not sure what happened out there just now, Roberta, but I'm pretty sure that the way to handle it isn't for you to go off and feel frightened all alone."

Her head popped up, proud and angry again. "What do you know about fear? You've probably never been afraid of anything in your whole life!"

He shook his head. "For four years I was so frightened that I started out each morning so sick to my stomach that if I'd been a girl, my parents would have thought I was pregnant. And I wasn't afraid of getting thrown by a camel, either, Roberta." He waited a moment, then tacked on gently, "Or even a horse."

Her face wrinkled up, but she valiantly quelled the threatening tears. Clay gave her a moment to collect herself and slipped his hand down her shoulder, then her arm, until it touched her hand.

To his surprise, she clenched it tightly.

"How did you know?" she whispered. "I never tell a soul. I'm ashamed for anyone to know."

He smiled kindly. "Roberta, girls who love horses for a year or two might outgrow them, but not a ranchwoman like yourself. From the first moment I saw you with Baby Bev, I knew you took to critters like a duck to water." His voice grew very soft, and the hand stroking her head grew very still. "But you turn green around the gills whenever anybody suggests you go riding."

Roberta's eyes were still red, but the only moisture on her face was perspiration. She looked shell-shocked, broken, ashamed. "It happened so long ago, Clay," she whispered. "It's not something I think about anymore. It was just...seeing you hit the ground like that, it all came rushing back. My neck even started to hurt. Psychosomatic, I know, but still...the pain was *real*."

Clay stroked her hand gently, trying to soothe her with his warmth. "Surely you've seen somebody thrown since you were hurt, Roberta. Anywhere there are horses and riders, it's inevitable."

She nodded. "I don't know why it struck me like that." Then her eyes met his, and he realized it wasn't coincidental that *his* fall had shaken her so badly. He mattered to Roberta Wheeler. He mattered quite a lot. The realization made him feel awed, somehow. Protective.

He put one arm around Roberta and pulled her closer. "Tell me if you want to. If you think it'll help."

As she nestled against him, he realized that she was just the right size for his big frame. Her short dark curls tickled his neck. The naturally sweet scent of her body filled his senses.

"I was a barrel racer. Our living room mantel bulged with trophies. I had a sorrel gelding named Flame who'd been my best friend since I was ten. We'd taken ribbons everywhere that summer, and this was just another show. Nothing special. Nothing different. No reason to push it. In fact, he might even have been going a little slow."

Clay ran his fingers through her hair. She snuggled closer.

"We did a figure eight around a barrel. We'd done it a thousand times. We doubled back, and he went down. Just like that. I don't know why. To this day I have no idea what happened. His leg just snapped and it folded up so fast that I couldn't jump clear before he fell. My knee was crushed beneath him. A few of my vertebrae cracked. He screamed. I screamed. My mother screamed. Then I blacked out."

He dropped a kiss on her forehead. He longed to take away the pain of the memory. The pain of the loss. And he knew the loss that she hadn't yet mentioned. Not just the loss of confidence, but the loss of the horse.

"My father never even called a vet. He didn't make the slightest effort to see if Flame could have been saved. The instant he realized that I was paralyzed from the waist down— I couldn't feel a thing below my hips—he shot Flame himself right on the spot." She closed her eyes for one tense moment, then faced him dry-eyed. "Fortunately I didn't find out until weeks later. But I've always wondered if things would have turned out differently if Flame and I could have recovered together. I mean—" her voice dropped to a cracking whisper "—I *couldn't* have refused to ride *Flame*. Do you understand? He wouldn't have understood. He would have thought I was mad at him. But when I found out he was gone and my parents were so protective of everything I did..."

She lifted the tail of her skirt to wipe the perspiration off her face and tried once more to get herself together. Clay kissed her temple—once, twice, three times so very gently—and wrapped his free hand around her waist. He wanted to pull her very close, to protect her from the hurt and the memory. He wanted to rewrite her past.

"I didn't actually *decide* that I'd never ride again. I mean, not in the beginning. The doctors were amazed that I'd beaten the odds and learned to walk. The therapy was—" she gulped at the memory "—pure hell, Clay." She closed her eyes and leaned against him. He pulled her closer, his arms like pillows against the punches life had brought her, cushions against her despair. He ached to help her erase the memory of those terrible years, but there seemed to be nothing he could do to help her.

"My directions were to take no chances. To learn how to do things again one step at a time. So that's what I did. And none of those steps ever seemed to take me back into a tack room. I tried to stay away from real-life horses and just read about them in my spare time."

Clay ran his forefinger down the line of her fine jaw and lifted her face gently. Her feelings about horses were foreign to him, but the notion of being trapped by adolescent fears was something he still understood. "And now you're afraid it's too late," he suggested.

She blinked back fresh tears, beating them yet again. Even shattered, Roberta seemed too strong to cry. "Oh, I *know* it's too late, Clay. It's been too late for years! I just didn't know that I could still be so frightened. Especially for somebody other than myself."

"I'm flattered," he said softly.

Roberta closed her eyes and turned away. In fact, she actually wiggled out of his grasp, as though his infinitely gentle touch had suddenly become intolerable.

"I really don't want to talk about this anymore," she told him. "I'm supposed to speak in twenty minutes. God, I wish there was somebody who could fill in for me!"

"I can't help you there," he replied, trying to cheer her up now that she'd decided to move on from her fright. "I could teach you to ride a horse again, Bobbie Jean, but I can't give a temperance lecture in a dress."

To his relief, she gave him a small smile. "Maybe you could give a speech on camels," she suggested. "You probably know more about their role in the west than anybody."

Clay didn't deny it, but neither did he volunteer to fill in for her. He would do anything he could to get Roberta back on track except for that! But if he could distract her with a personal demonstration of some of Lieutenant Beale's thoughts, it was no skin off his nose. Giving a public speech was one thing; this was just talking to a friend.

Determined to cheer her up, Clay rose and pretended to tip his nonexistent cap. "Lieutenant Edward Beale, U.S. Army, ma'am, at your service," he introduced himself, pleased to see Roberta grin. "I'm here in town to plead the cause of the U.S. Camel Corps. I firmly believe that these fleet-footed beasts will change the face of the American West."

"Do you now?" she asked valiantly, trying to follow his lead despite the lingering anguish on her face. "And what can those clumsy oafs possibly have to recommend them?"

"Why, they have everything to recommend them!" he declared, gesturing dramatically as though he were on a train platform. "They carry up to fifteen gallons of emergency water in their stomachs. They can live off of mesquite and cactus, even the spines! They carry up to a thousand pounds and go a hundred miles from sunup to sundown! Now, I ask you, missy, can any Army mule beat that?"

It only took a moment for him to get into the role. Even after all those years, Mr. Carey's excruciating lessons stayed with him. He'd been trained to give ten-minute extemporaneous speeches, and he'd never had trouble coming up with intelligent introductions, conclusions or contentions. But in those days—those tender years when Roberta was learning to walk again—he'd been fighting a battle of his own, a battle that had destroyed his sense of self-worth and cemented his lifelong hostility toward his overbearing mother.

He'd been trying desperately to overcome his stutter.

IN THE END, Roberta became Carry Nation again, getting into the act with the appropriate fire and brimstone. Clay, busy with afternoon camel races, wasn't around to heckle her, but another man—the drunk who had bad-mouthed her that morning—did enough name-calling for half a dozen cowboys. He appeared to have consumed considerably more alcohol, and it was exceedingly evident that he was no longer baiting her just for fun.

He stripped most of the pleasure from Roberta's performance. Mercifully most of the crowd thought he was part of the act, so she was able to carry on. But her speech lacked the zest of her morning performance, and she returned to her hotel room for an afternoon rest feeling resentful and utterly drained.

Still, she took careful notes on the incident for Charles. He would want to know how the temperance lecture was received, and he would not be happy with her report. In fact, if this experience were repeated very often, she knew that he'd tell her to forget Carry Nation and stick with something less controversial. His parting words when she'd seen him last were something to the order of "Remember that you're serving as a test case for our students. In each setting, try to think of how one of them would cope." At the moment, his warning wasn't particularly reassuring.

But Roberta knew that her negative feelings about the afternoon had less to do with the drunk than they had to do with Clay. Well, not Clay himself, but Clay's spill. It had shaken the rafters of her memory, rattled the hiding place of her postriding days. How desperately she longed to ride again! How terrified she was by the very notion!

Clay understood. Before she'd ever so much as breathed a word of her experience, he had known about her accident, known how the memory lingered, known that she could never quite extinguish her longing to ride again.

He had also known that she wanted him.

This afternoon his touch had been tender, soothing . . . and platonic in intent. Yet it had quelled her anguish and stoked the fires she'd tried to bank ever since the first time he'd touched her face in Patchwork. Roberta had been deeply moved by Clay's gentleness—yet she could not deny the fact that she still wanted far more from him than comfort.

CLAY REACHED the giant barn set aside for Saturday evening's "Happy Birthday Little Horn" party around nine o'clock, when everything had been underway for nearly an hour. He was riding Velvet and wearing his cavalry lieutenant's uniform. After all, he was Clayton Gann, the Camel Man, every day of the year. An 1850s costume ball required a change of sorts.

He didn't need to go to the party; he knew that. There were plenty of people here to make the event a success, including four of his own men. But he knew that Roberta would be there.

Roberta would be waiting for him.

He spotted her almost at once. She wasn't dressed in sober gray as Carry Nation, but was wearing the beguiling low-cut blue-green taffeta number she'd sported while playing her young-lady-on-the-town-with-an-officer-gentleman role in Patchwork. Her head erect, she was apparently lecturing the man in front of her...a fellow dressed in sheepskin chaps and vest. He'd seen the man before...he was the drunk who'd been hassling Roberta just that morning. Clay hoped to God he wasn't determined to hassle her now.

He moved toward her slowly, keeping out of sight. He realized it was remotely possible that she wasn't planning to meet him here this evening. He could hardly say that they'd made it a date; this afternoon he'd gotten cold feet before he could mention the party. For all Clay knew, this fellow could be her date. He certainly seemed to be gripping her arm possessively.

Off to his right, Warner was kicking up his heels with a middle-aged gal wearing a sheriff's outfit—badge, six guns, the whole nine yards—and George and Roscoe were nursing drinks at the makeshift bar. He couldn't reconcile his baffling feeling he had that he didn't want them anywhere near Roberta. It wasn't that he didn't trust them, and the truth was, he liked them quite a lot. But his cowboys were emphatic reminders of the difference between his world and hers, and tonight he didn't want to think about that gulf. He wanted only to hold her close.

And then he saw it—the flicker of motion, the backward tug of Roberta's elbow as she took a step back from the man who gripped her. She was trying to get away.

Clay should have been pleased, but something in the exchange troubled him. It took him a moment to discern what it was.

Roberta was frightened.

Not the way she'd been frightened this afternoon, not deep-down-to-her-toes scared. But she was uneasy. She kept stepping back, and the other man kept following her. It had never occurred to Clay that there was anything Roberta couldn't handle; he expected her to deliver a swift uppercut to any unruly hooligan. But clearly she was struggling to keep her poise. It was a struggle he was not about to let her lose.

In three long strides Clay was by her side, possessively clenching one arm around her waist and taking charge of the situation in the best way he knew how.

"Why, there you are, my l'il sweet petunia," he drawled, realizing with sharpening alarm that the drunk wore an ugly snarl on his face, which had not been there that morning. "I don't believe Ah've met yer friend." Trying to look as intimidating as possible, he saluted the other man, whose drunken breath quickly assailed him. "Lieutenant Edward Beale, U.S. First Dragoons," he introduced himself. "And you are . . . ?"

"Here aheada you, so get out th' way," the drunk growled. "Me an' th' broad was just gettin' chummy."

Roberta ignored him. Leaning into Clay's embrace, she said pointedly, "I'm so glad to see you, Lieutenant. You're late."

Clay didn't need to see her eyes to hear the gratitude in her slightly shaky voice. She really had needed help! He tightened his grip around her waist as he apologized. "So sorry Ah was detained by Army business, sweet pea. Ah do hope you saved the first dance for me."

"Why, of course, Lieutenant," she replied with dignity. "I've never danced with another man since we became engaged."

To the other man, who was still glowering, Clay said curtly, "If you'll excuse us—"

"Like hell I will! I was here first. Me an' her was just gettin' cozy when you showed up."

It was a tiny thing, the shiver that ran down Roberta's spine. But Clay felt it, felt her fear, her anger, and a streak of protectiveness surged fiercely within him. In a voice he hardly knew, he suddenly snapped, "Look, pal, I've tried to be nice, but this is my woman, and I'm telling you to keep clear."

He met the man's eyes for a long, angry moment. At last the drunk dropped his blurry gaze. "Well, we was just chattin'," he muttered as he stumbled off.

Clay didn't answer. He just whisked Roberta away. They didn't talk as he tugged her into the sea of dancers.

He took her hand and slipped his free arm around her waist as he tried to find the tempo. He was no great shakes as a dancer, but at the moment, bouncing to the old country two-step was about the best way he could hope to distract her from the ugly scene. He was still angry with the drunk, but more than that, he was embarrassed. He'd been determined to handle the situation judiciously, but in the end he'd behaved just as his father had that time in Kansas. He couldn't have given Roberta a better demonstration of the kind of "Neanderthal" behavior that separated his world from her ivy league one if he'd planned it.

"Clay?" she said, her voice audible only because her lips were an inch from his ear. Her warm breath caressed his throat. "Thank you. That man came to my lecture again this afternoon and caused quite a ruckus. And he's a lot more drunk now than he was then."

He pulled her closer. "I'm sorry if I embarrassed you," he admitted. The confession was difficult even though he couldn't see her face. "I wasn't sure you'd want my help. I was afraid you'd tell me to mind my own business."

"Well, I could have handled him, of course," she answered stoutly. "But it would have required an unpleasant scene."

Heartened by her pluckiness, he grinned and said, "That's my girl."

"Woman," she corrected him with her usual aplomb, proving she was back on top of things. "I haven't been anybody's 'girl' in a long time."

Suddenly he remembered just what he'd said to the drunk; he realized the implication of Roberta's words as well. She must have realized it, too, because suddenly she was pulling back a bit, saying, "What I mean is—"

"I know what you mean."

But suddenly he didn't know what *he* meant. He didn't know what he wanted. He didn't know what to do.

The music stopped. His boots ceased to clatter across the floor. Roberta's long skirts stopped swaying.

His cheek almost met hers; he could feel her warm breath on his chin. The female body in his arms was alive, warm, swaying toward him. He wanted her. He knew she wanted him.

And suddenly he knew he couldn't pretend anymore. Things were happening too fast. He wanted this woman, wanted her in a way he'd never wanted a woman before. She lifted her head until their eyes met. If their lips had been an inch closer, they would have touched. Desire and muted hope radiated from her mouth to his. His whole body felt as though it were crumbling, melting in her flames.

His hands slid up to cradle her face, and he could feel her trembling. Every instinct in his body called out for him to pull her closer, to ignore the throbbing crush of bodies that still filled the dance floor.

And then he realized, as surely as if he'd signed a pledge in blood, that if he kissed Roberta now he'd pull her out the door, down the steps, inside his trailer... where she'd surely spend the night.

It would be wonderful; it would be glorious. It would happen too fast for either one of them to think about tomorrow, about where they'd both be heading then—Roberta back to the intellectual world where doctorates were as common as colds, Clay back to a ranch like the one Roberta had fled as a frightened teen.

And that was when he remembered why it would never work, why he had to protect them both from the despair and mutual destruction that would surely precipitate their parting. The Roberta he wanted was only a mirage, a woman on a platform, a woman whose love he might be lucky enough to win, but whose respect he could surely never keep.

Here, during a lonely weekend, Roberta might want him enough to share a tender moment or two. But back home, inside the hallowed university walls, he knew she'd be ashamed of him. She didn't want a cowboy for a lover, and Clay didn't want Roberta Jean Wheeler, Ph.D.

He wanted a Texas girl. He wanted Bobbie Jean.

CHAPTER SEVEN

SHE WAITED FOR HIM all night.

Even now, after a week of normal classes back in Tucson, she couldn't believe he hadn't come. Roberta was no expert on the needs of men, but she was certain she'd seen genuine hunger in Clay's eyes that night on the rustic dance floor. She was certain he'd ached for her every bit as much as she'd ached for him.

It wasn't easy to accept the fact that she'd been wrong. It was even harder to accept the fact that she'd fallen flat on her face for a man who apparently was unmoved by her incipient love for him.

For days Roberta had shied away from that awesome name for her feelings for Clay, tried desperately to believe those feelings couldn't possibly run that deep. But she knew that the wild, crashing joy she'd felt on the dance floor—not to mention the absolute hollowness of her soul since then—spoke of a powerful cluster of emotions that outstripped anything she'd ever felt before. Whatever it was, she didn't like it, and she desperately wished that the cacophony of feelings would cease to plague her.

"Roberta? Roberta, are you still with us?"

She glanced up nervously, surprised to realize that she was still in the faculty lounge where she generally ate her weekday lunch. In fact, everything was pretty much the way it always was, except for the absence of two secretaries who were out with the viral laryngitis that was making the rounds. Stella, the chatty redhead who taught Asian history, was chewing the ears off of Henry Oliver, who specialized in World War II. The two women who shared an office and most of the Latin American history courses were splitting a sandwich near the window, and Charles, who ate in the lounge as often as not, was sitting directly across the table from Roberta.

She realized, with a start, that she hadn't noticed him come in and had no recollection of greeting him. No wonder he was pressing for a bit more attention.

"Uh, hello, Charles. How are things going today?"

He gave her a surprisingly supportive smile. "Stella just asked me that question and I answered it in great detail. I must have put you to sleep."

Roberta flushed. Aside from the fact that Charles was exactly the sort of man she believed she should marry, he was her boss—her immediate supervisor, anyway—and Roberta was keenly aware that offending him was both inappropriate and imprudent.

"I'm sorry, Charles. I was . . . off somewhere else. I didn't hear you come in at all, and I'd be happy to listen to whatever you want to tell me about your day."

He smiled again. *That makes twice in one day,* she noted absently. *He's already over his quota.*

His smile was nothing like Clay's. When Clay smiled, his whole face lit up. He threw his head back and gestured with his hands, big, sturdy hands, which could. . . .

"Are you feeling all right, Roberta?" Charles asked solicitously. "You seem to keep drifting away."

She felt a rush of heat color her cheeks. Silently she cursed Clay as she maintained, "I've just got a lot on my mind, Charles. Is there something important you wanted to say?"

He looked almost offended. "I wanted to discuss your last chautauqua, but I guess this isn't the time or place."

Instantly Roberta snapped to attention, thrusting Clay out of her head. Was it possible that Charles had already heard about her problems with the drunk? Would it influence his feelings about letting grad students participate? "Let's make an appointment, Charles," she suggested brightly. "I don't have any classes this afternoon and I'm free tomorrow morning until ten."

"And I'm busy until noon," he answered without missing a beat, "so why don't we meet at Christie's around one?"

"Christie's?" Roberta repeated blankly. Christie's was a very nice, almost lavish restaurant downtown. The food was excellent and the service superb, but it was neither a convenient nor typical choice for a business engagement. "Wouldn't it be easier to talk in your office?"

Again he smiled.

That makes three times today, computed the counter in her head. Granted, he had been warm and complimentary the last few times they'd talked, but there was something different about his smile today.

"It would be easier, Roberta, but not nearly as pleasant," he explained. Then his voice dropped slightly as he confessed, "I was looking forward to the opportunity to engage in some personal conversation with you undisturbed."

His pale blue eyes met hers with an expression she'd never read in them before. It was not a plea, exactly—

Charles did not know how to beg—but it was a request, or maybe an invitation, for something more personal than taking on a committee chairpersonship or doing a rush job turning in her grades. *My God, I think he's asking me for a date!* Roberta realized belatedly. How long had she waited for this moment? How hopelessly had she believed it would never come to pass? Why wasn't she feeling deliriously excited that it finally had?

Apparently she hesitated too long, because Charles averted his eyes as he said discreetly, "Of course, if you'd prefer to confer briefly in my office, that would be fine, too."

For a moment Clay's face swam before her, Clay's face shining with reckless joy as he galloped along doing rope tricks on a camel... Clay's face gentle with sympathy as he cuddled a female desperately fighting tears because she no longer had the courage to ride.

If she had a choice between them, she realized—logic or no logic—she'd choose Clay over any man. But she *didn't* have a choice. Clay didn't want her. And it was just remotely possible that Charles—whom she respected highly—did.

"I'd be delighted to meet you at Christie's tomorrow," she warmly agreed, feeling a surge of pleasure as Charles's eyes swept back up to meet hers in poorly concealed relief. "I'll be there with bells on at one."

ROBERTA WORE a white summer dress with fluttery wing sleeves when she lunched with Charles. In honor of the occasion, she dabbed on a bit of eye shadow and dug out her only tube of lipstick. She even looked over her collection of earrings—three pairs—and put on the tiny pearls.

Charles looked the way he always did—immaculate in a black suit and tie. His blond hair all but shimmered in the sunlight drifting in from the dramatic window on the wall, which was flanked by green plants of all shapes and sizes. It made him look bigger than life... like the king fish in a giant aquarium.

"I'm glad you could spare the time to meet with me, Roberta," he said formally, making her wonder, for the hundredth time, if he'd actually intended this to be a business meeting or a date. "I have three things to discuss with you today."

That hardly sounds auspicious, she told herself, pasting on the smile she kept handy for such moments. *If he thinks all this swank will make up for pulling the plug on my program, he's in for a big surprise.*

But Charles didn't seem to want to talk about her chautauqua program right away. First he tried to order for Roberta—backing off when she insisted that she could choose for herself—and then he informed her that he'd found an excellent summer intern to assist her.

"Marla Stevenson is one of our best. She's a bit starry-eyed and garrulous at times, but her scholarship is superb. She comes from a Texas home that frowns upon female academics, so I think your role-modeling will be vital to her success."

Roberta thought that was overstating the case a bit, and she also wanted to protest that not all Texas parents were allergic to school just because hers and Marla's were. Instead she said, "She sounds fine, Charles. One of my classes for the summer term if fairly traditional and one relies heavily on my chautauqua approach. The combination should give her a good balance."

Charles sipped his coffee—black, no sugar, a touch of cream—as he soberly studied Roberta. His intensity was making her nervous. In fact, he almost seemed edgy himself, and that exacerbated her own tension.

"Speaking of your 'chautauqua approach,'" he said quietly, "how did it go in Little Horn?"

Oh, no, here it comes, she thought grimly. She debated sidestepping the drunk altogether, but she knew she couldn't. Especially if he'd heard about it from some other source.

"Oh, it was fine, Charles. I ran into a couple of minor problems using Carry Nation—one drunk took umbrage and one woman who was married to an alcoholic tried to turn my speech into a therapy session—but other than that it went fine. Actually I think Susan B. Anthony goes over better, though. The rights of women are—"

"A drunk, you say?" His tone was stern. "How, exactly, did he voice his displeasure?"

This man is too sly, she realized unhappily. *Can't pull much over on him.*

"Well, he said it was a free country, a man could drink if he felt like it, that sort of thing. Actually—" it was the truth "—it sort of fit right into the usual pattern of nineteenth-century heckling. Sometimes my friends have heckled me voluntarily to get things moving. He just sort of hurried things along."

Roberta sipped her water, wishing the waiter would appear with a timely interruption. But there was no reprieve, just Charles staring at her quietly.

"And that was the end of it?"

She would have been okay if she hadn't met his eyes. They were stern—department-head stern—but there was something else in them that she couldn't believe and she couldn't ignore. He looked concerned, genuinely concerned. The way Clay had looked when he'd rescued her from the drunk at the dance.

It startled her, softened her, made her remember all the reasons she'd once hoped she'd fall in love with him... once hoped he'd fall in love with her. Painfully she remembered how Clay had turned away, rejected her not once but several times, and she knew, with sudden clarity, that her future lay clad not in some dusty buckskin jacket but in the flawless suit dead ahead.

"He harassed me at an 1850s costume ball, Charles," she guilelessly confessed. "I was uncomfortable, but I kept him at bay. Then another man gave me a hand."

Charles didn't ask about the other man, the Good Samaritan. Nor did he let her squirm away. "Did he hurt you? Frighten you? Are you okay?" Honest concern tightened his voice. He almost looked afraid.

"It wasn't that bad, Charles, honestly," she assured him, touched by his alarm. "I'd almost forgotten about it till you brought it up."

He sat back stiffly, laying both hands out flat on the table as though to steady himself. "I presume it's recorded in your official report."

She swallowed hard. "Well, I did mention it, Charles, but—"

"Has anything like this ever happened before?"

"No."

"But you've never gone anywhere the office has arranged before, have you? You always spoke at the invitation of a specific friend."

"Well, that's true, Charles, but—"

"A student could not have handled that. We could have been sued."

"Oh,Charles, you're overreacting!" A sudden panic shot through her heart. He couldn't be thinking of axing her program! She'd barely had a chance to start! "The heckling is part of the chautauqua experience. Besides, a group of students would always be together, with me to supervise. They'd be in no more danger than exchange students in Europe, Charles."

He couldn't argue that. Still, he eyed her quietly as he said, "I don't like the idea of you making this tour alone. If you had any kind of a problem, there would be no one to help you."

Suddenly she saw Clay coming to her side after her scare when he fell; she could feel his gentle hand on her head. A keen wave of gratitude for the marvelous understanding Clay had shown swept over her. "I'm not alone, Charles, not really," she told him truthfully. "I have a friend who makes the same circuit every year."

He digested this information, then soberly said: "I don't like this, Roberta. If you have any more trouble—any kind at all— I want you to let me know. I've always had some reservations about this idea of traipsing about the countryside. Your chautauquas in the classroom are creative, effective, maybe even brilliant. But out on the road..." He shook his head. "Honestly, Roberta, I just don't know."

Roberta found herself tugging tiny pieces off of her napkin and tossing them in her lap. She struggled to get control of herself, then said firmly, "Trust me, Charles. Please. It'll all work out."

Their eyes met, debated. Roberta refused to look away. At last he said, "Keep on your schedule. Keep copious notes." His voice was firm. "If anything like this happens again—any trouble at all— I'll cancel the rest of the tour."

Roberta swallowed hard. "There will be no problems," she promised him.

"I hope not. But if there are, don't play games with me, Roberta. You've got to let me know."

She couldn't hold his gaze any longer. He was the head of the department. She could influence him, beg him, lie to him if it came to that, but she couldn't overrule him. "I'll keep you posted, Charles," she promised.

Over the course of their conversation her interest in the meal had vanished, as had her foolish expectation that Charles had chosen Christie's because he'd considered this a quasi-date. Desperately wishing that the waiter would arrive to put her out of her misery, she asked a bit too harshly, "You said you had three things to tell me, Charles. We've covered one and two. What's number three?"

To her amazement, Charles's neck suddenly turned bright red. He glanced at his coffee, at her plundered napkin, then slowly lifted his eyes to her face. "I wanted to ask you," he said very carefully, each syllable a confession of his uncertainty, "if you might want to go out to dinner with me on Saturday night."

For the first time in her life, Roberta Wheeler was rendered absolutely mute.

ROBERTA DID NOT COME to Marshall, Montana. Of course, Clay had no particular reason to believe that she would and a very good reason to hope that she wouldn't. Still, he felt a keen sting of disappointment when he realized that he'd be spending the entire weekend without sharing a single laugh with such a special friend.

And she *was* special. Of that he had no doubt. That was the trouble, in fact. She was too special for a cowboy: too bright, too capable, too sure of who she was and what she wanted. He wasn't sure he could ever keep up with her. At a pleasant weekend summer fair, they seemed like equals, and their real lives back home didn't seem to matter. But he knew only too well that when summer was over, whatever glorious times they'd spent together would seem as illusory as a mirage.

Camel jockey Irene Wileman, on the other hand, was about as solid as a woman could be. She didn't just hail from a Texas ranch or pretend to be a cowgirl when it suited her. She was an old hand and made no bones about it. Clay had known her for years but had never been romantically inclined in her direction; now he wondered if a meaningful relationship with a good-hearted woman with an education like his own might help push Roberta from his mind. He spent most of Saturday afternoon in Marshall palling around with Irene, trying to convince himself that maybe there could be more than friendship between them. But he couldn't even rev up the spirit to make a pass at her, which was a good thing since it turned out she had a hot date for Saturday night anyway. He spent the evening playing penny-ante gin rummy with Ozzie, and wondering what Roberta was doing.

He tried not to think about the fact that she may well have had a date herself that night. If she did, Clay knew he had nobody to blame but himself.

"I ACTUALLY HAD A DATE with Charles, Tess," Roberta told her friend when they talked on the phone on Sunday afternoon. They'd already discussed Brady, J.J., the growing number of tourists flocking to Patchwork and the Hendersons' ongoing concern that Ira might not go to college in September, despite the several applications he'd sent out.

"Last week when we went out to lunch, we mainly talked about the chautauqua tour and my graduate summer intern, but then he shocked my socks off by asking me out to dinner at a posh spot with a dance floor. I went, and we had a great time."

There was a moment's silence before Tess said, "That's . . . great, I guess. I mean, you always thought he'd be perfect for you."

Roberta heard the hesitation in Tess's voice, a hesitation that matched the subdued pleasure in her heart. "You don't sound very thrilled."

"I'm just surprised, I guess. I had the definite feeling that you had your sights on somebody else."

Roberta exhaled a long sigh. "If you mean Clay, let me bring you up-to-date. I made it clear that I was interested, and he made it clear that he was *not*. It was the better part of valor for me to go my own way."

"Oh, Roberta, I'm sorry," Tess said gently.

"So am I." *Sorrier than I can possibly say.* "But what is, is, I always say. Clay is out and Charles is in. You know Charles is far more appropriate for me anyway."

"Yes, he is," Tess agreed, though she didn't sound entirely convinced. "And we both know how important propriety has always been to you."

The words were spoken tongue in cheek, but Roberta didn't like them anyway. "We have a lot in common, Tess, you know that," she reminded her friend. "There are no jagged edges to our lives."

"I know that. I also know that never, in all the time I've known you, have you ever *glowed* when you mentioned that man's name. And every time you mention Clay, you just—"

"Tess, he doesn't want me!" she snapped with more vigor than she'd intended. "It's not like I'm choosing Charles over Clay. I'm choosing Charles over nothing!"

The words seemed stark and harsh, and she wondered, for the first time, if she was really being fair to Charles. Oh, she admired him a great deal and she'd wanted their relationship to blossom for some time. But her feelings for him were so tepid compared to what she felt for Clay! So logical. So intellectual. So tame.

She'd felt no throb when he'd held her gingerly while they danced; she'd been almost relieved that he hadn't kissed her. Of course, Charles was her supervisor and her colleague, so he remained discreet in public and equally respectful when they were alone. He did not touch her unless he was helping her put on her coat or get out of his Mercedes.

There had been a time, Roberta recalled dimly, when she would have longed for a more vivid demonstration of his feelings—if only to erase Clay from her thoughts. But to her surprise, Charles's flattering attention had done nothing whatsoever to ease her longing for the other man. In her mind she was certain that dating Charles was the right thing to do; marrying him would be wiser yet. Getting closer to Clay was clearly out of the question. So why was it that Tess's probing questions left her so uneasy?

After another long silence, Tess asked, "When are you seeing Charles again?"

"He asked me to go see a musical with him next weekend. *The Phantom of the Opera*. It should be very nice."

"I'm sure it will," said Tess. "Speaking of operas, or opera houses, at least, ours is coming along rather nicely. We've got three bids to finish remodeling it and Brady says we'll make the final decision in a few days. I'm still hoping that you can make your debut onstage during the sesquicentennial weekend."

Roberta had almost forgotten the massive parade and festivities scheduled for November when tiny Redpoint, Colorado would celebrate its one hundred and fiftieth anniversary. Brady and Tess were planning to enter a group of wagons in the parade and hoped to kick off the opera house that same weekend.

"You want me to give a solo speech or did you have some kind of a play in mind?"

"A play would be terrific, but I don't think we can pull it off without hiring somebody. You and Clay are the only people we know with backgrounds in drama, and both of you had training more geared to monologues."

"Clay's had speech training?" she asked with interest, wondering why he'd never mentioned it. She recalled how quickly she'd lost his interest when the subject of debate had come up over the dinner they'd shared in Patchwork. She'd assumed then that he'd had no similar training. In retrospect, she realized that the polish of his impromptu Lieutenant Beale speech after she fell apart in Little Horn should have tipped her off.

"Yes, he was a debater like you. Well, he was on the debate team in high school, not college, but from what he's said I gather it was a very demanding program so I imagine it was about the same. He's volunteered to traipse about as Lieutenant Beale that weekend, but I haven't asked him about giving a speech."

For a moment Roberta pondered the evening she and Clay had "traipsed about" together in Patchwork—not to mention the night they'd danced in Little Horn—and she wondered what would happen when they met again. She'd promised Charles that she had a "friend" who would be at all of her circuit stops, but she really had no firm notion of when she'd encounter Clay again.

Or whether he'd do his best to keep his distance.

Still, she didn't feel that she'd misrepresented her case to Charles. No matter how Clay might be feeling toward her—which was always anybody's guess— Roberta had no doubt that in a pinch, he'd come through for her. Again.

"I wish there were some way to pay Clay back for all he's done for us," Tess mused. "He's filled in for Brady on so many wagon trains, referred customers to us, given advice on almost everything over the years. He's a crucial link in this convoluted system."

Roberta felt a tug of sorrow inside, a tiny breath of loss. She didn't want to hear a litany of Clay's virtues. "I don't need a list of his credentials, Tess," she declared a bit roughly. "I need to forget the damn man."

"Are you sure, Roberta? Are you absolutely certain he feels nothing for you?"

Robert thought a moment, tried to recall the exact look on his face when he'd last called her his "li'l sweet petunia." That had been a joke. She tried to recall the tone of his voice when he'd told the drunk that she was his woman. That had been a defensive technique; he would have done the same for anyone. She tried to recall the look in his eyes when that last dance had ended, when he'd all but sizzled with desire.

That must have been her imagination, because if his true need for her had matched his body language, he never would have let her greet sunrise in the aching emptiness of that chilly hotel room bed.

The only thing I'm sure of, she promised herself fiercely, *is that I'll never wait up all night for him again.*

DURING MAY, Clay took the camels to three different tiny western communities. Each one had a parade, a dance and scores of creative folk art items for sale. Not a single one had a scheduled chautauqua.

The first time, in Marshall, he'd told himself it was just as well. The second time he'd told himself it didn't matter. The third time he'd packed along a gripping Richard Martin Stern novel to keep the evenings full. By then he'd stopped lying to himself.

He desperately missed Roberta.

He didn't know how to get in touch with her, but that problem could have been resolved with a thirty-second phone call to Patchwork. It would have involved admitting his feelings to Tess and Brady, of course, but that he could have endured. The trouble lay with taking the next step—admitting his feelings to Roberta.

What was he supposed to say? If he just happened to run into her in some town on the circuit it would be easy to play it by ear. But if he tracked her down in Tucson and made a big fuss about it, he would be declaring himself somehow. And he wasn't at all sure what he wanted to declare.

The only thing he was sure of was that if Roberta didn't show up in Kresky, Utah—the next time Susan B. Anthony's name showed up on his official schedule of events—he was going to have to make some hard decisions. Decisions that didn't make much sense.

IT WAS THE MIDDLE OF MAY when bright-eyed, brown-haired Marla Stevenson first showed up at Roberta's office. Despite her obvious sniffling from a bad cold and her attendant laryngitis, her eyes sparkled and her smile was wide.

"I'm thrilled to be assigned to you this summer, Dr. Wheeler," she declared in a raspy whisper, which she explained was all the voice she'd been able to muster since she'd come down with the cold.

Roberta wasn't surprised; the same symptoms had been making the rounds of her colleagues and students for the past two months. Trying to ignore the girl's unavoidable squawk, she assured her, "I'm delighted to have you with me, Marla. I understand you're from Texas, too."

The young woman grinned. "Lubbock. Dr. Trumbull said you're from Fort Worth."

"That general area," Roberta corrected her. Actually the nearest small town to her father's ranch was one nobody had ever heard of. "I'll be speaking near Lubbock in August," she told her new assistant. "Have you ever heard of a wide spot in the road called Three Teeth?"

Marla nodded and laughed. "You bet. It's only a hundred miles or so from Lubbock, named after a local who kept losing his teeth in fights. You know, Dr. Wheeler, I'll be back home by August. Maybe I could come hear you speak?"

Roberta had never had a student appear in a roadside audience, and she wondered if it would be good or bad. Recalling her episode with the drunk—and Charles's keen apprehension about any future troubles—she decided that maybe it would be safer not to have anybody from the university observe her performances on the road.

"You don't have to wait until then to see me give a chautauqua, Marla," she assured the eager young woman. "You can watch me in action right here."

"This summer?"

"Absolutely. I'll be teaching two classes this term. One is a freshman general history class and one is a senior seminar on Women and the West. The first will have weekly homework, which I'll expect you to help me grade. The second will involve some rather, uh, unorthodox approaches to the teaching of history."

Marla grinned. "I know. I've heard some fascinating things about your classes! I'm hoping to sign up for your chautauqua tour next summer when you open it up to grad students."

Roberta was pleased with the compliment—and the obvious message that the news of her project was getting around—but she had to be honest with the young woman. "There is no traveling chautauqua class lined up for next summer yet, Marla. Dr. Trumbull has only agreed to *consider* the possibility pending my report this year. There are a number of logistical factors that still need to be worked out."

Actually Roberta didn't intend for anything to stand in the way of her graduate chautauqua circuit, but Charles was still feeling uneasy about her tour. Roberta had repeatedly reminded him that her plan was no more risky than a semester in France or an Egyptian archeology dig—both of which were available to students at T.S.U.—but it seemed he was more afraid of drunken cowboys than mysterious foreigners.

"Honestly, Charles," she'd told him once. "This is 1990. It's not as though these towns will be full of wild cowpokes who just rode into Abilene with the longhorns."

"The year makes no difference," he'd pointed out sagely. "The masses never change."

Roberta couldn't argue with that too vigorously, but she knew that the bourgeois notion was precisely the sort of intellectual snobbery of which Clay had once accused her. It made her uncomfortable to see the same feature in a man she greatly admired and had been eager to date.

Now, after three evening dates and five working lunches, she was having trouble summoning her earlier enthusiasm for Charles. She enjoyed their time together; he was an urbane host and an intellectually stimulating companion. But she felt no breathlessness when he touched her arm or shoulder, and suffered no great anguish when he failed to touch her elsewhere. With Clay, just the look in his eyes had been enough to make her crazy.

But Clay doesn't want me, she reminded herself every time his memory stole the pleasure from her time with Charles. *I asked him outright and he turned away. There's no maybe about it, I have to let him go.*

"Dr. Wheeler?" prodded Marla, as though she'd said Roberta's name before. "Is there anything special you want me to do before summer session starts?"

Roberta shook her head. The only special thing she wanted was to see Clay Gann smiling a "How desperately I've missed you, Bobbie Jean" greeting, and that was something that was clearly not meant to be.

A WEEK BEFORE her scheduled trip to Kresky, Roberta came down with a sore throat and a cold—thanks to Marla, she was certain. She was not terribly ill, however, and by the time she crossed the Utah state line on Friday afternoon, she felt perfectly normal, except for one thing: she had no voice whatsoever.

She whispered loudly at cashiers. She croaked at gas station attendants like a sore-throated toad. She pointed to menus for waitresses and smiled mutely at anybody else who tried to carry on a sensible conversation.

For six days she had pretended that she'd be well enough to speak in Kresky, but by the time she reached the tiny town the next morning, she realized that there was no way on earth she was going to be able to harangue a crowd by three o'clock that afternoon.

The spector of Charles's response to her failure filled her with trepidation. He'd made it so clear that there could be no more problems of any kind! This was a different problem than the one she'd had with the drunk, of course, but it emphasized the frailty of her organization. He'd nearly pulled the plug on her plans after that incident in Little Horn, and if she reported a no-show and had an angry sponsor...

Well, that just couldn't happen. Somehow, some way, she was going to have to find a substitute speaker. Somebody who could give her prepared speech...or some other chautauqua that fit in to the town's Old Western Days celebration. Any subject would do: abolition, states' rights, the Monroe Doctrine.

Or, perhaps—yes, oh yes!—the need for a U.S. Army Camel Corps.

It was a miracle that she happened to know a man who would be in town that very weekend who always traveled with a cavalry officer's uniform in his trailer closet. The only question was whether or not Roberta could find the courage to ask him to do her a favor without revealing how desperately she longed for his touch.

CHAPTER EIGHT

CLAY HAD JUST FINISHED supervising the first round of camel races when he heard the rap on his trailer door. He'd been expecting Ozzie, but there was too much power in the knock for his caller to be Oz. Lately the boy had been acting even more timid than usual.

He took the three steps from the tiny kitchen to the door and pulled it open, intending to say howdy to his unexpected guest after he tugged the nearly boiling kettle off the stove. But one glance at the broad-browed bonnet and ankle-length full skirt was enough to stop him in his tracks. His stomach did a neat three-hundred-and-sixty degree somersault as he joyfully realized that his caller was Roberta.

It had been six long weeks since he'd seen her. Six long weeks of second-guessing his decision to keep his distance from her that night at the 1850s ball, six long weeks of rising need to see her face, touch her hands, hold her in his arms.

Coffee plans forgotten, he opened the door a bit wider and gave her an unabashedly welcoming grin.

"Bobbie Jean. My, my," he greeted her playfully. "Aren't you a sight for sore eyes."

Roberta smiled. It wasn't a nervous smile or a hesitant smile or even a questioning one. Her radiant grin cast light on every corner of her strong-boned face. He had the strangest feeling that his smile had warmed her like the morning sun.

"It's good to see you, too, Clay," she told him softly. At least, he thought that was what she said. Her voice was a hoarse mixture of whispery speech and air. He practically had to read her lips to decipher her meaning.

"Got a touch of laryngitis, I see," he teased her.

"More than a touch," she croaked. "I can't talk at all."

Clay chuckled. "Well, don't that beat all. A silent female. I reckon you'll just have to do all the listening, then." He studied her closely as she continued to beam at him. "Or then again, maybe we could find something else to do besides talk."

Her smile faded just slightly as she appeared to ponder his words. But her eyes were still bright as she rasped, "Maybe we can talk later. Right now I came to ask you a favor."

He might have hidden his disappointment from Roberta, but he couldn't hide it from himself. Oh, he was glad to help Roberta out, glad that she felt sufficiently at ease with him to seek him out for help. But after all the time they'd been apart, all his mounting frustration, all of his... well, second thoughts about whether or not it might be worth the risk of throwing caution to the winds to spend some time with her... a visit just to ask a favor was a bit of a letdown.

Over this past month, he had just about convinced himself that he'd made a grave mistake pushing her away the last time they'd been together. At the very least he'd decided to take the risk of spending some more time with her, savoring the moments fate handed him, exploring the possibilities that somehow seemed more likely than they had seemed before. But he'd been banking on his memory of Roberta's feelings for him. And she had—surely!—been eager enough to further their acquaintance in Little Horn. But it had never occurred to him until this very moment that in the month that had passed since then, her feelings might have changed.

By now she could even be seeing someone else.

Clay's eyes sought hers, seeking confirmation of his dearest hope: that she hadn't just come to him for help. Her gaze was proud, determined... and despite the radiant smile he'd seen a few moments before, he could see now that she was uneasy.

So was he.

Before he could stop himself, Clay blurted out, "It's been a long time since we've been together, Bobbie Jean. Before we get down to negotiating favors, don't you think you ought to kiss me hello?"

He threw out the challenge only casually... at least that was what he told himself. But as Roberta casually lifted her lips to his cheek, he suddenly realized that he wasn't in the market for a platonic peck. He wanted far more from Roberta, and it was time to tell her so.

And then, for no reason that he could fathom, Roberta didn't kiss his cheek at all. Her soft, full lips found his instead.

It was a brief kiss, a chaste kiss, a kiss that whetted his appetite and made his heart cry out for more. She pulled away before he had a chance to respond, but not before his strong hands found her waist and steadied her; he desperately fought the urge to pull her closer.

He took a deep breath to still the sudden trembling. To his surprise, it did no good. He considered himself a strong man, a man of great control, but he could not stop from shaking. And he could not step away.

Clay didn't recognize his own low tone when he huskily confessed, "That's not quite how I pictured our first kiss, Bobbie Jean."

This time something new flickered in Roberta's hazel eyes... a hint of hunger, a hint of fear? But though she straightened, she did not pull away. Her eyes met his boldly as she asked in today's raspy tone, "How... exactly... did you imagine it, Clay?"

One hand lifted to stroke her cheek. The other swept around her back to pull her close against him. "I don't rightly recall all the details—" he took another deep breath "—but I think it was something like this."

Hungrily he took her mouth—with strength and need and tenderness—and made it his own. Her moist lips met Clay's, then parted as his tongue sought entrance to the private reaches of her delicate mouth.

They melded together as though they'd kissed a thousand times before. There was no hesitation, no question, no restraint. He wanted her and he knew she wanted him. He was done asking questions about right and wrong and practical, and as far as Clay could tell, so was she.

"Roberta," he whispered against her mouth as he pulled her tightly against him. "It's been so damn hard."

"Oh, Clay." Her voice was barely a whisper now against the shimmering moisture of his throat. Her arms snaked around his waist, then lifted to tug on his shoulders. He could feel her breasts press into his chest. "It's you I want, Clay," she confessed. Her voice broke, not just with laryngitis but with emotion. "Please don't change your mind again."

He shook his head, suddenly afraid to speak. His hand swept over her bonneted head, tugging loose the straps as he stroked her ear and fingered her curly hair. His lips found hers again, then her cheek, her jaw and the hollow of her throat. Her strong feminine hands left his shoulders, cradled his neck and embraced his head.

Clay kissed her again—kissed her hard. Suddenly they were pressed together, thigh to thigh, breathing too fast and starting to sweat in the closed space of the trailer.

"Roberta?" he whispered against her hair. It wasn't a question, not really. It was a request for confirmation that he was right in his interpretation of her desire.

She pressed against him, pulling his head down hard for another searching kiss. He slid one hand down her shoulder and over the upper curve of her breast. She arched upward, her nipple seeking his hand. He gave her what she wanted.

But only for a second. Even as his fingers stroked her, he whispered in frustration, "Ozzie'll be knocking on that door any second. I think we're going to be sorry if we—" he took in a deep breath "—don't wait till a little later to finish saying howdy."

He heard her moan softly. She did not move away, but she stopped pressing against him—just held him with her strong arms.

"You're sure it's just Ozzie?" she whispered. "You're not just making another excuse to send me away?"

"Oh, Roberta!" He kissed her again, letting his lips answer the question more forcefully than any words could have. "I'm done sending you away. I'm done counting the days wondering what will happen when I see you again. I'm done going to sleep every night trying to get up the gumption to call Brady and ask for your number and address."

She pulled back then, her fingers still threaded in his hair, her nipple still alert beneath his stroking thumb. "Clay, if you felt that way, why didn't you call? Do you have any idea how—" She broke off then, swallowing a sigh of frustration. Suddenly she covered his hand with her own and gently pulled it away. "I can't take much more of that right now. Not if we...have to wait."

He grinned. He loved the idea of his high-strung filly panting for him. A few more minutes of frustration wouldn't hurt her. When he did minister to her needs—as soon as Ozzie gave him his midday report on the camels—she'd have no complaints about the wait.

With one last stroke, more tender than erotic, he slipped both arms around Roberta and cradled her gently. His timing couldn't have been better. Almost at once Ozzie knocked on the door.

Roberta jumped back as though she'd heard a gunshot.

"Shhh. I told you Ozzie was coming. Don't look like you've got anything to hide."

They shared a secret, power-charged grin as they reluctantly released each other and struggled for calm.

"It's open!" Clay called out, unwilling to turn his back on Roberta long enough to answer the door.

An instant later Ozzie poked his head inside the trailer. "Clay, I just—" The boy stopped as he spied Roberta. "Uh, hello, R-R-Roberta," he stammered. "N-n-nice to see you."

"Hello, Ozzie." Her whisper wasn't particularly warm, but neither was it chilling.

Still, her raspy tone was odd enough that Clay felt compelled to explain, "Roberta's got laryngitis, Ozzie. She doesn't feel much like talking."

Ozzie looked relieved. "Uh... that's t-t-too bad."

Roberta shrugged, as though to say it were nothing, then swiveled her glance back to Clay.

A flash of desire zigzagged from her eyes to his, and he felt the need for her wash over his whole body. Tensely he asked Ozzie, "What's the word?"

"I, uh, just w-w-wanted to know if you wanted to check on the camels before the next race. Warner checked on Luscious Laura after she r-r-ran into the fence this morning and he says sh-sh-she's okay. Do you w-w-want her to run this afternoon?"

Clay replied evenly, "Give Laura the rest of the day off. She seemed all right when I looked at her just before lunch, but if you see any sign of a problem, let me know."

"Okay," said Ozzie, his face slightly red.

"Is that all?"

"Uh... I guess so. We can get the camels ready without you."

Clay shot him a commanding glance. "Do that."

Ozzie retreated without further ado, and Clay locked the trailer door behind him. He knew the boy would be curious, but he didn't feel he had to explain every move he made. It would be obvious to all of his men soon enough that he'd found a special friend. Right now he wanted to savor the moment in privacy.

But at the moment there wasn't much to savor, because when he turned back to Roberta she was retying the strings on her bonnet as though she were a prudent nineteenth-century virgin. She'd actually taken a few steps toward the kitchen; his bed was at the opposite end of the trailer.

He knew better than to reach for her quickly, to risk offending her by trying too bluntly to recapture the moment they'd lost. As casually as he was able, he took a seat on the small bench sandwiched against one wall of the trailer and motioned for her to do the same. She did so, gingerly, scooping up her voluminous skirts when they threatened to spill over his knee. Quietly he took her hand, and she clung to him with heartening eagerness.

He only kissed her once before she said softly, "Before we... get carried away—" they shared a mutually erotic grin "—I need to discuss something with you."

At first he thought she was about to bring up birth control, but in an instant he realized that her mind was on something else altogether.

"Clay, I need to ask you to do me a favor."

He tried to quiet his own arousal and concentrate on her words. She looked remarkably serious for somebody asking for a casual favor. With a false show of calm, he said, "You mentioned something about that when you came in."

"Yes. It's terribly important to me, Clay, or I wouldn't ask. Especially now," she added as she stroked his jaw. Her voice was still a strained whisper, punctuated by an occasional barked syllable or two. "And I really don't think it'll be that hard for you."

He squeezed her fingers gently, restraining the urge to pull her back into his arms. After all that had happened between them—and all that hadn't—over the past few months, he was surprised that she was so willing to take time out at a moment like this to start talking about something prosaic. There was an awkwardness between them now that hadn't been there before. He hoped it was just a first-kiss transition phase that another embrace or two would clear up, but he knew he had to get this favor-asking out of the way.

"Whatever it is, you know I'll help you, Roberta," he assured her. "Shoot."

She sighed in relief, then touched her throat. "I'm supposed to speak in three hours," she croaked. "There's just no way. But Charles has made it crystal clear that I can't report any more foul-ups. He was really upset about what happened in Little Horn."

For a moment he thought she was referring to her ringside hysteria, then realized that she meant the unpleasant episode with the drunk.

"If I don't provide a substitute, the fellow in charge of entertainment is going to have a fit and it'll get back to Charles," she explained, her grip tightening. "I need a fill-in, Clay."

Clay was dismayed. He'd meant what he said about helping her, but he couldn't possibly see what he could do. "Roberta...wow, you've got me stumped," he admitted. "The only woman I know in town this weekend well enough to ask for help is Irene Wileman, one of the camel jockeys. She's solid as a rock and hell on horseback, but I can't see her making a speech. I doubt that she knows enough about history to fake a role as Susan B."

Roberta shook her head. "I don't want somebody else to be Susan. Only a professional actor could master a new role in a few hours. I need somebody to give a chautauqua he's done before." Her eyes were big now, imploring. "Somebody who can take on a persona that it's easy for him to be."

A strange, quicksandy feeling began to stir within Clay. He wasn't sure what she was getting at, but he didn't like the way she kept saying "he."

"I don't know any men who give chautauquas, either, Roberta. You're the only traveling orator I know."

She shook her head, squeezed his hand and moved an inch closer. She laid one earnest hand on his thigh, instantly arousing him. "If you have your uniform with you," she rasped, "you could be Lieutenant Beale."

He stared at her, his mouth slack. Arousal vanished and nausea took its place. "I only walk around in costume to lend ambience. I don't—"

"That's not true! You play his part with words all the time! And that time I was so scared when Violet threw you, you gave me a whole speech off the top of your head! That's all you'd have to tell the crowd. I bet you've given folks that lecture on the value of camels a thousand times. It would be a snap."

Clay did not answer. He could not speak.

"Besides, you've been trained to speak off the cuff. I know it's been a long time, but once you've gone through the debate mill, you never forget. It all comes back."

You never forget. It all comes back, he groaned to himself. *God, yes, you never forget. It's been twenty-six years, and just the thought of giving a speech splinters my stomach, cuts off my air....*

"No," he choked out. "It wouldn't work."

Remnants of hope shadowed her eyes. Frustration darkened her shadowed lids. "Please, Clay. I'm desperate! It doesn't have to be perfect! I know you can do it!"

"You know nothing of the kind!" he snapped. "You're the one who got trophies for giving speeches. Not me!"

He felt panicky, trapped, ashamed. How could he tell her that he was *afraid* to do something she did so effortlessly? Worse yet, how could he tell her why? From her comments about Ozzie, he knew she had little patience with speech impediments. Granted, his was in the past, but he could only imagine her reaction to the news that he'd been a childhood stutterer. It would be even worse than her reaction to the news that he'd barely finished high school.

Suddenly his fear made him angry, and his anger made him suspicious. Mentally he retraced the last minutes between them since she'd arrived at his trailer—minutes that were completely different from any time they'd ever spent together before. He tried to recall how it had happened...who had made the first move. All he could remember was that searing hello kiss and her bald request for a favor—almost in the same breath, as he recalled.

"Is that what all this is about?" he barked, thrusting her beseeching hand from his taut thigh as he grappled with the sudden fear that he might have been used. How many times had he seen his mother play those games on his dad! Sweet-talking him to persuade him to do whatever she wanted him to do. "We've never been anything but friends before, but suddenly you need a favor and you can't get enough of my hands?"

Pink dappled Roberta's cheeks as she rose and wrenched herself away. "We've never been anything but friends because *you* didn't want me as a lover!" she croaked, her voice breaking painfully on the half-whispered words. "And *you* asked me to kiss you the moment I came in!"

"And you opposed the idea?" he shot back.

She swallowed hard and looked out the window toward the sage-dotted hills. He could tell she was fighting tears. But he knew she wouldn't cry; he knew how tough she could be. "I thought you'd had a change of heart," she whispered hoarsely. "I guess I read you wrong."

She started for the door then, but Clay caught her elbow as she whipped past him. She didn't fight him, didn't try to pull away. He felt stupid and sheepish, and he knew he was letting his past cloud his present judgment. He couldn't possibly give a speech—even for Roberta—but that was no reason to toss in the towel and push her away.

"I'm sorry, Roberta," he said softly, his grip loosening, easing into a caress. "I had no call to make accusations."

She met his eyes boldly. "Then why did you? Do I strike you as a catty sort of woman?"

He shook his head. "I don't think you're capable of guile."

"Is that a compliment?"

Slowly he nodded. "Yes, it is. I've got lots of other compliments stored up for you if you're in the mood to hear them."

She did not bat an eyelash. "Maybe some other time, Clay. Right now I want to know why you're making wild accusations, not to mention why you're refusing to do something so simple when I need your help so desperately."

He wouldn't have thought a person could plead with dignity when her voice was so shattered, but Roberta managed it. Her expression was proud, clear, straightforward. He longed to answer her questions with equal integrity, and he cursed his own dark fears.

"I grew up with a woman who tried to recreate the world in her own image," he admitted slowly. "She feigned affection when it pleased her. I don't think she really knew how to love."

Roberta's expression softened ever so slightly. "I'm sorry, Clay."

"She belittled everything that mattered to my father. Everything that mattered to me. She wanted a senator for a son, or a bank president at the very least. She hammered school down my throat so hard I gagged on it. She made me take debate for four terrible years, even though she knew it had given me an ulcer."

There was more, much more, but that was enough for now. He'd told the truth—or at least a glimmer of it—and if she handled that much with sympathy, maybe he could chance the rest of it someday.

"You hated debate?" Roberta asked, as though the notion was inconceivable to her.

He nodded.

"But you were good at it anyway."

He shook his head. "I was not good. I was terrible."

"I don't believe that. I've heard the way you express yourself. Even in the most casual presentation, your ideas are clear and organized, Clay. Fascinating and funny. You're a wordsmith. You play with words, whether you're taking the role of Clay Gann or Beale or the Camel Man. Nobody does that who isn't a natural born talker."

He could not meet her eyes. "I can talk. One-on-one. You're talking about speaking to a crowd. That's a different thing altogether."

"All you have to do is pretend you're talking to me, just the way you did before."

Sadly his eyes met hers. "No."

"Dammit, Clay, you know how to do it! I know you want to get back at your mother, but the one you're hurting now is *me*!"

Clay took her hand, pulling her closer. "I'm not trying to punish you. Or even her. I just—"

"Listen to me, Clay," she begged. She was whispering now, as though her voice had completely failed her. "This summer program means everything to me, and Charles will ax it if anything goes wrong! Do you think I would have come here and begged for your help if I hadn't need it desperately? I didn't know you'd be glad to see me. I was afraid you'd be embarrassed after...well, after the way we parted. I spent hours trying to decide if I had the courage to come to you. I finally decided that you were a kind man who would help out a stranger if he could. The only thing I doubted was whether I could find the courage to face a man who'd so clearly turned me away. I never for a minute really believed you'd say no."

Clay dropped his gaze. His shame—the old shame, coupled with some new variety—very nearly rendered him mute. Keenly he recalled the first weekend they'd met, when Roberta had revealed to him how often men had rejected her for being herself. And he'd done the same thing, not just in Patchwork but also in Little Horn. He knew what courage it had taken her to come to him for any reason. But she'd done it, damn her. She'd shown him true guts.

"Okay," he whispered, his gaze on the floor. His tone sounded more strained than Roberta's.

"Okay?" Disbelief streaked her raspy voice.

"I said okay!" he snapped, his eyes flitting past hers. He could not bear to face her, could not risk letting her see the terror mounting inside him. "Just tell me when and where, then get out of here and let me get ready."

"Oh, Clay—" she reached up to cup his face with both her hands "—thank you, thank you, thank you! I know you'll do a wonderful job. If you need any help preparing your—"

"I don't need a speech coach," he snapped, pulling away from her. Later—a lifetime later, after it was over—he could concentrate on those soft, strong hands and the feel of those lips upon his mouth. But now he turned away abruptly, before he could risk the inevitable kiss. He couldn't think about kisses, let alone concentrate on Roberta.

He was going into battle, and he needed time to arm.

CHAPTER NINE

THE NEXT TIME Ozzie saw Clay, it was three o'clock and he was dressed in his cavalry officer's uniform. He was standing in front of the trailer looking glazed. A dull shine moistened his face, and tiny pools of sweat glistened along his upper lip and beaded his mustache.

"Clay?" Ozzie asked, sensing that something was terribly wrong. "Are you sick?"

Clay stared at him. Actually Clay stared through him, or past him, or beyond him to some imaginary beast on the other side. Ozzie was sure it was imaginary because there was no one and no thing remotely near him, yet Clay was studying the air with clenched fists and grinding jaw.

Ozzie was scared. Not afraid-that-somebody-would-laugh-at-his-stutter scared, but really deep-down-inside scared. Clay was his rock, and if something was wrong with Clay, then something was wrong with his world. And it only took one glimpse at Clay to see that something was terribly wrong.

Cautiously he laid one hand on Clay's arm. "Clay? T-t-talk to me. What's going on?"

Clay stared at him, actually met his eyes this time. "I'm going to give a speech, Oz. I'm filling in for Roberta. I'm going to be Lieutenant Beale."

"A *sp-sp-speech*?" stammered Ozzie. "In front of *p-p-people*?"

Clay swallowed hard. He took several deep breaths. "I'm a trained speaker. I'm going to talk about camels. I know what to say."

Ozzie shook his head. "I thought you d-d-didn't want to give a speech ever again."

Clay tugged on his scarf. He closed his eyes and shuddered. "I don't."

"Then w-w-why are you doing this to yourself?"

Clay grimaced. He straightened slowly, as though he might be ruled by something more than fear. "She's counting on me, Ozzie." His voice was quiet now, but clear. Ozzie could see him getting a grip on himself, see his courage rise and strengthen.

Ozzie was awed. Quietly he murmured, "But Clay... aren't you sc-sc-scared?"

Clay did not deny it. But he did not wilt. He did not buckle. Instead he said softly, "There are some things more important than fear, Ozzie. Some things that can make you rise above it." As he started off for the platform he declared with increasing conviction, "There are some things a man simply has to do."

ROBERTA WAS in the crowd, watching and waiting, when Clay marched up to the platform with all the regal bearing befitting an Army officer in 1860. He had asked her not to speak to him before the speech, nor to interfere in any way. She still did not understand his great resistance to helping her out; she did not want to believe that Clay was pigheaded enough to carry a prejudice against public speaking after all these years. Then again, she knew he was downright hostile about academia. She could still recall the way he'd bristled when she'd started to talk about her doctorate the first night they met; in fact, it seemed to her that he bristled whenever she mentioned her work. And every time Charles popped into the conversation, the hair on the back of Clay's neck seemed to stand straight up.

Charles, she knew, would never have hesitated to take over a podium for any staff member or friend. He was good at speaking. In fact, he was good at almost everything. So far the only thing she'd ever seen him fail to accomplish was the one goal he didn't even realize loomed before him: making Roberta forget about Clay Gann. It was something she was increasingly sure he could never do.

Roberta wasn't given to flights of poetic fancy, but the simple truth was that Clay had rendered her absolutely powerless in those few breathless moments before Ozzie had arrived. She had never wanted anything—not even the trophies she'd collected as a rider—the way she'd wanted to make love to that man. Even now, when she was ostensibly ready to forget that aberrant moment, the mere thought of his hand on her breast left her shaking.

She didn't know what was going to happen when the speech was over. She didn't know if he would still be angry or suspicious... or even interested in her at all. The only thing she was sure of was that she had to know—positively, absolutely—that there was no hope whatsoever for a relationship with Clay before she gave herself to Charles.

And even then, she realized bleakly as the sight of the crisply-clad cavalry officer marching assertively up to the red-white-and-blue draped podium gave her heart a lurch, *poor Charles wouldn't stand a chance.*

But for all his regal carriage, when Clay reached the podium, he stared out at the crowd as though he were trying to get his bearings. In fact, he stared so long that a few people began to get restless, and Roberta had a sudden stomach-dropping instant during which she wondered if Clay might have blanked out momentarily. Stage fright, she knew, could do that to some people. But surely somebody of Clay's presence would never have a moment of such fear!

And then he started speaking. His voice was low, dramatic, and perfectly captured the pitch of an Army officer deeply committed to a cause. His gestures were fluent, remarkably natural. Her stomach began to unknot itself as she realized that he was going to do just fine.

"Ya'll might hear that camels are an obstreperous lot," Clay drawled, exaggerating the southern accent for dramatic effect. "But ladies and gents, it just ain't so. If you're good to a camel, he'll be as faithful to you as your best horse. Believe me, I know whereof I speak. I've got the most loyal camel in the world waiting for me back at the barn."

Roberta wondered if he was referring specifically to Violet. The two of them had an unusual relationship that was quite different from the one she'd had with Flame. She and Flame had been partners. Best friends. They had adored each other. Clay and Violet, on the other hand, maintained a well-restrained mutual respect. She wasn't sure she'd go so far as to call it affection.

"Now there is no more practical way to get across the desert than on a camel," Clay maintained. "A camel can carry a thousand pounds across the desert and cover a hundred miles in a single day. It can live on desert shrubs. The last time we crossed the Mojave with a camel herd, the camels carried enough water and food for the horses, mules and men but never drank one drop nor took a mouthful of the hay. Each beast was a veritable traveling machine!"

He went on for twenty minutes, extolling the virtues of the gangly beasts and bragging a bit about his own desert exploits on camelback. He played his part so perfectly that at times even Roberta forgot she was listening to Clay perform. But she couldn't forget the uneasiness she still read in his beautiful gray eyes. She didn't think that a stranger would discern the tension that racked every inch of his body, but to someone who cared for him deeply, it was all too clear.

When Clay finished, he did not wait around for congratulations and hurrahs. His eyes did not search the crowd for Roberta. He marched off the stage, shaking the hands of those people who pressed him, until he could finally break away. She followed him back to the trailer, but she was so far behind him that he'd already opened the trailer door when she arrived. He hadn't had time to close it before she slipped inside.

When he didn't turn around to greet her—or even acknowledge her presence—she felt a quiet twist of panic inside. It was that moment—that hurtful, terribly frightening moment—that told her as nothing else had how desperately she truly cared for Clay. His rejection in Little Horn had been unbearable. If he pushed her away after this afternoon...well, if he pushed her away again, there really would be nothing left to say.

Keep it steady, Roberta, she cautioned herself. *He did you a big favor; common courtesy requires a big display of gratitude. Get it over with, and if that's all he wants from you, swallow your pride and be on your way.*

"Clay, you were terrific!" she gushed in her whispery voice, lightly gripping his elbow as she forced a tremulous smile. "I knew it would all come back to you. You just fell into the role! Seriously, now, aren't you glad you did it?"

It was sometime during the next few seconds—the next few utterly silent seconds—that she realized Clay was staring at her blankly. She also realized that he was trembling violently...so violently that his tremors were shaking her hand right along with his arm. His lips were white, dry and tight. Sweat poured down his face and dripped on his collar. He was breathing in short, terrifying gasps.

"Oh, God," she whispered, suddenly awash with fear and shame. While she'd been bemoaning her own fate, poor Clay hadn't been ignoring her—he'd been fighting for his life! She had no idea what was wrong with him, but he looked as if he might be suffering respiratory failure or cardiac arrest.

"Clay, sit down," she said with all the tense calm she could muster. "I'm going to go get some help. The paramedics are just on the other side of the—"

"No!" It was a strangled yelp, fierce and desperate, almost lost in his effort to get air.

She was thrilled that he was still able to talk, but she was not about to heed his command. "Clay, I don't have time to argue! You need a doctor. You need—"

He grabbed her arm with superhuman strength and dragged her forcibly from the door. Still gasping, he slammed it shut and leaned heavily against it, blocking her escape. "If you want to help me, sit down and shut up!" he ordered her, each word punctuated by a breathless gasp. "I know what's wrong with me. It's happened many times before, and it's not physical. When I calm down I'll be all right!"

Then he closed his eyes. He tugged loose his collar with desperate hands. He gasped and trembled, but less violently now. It was Roberta who was losing control.

She did not speak; she did not move. She was still uncertain whether or not his situation was medically precarious, but she had no doubt that she could not physically move him from the door; if she tried, she would only aggravate his condition. She took heart as she watched his breathing slowly grow more stable. Desperate to do something to help him, she found a glass in his trailer cupboard and filled it with water. Careful not to crowd him, she took a step closer and held it within easy reach of his hand.

He opened his eyes, blinked once or twice, then took the glass. He drank about half of it, then poured the rest over his head. He unbuttoned his jacket and tossed it off. Again he took a handful of deep breaths. At last he sat down on the bench and began to pull his boots off.

Roberta was fighting tears by then. She knew—in the deepest reaches of her heart—the magnitude of what Clay had done for her. She'd interpreted his initial resistance as obstinacy, indifference, maybe, when in reality he'd been fighting sheer terror! She knew it made no sense, but how many phobias really did? Her own terror of horseback riding was no more logical. Competition barrel racing was a far cry from taking a leisurely afternoon ride on a baby-proof pony, but her own shivering panic wouldn't even let her attempt that much anymore. Clearly Clay viewed public speaking with a similar brand of panic.

The trailer remained silent for a good five minutes before Clay's voice, soft and apologetic, drifted to her softly. "I'm sorry, Roberta. I didn't mean to bark at you." His eyes met hers. They were sad gray eyes, eyes full of shame. "I told you to keep your distance until it was over. I knew it would be like this."

Roberta, who had been hovering helplessly by the sink, now gingerly took a seat at the small kitchen table. She felt helpless, confused, ashamed. Never in her most desperate moments would she have forced Clay to endure such pain just to save her chautauqua program. She'd never even imagined he was capable of such fright. How had she managed to coerce him into doing something that he'd known ahead of time would shake him to his core? And how could she have been too insensitive to realize it? Hadn't he told her he didn't want to give the speech at least half a dozen times?

Roberta wasn't quite sure what to say, and with her voice so raspy, there was no smooth way to say it. "I thought you'd want me to join you as soon as your speech was over," was all she could say.

He shook his head. "I used to need at least half an hour after I'd finished each speech before I felt even close to normal. When I was a kid, I lost my lunch after most of my presentations. I vowed I'd get through this one without falling apart, and I guess I can be grateful that I held together until I got out of sight of the crowd." His voice dropped to a near whisper. "I just wish to God I could have kept you from seeing me this way."

Now shame tightened the loop of guilt around Roberta's heart. How *could* she have been so blind and self-centered?

"Clay, I'm so sorry," she rasped as gently as her hoarse tone would allow. "I had no idea it would affect you this way. When you told me you hated public speaking, I just thought you hated the memory of your mother and your coach."

He shook his head. He rubbed his temples, his forehead, his eyes. "I hate the memory, all right. I hate the memory of talking like Ozzie. As if it weren't bad enough that everybody laughed at me when I carried on a regular conversation, I had to become a target every time I got up onstage."

He watched her then, as though her reaction to his news meant life or death to him. And suddenly she saw the big picture, the big picture that included a stuttering child and a young man who refused to go to college. A proud cowboy with a keen mind. A man who was unquestionably her intellectual equal even though he'd never be her academic peer.

Maybe he's uneasy about the difference in your backgrounds, Roberta, she suddenly heard Tess say: *Maybe he doesn't think a woman of your education would be interested in a man like him.*

She didn't know if Tess was right, but she realized that it was a very strong possibility. He'd told her—not so very long ago—that he wasn't interested in pursuing a relationship that had no future. She'd thought he'd worked that through, but maybe...

No maybe about it, she realized swiftly. *It's my education that's always stood in the way.*

Suddenly determined that nothing could block the path between them, Roberta stood slowly, laid both hands on Clay's shoulders and began to rub the tension that still lingered there.

"I wish you'd told me earlier," she whispered. "I never would have forced you into doing this."

He shook his head. He did not turn around to face her. "I didn't want you to know. I didn't want you to know I was a coward."

She stopped rubbing to sit down close beside him. Very, *very* close beside him.

"You're not a coward, Clay. It takes a lot of courage for a man with your fear to do what you just did."

He did not move away from her, but he did not draw her nearer. At last he looked her in the eye. "Almost as much courage as it would take you to ride a camel," he suggested softly. "Or even a horse."

Roberta didn't answer the challenge. She had her mind on other things. "Life requires all kinds of courage," she admitted a bit tremulously. "For me it would be very hard to risk falling in love with you."

He turned quickly to face her, eyebrows raised, eyes wide with shock. For a moment he just studied Roberta, clearly weighing her words. Then, slowly, he rested his chin against her temple. She could feel his mustache brush her hair, his throat pulse against her skin. His voice caressed her senses. "Maybe you shouldn't do it."

"Maybe it's too late," she confessed.

Roberta couldn't see him then, not really. But she felt the strong male hand caress her cheek, felt it slip deeply into her hair. Her scalp tingled with sensual awareness. Unconsciously she snuggled closer.

Later, she was never certain what happened next. It was possible that Clay put his free hand on her cheek and nudged her mouth toward his before she turned and kissed him; it was possible that he cupped her face only after she'd hungrily claimed his lips. It was even possible that they'd both sensed the inevitable at exactly the same time. The only thing she was sure of was that from the moment their mouths joined, there was no turning back.

As Clay's strong hands cradled her head, Roberta circled his waist with eager arms, clutching the smooth, tight muscles that rippled over his ribs. She reveled in the teasing search of his tongue against her lips and its ultimate plunge deep within her sensitive mouth, and she gulped back a whimper when his urgent fingers slipped down to stroke the side of one breast.

"Clay," she moaned softly, pressing herself against him.

"I sure hope that's 'Clay, yes' and not 'Clay, no,'" she heard him whisper as he broke off the searching kiss. "I'd never press you, Bobbie Jean, not for the world. I want you clear down to the tips of my toes, but if we're headed somewhere you're not ready to go, please tell me now before I—"

Roberta covered his hand with her own and pulled it over the aching center of her breast. "Does that answer your question?" she asked a bit breathlessly.

Clay grinned. She could see his clean white teeth, his inviting tongue, the beginning of his five o'clock shadow starting to grow. His mahogany mustache heightened his rugged masculinity. She felt his fingertips slid back and forth over her dress, deftly localizing the sensitive point of her fully erect nipple despite the layers of Susan B. Anthony's notion of fashion and her own modern bra.

"Is that what you had in mind?" he asked.

Now it was Roberta's turn to grin. "I'd say you're on the right path, Lieutenant."

Suddenly Clay was kissing her again, with a slow but intense kind of urgency that let her know that she wasn't the only one who wanted to be stroked. To her surprise, she realized that she was a little shy about taking the next obvious step—undoing his pants and warming him in her hands. She wasn't afraid to touch him; she was simply afraid she'd do it wrong. It had been so long that she barely remembered the rudiments of lovemaking... so long that she'd had no reason to think about birth control for years. Somehow she'd have to find a tactful way to mention that to Clay before things went much farther. He was a resourceful man, and she was certain he could find a way to work around that small problem.

With relief she suddenly remembered that Clay was wearing his cavalry trousers, which in keeping with nineteenth-century technology, were held together with buttons. "I'm not quite sure how to undress you," she said honestly. "I've never tackled a pair of pants quite like these."

Clay chuckled, abruptly releasing her yearning breast. Somehow the absence of his hand was even more exciting than its presence, and Roberta became acutely aware of how urgent her arousal had become.

Her heart began to thump almost painfully as Clay stood, but before her doubts got the better of her, he reached for her hand. "Considering that we're both tangled up in costumes, it might be easier if we got out of these convoluted things ourselves," he observed straightforwardly. "I'll lock the door and meet you at the bed in thirty seconds."

He did as he promised, and by the time Roberta spotted his head beside the double bed, which rested only three feet from the trailer's ceiling, she was already naked and waiting for him.

Roberta had a sudden longing for darkness. She was not afraid for him to see her body in the sense that she was a woman and he was a man, but she was embarrassed by her own shortcomings—she was so husky, so strong. Suddenly she longed for a frail and feminine body that a man would long to cradle.

He stared at her for so long that she began to tremble—in anticipation and a bit of fear that her body might disappoint him. Partly to fill the silence, she blurted artlessly, "I'm not on any kind of birth control, Clay. It's...been a long time." *Great, Roberta,* she chided herself. *You had to tell him, but you couldn't have put it any worse if you tried.*

A gentle smile curved Clay's lips as he handed her a blue foil-wrapped square. "I suspected that might be the case, so I came prepared."

Roberta wasn't sure what to say. Did he just keep these things in the trailer so he'd be covered whenever some eager female stumbled in? She gazed at him, half grateful, half haunted, until he answered her unspoken question. "I stopped at the drugstore the day I got the list of events for Kresky. No reason to waste my money for a weekend without a scheduled chautauqua."

She got it then, the quiet confession that she was indeed special to him, that he'd missed her as much as she'd missed him. She reached out to touch his face, lightly tugging on the spiky edge of his mustache, meeting his eyes with fresh courage.

Carefully Roberta tucked the square under her pillow where she could get it in a hurry, then suggested a bit awkwardly, "I guess we should pick up where we left off."

Clay grinned, openly studying her taut and tingling breasts. "I have a notoriously poor memory," he confessed in a low, husky voice. "Was it this one?" He tapped her left nipple with his forefinger, pressed on it slightly, then circled it. Just as Roberta closed her eyes against the hunger, he abandoned that nipple and moved to the other one, seizing it lightly with his thumb and all four fingers. "Or was it this one?" he asked nonchalantly, ever so gently pulling it in tiny, erotic twists that electrified her woman's core.

"It was that one," she forced out with a husky moan.

"Which one?" he teased her again, relinquishing the second nipple to go back to the first. Before Roberta had time to whimper her frustration, he lowered his head and embraced the nearest nipple with the moist warmth of his lips. At the same time he used his palm to press wildly erotic circles around the other one.

Roberta started to tremble. She found herself clutching Clay's shaggy brown hair and pulling him closer. Instinctively she clung to his shoulders and kissed his chest. She stroked his back and his waist but could get no further because he still stood on the step next to the raised bed only a few feet below the trailer's ceiling. Constrained by no such limitation, Clay's hand slid off her breast, down her ribs, over her stomach and crawled toward her thigh. Each separate finger carved a tiny contrail of anticipation through the path of dark hair that blocked his way.

Abruptly Roberta's own desire overwhelmed her earlier hesitation. She rolled to the edge of the bed and reached out hungrily for Clay's sexual center, celebrating the rich satisfaction of hearing his startled, joyful gasp. It was a gasp that transformed itself into a wildly urgent moan when Roberta's lips replaced her hand a moment later. In a second Clay was trembling so hard he could barely stand up.

"Get up here," Roberta commanded, yielding her grip to reach for the blue square.

She didn't have to tell him twice. In a single breathless moment, she tore off the corner of the packet as Clay lifted himself up on the bed and pressed urgently close. She sheathed him with the condom, then sheathed him with herself.

Clay's arms came around her tightly as she locked her legs around his thighs. She felt his kisses on her neck, her collarbone, the pulse of her throat. One massive hand found her breast again. The other was trapped a moment later by his hot tongue.

After that she didn't know where she was, and she didn't care. She knew only that paradise was this moment, in Clay's bed, in Clay's arms, in Clay's life, and nothing she'd ever learned in history could rival this majestic moment in real life.

She had found something even more incredible than the joy of teaching history or the thrill of delivering chautauquas, something more fantastic than being the proud owner of a Ph.D. She wasn't just Dr. Robert Jean Wheeler anymore.

She was Clay Gann's woman, Bobbie Jean.

IT WAS LATE AFTERNOON when Clay heard the knock at the door, but he did not answer it. Unless the camel barn was burning down, he refused to be disturbed. He was lying, still naked, with the strongest woman he'd ever known, and he felt the happiness deep in his bones.

It had been quite a day, starting out with mundane worries about his camels and anxious anticipation as he'd waited for Roberta to arrive in town. He'd surrendered to her the instant she'd reached his trailer, only to fear he'd been played for a chump. Then he'd survived a pubic oration—his first in over twenty-five years—and realized, in hindsight, that he really hadn't done half bad. And then, incredibly—his eyes swept over the magnificent woman who still lay snuggled next to him—there was Roberta.

He had always known that their lovemaking would be perfect. He knew he had pleased her greatly, and he still trembled with the memory of how deeply she'd pleased *him*. The only thing that could make the moment more perfect was the false assurance that they could now look toward an untrammeled future together. But Clay knew that the differences between them were still too great to ignore.

Oh, they could set them aside for a few fun weekends; they could enjoy a summer of delight. But sooner or later, the day would come when Roberta would look at him through the eyes of her friends and see an unlettered cowboy, and it would all come to an end. But that was a long way off, he desperately hoped, and he refused to worry about it during this pristine afternoon when his body still tightened and tensed from her nearness.

But then the knocking started again, and a voice far away called, "Hey, don't bug the boss! He's got company in there!" It was Roscoe's voice, protective and a bit amused.

Outside the door came another voice, Warner's. "You're kiddin' me! Clay never takes heeda them girls what drool all over us after a show. He allus leaves 'em to me!"

Roscoe's voice, still hushed, a bit distant, drifted through the walls again.

"It's not one of them girls! It's that professor lady. Now you get away from there!"

Warner chuckled again, and by this time Clay was ready to pound on the wall in warning. Roberta wasn't a kid, and she wasn't likely to be embarrassed that his men knew they'd made love, but that didn't mean she was likely to enjoy hearing them joke about her.

"The professor? That egghead? You gotta be kidding! She don't even ride!" He chuckled, then added, "At least not four-footed critters. Besides, she's too smart for him!"

That did it. Clay pounded on the wall in certain warning, and Warner called back, "Okay, I get the message!" and wandered off.

The trailer was silent for a moment. There seemed to be a gulf in the center of the bed . . . a gulf Clay was determined to cross over.

He turned to gaze at Roberta, surprised at the warmth that surged through him. She smiled. When he reached out gingerly to touch her hair, she rolled eagerly into his embrace as though she'd been waiting for the slightest invitation. Hungrily he drew her close. Another half hour passed in sweet intimacy before they once again lay quietly intertwined.

They spent most of the weekend the same way. They got up for meals and mandatory camel care, but they skipped all the pubic hoopla. On Sunday afternoon, Roberta joined Clay's men in leading camels back and forth from the arena, and he noticed that she started giving the greenhorn jockeys specific advice about how to control the unruly beasts.

Clay knew that she longed to tackle one of the boisterous critters herself, and he knew that someday he'd have to help her find the courage to climb on board. Aside from the fact that he couldn't imagine having a long-term relationship with a woman who wasn't at home in the saddle, he knew that until Roberta licked her riding fear, she would never feel healed and completely whole.

Clay knew only too well that gnawing feeling of inadequacy with which his private fears still crippled him. If public speaking had been his only problem he could have chalked it up to common stage fright, or maybe the leftover effects of childhood stuttering. But he still quailed at the notion of *any* overt academic endeavor. He dreaded being graded, being judged in any school-like setting—and he was certain that he'd endure many such situations if he spent much time with Roberta.

How often would he be expected to make small talk with other proud professors? How would she judge his letters to her—misspellings, grammatical errors and all? How long would it take her to nudge him toward more schooling, to urge him to sound more sophisticated, to give the illusion that he was an educated man?

How long would it take her to start carping like his mother—making his mother's demands?

Clay had never been able to meet his mother's expectations, and he was certain that he'd fall short of Roberta's. He was a cowboy, not an academician. He couldn't live up to the standards of a highly educated woman even if he wanted to.

It was early Sunday evening and long past time for both of them to leave Utah when Clay realized that they had not really talked about the future. But this make-believe weekend had to come to an end. Clay had to take his camels back to Fort Collins by way of Patchwork, where they'd have some time to stretch out and graze, and Roberta had to drive all the way back to Tucson and get some sleep before teaching class on Monday morning. Despite the men's audible joshing outside the trailer—they were growing restless now—neither one of them seemed able to say goodbye.

They lay in bed in the trailer, side by side, covered by a single sheet. For a long time they'd both been silent, and now Clay was almost afraid to bring the moment to an end, almost afraid to speak.

"I was so sure I'd disappoint you," Roberta finally mumbled in that husky voice, which he hoped was not so much the result of laryngitis as freshly remembered passion. "Ever since the dance in Little Horn, I thought you'd decided that you really didn't want to make love with me."

Clay shook his head, then kissed her softly just below her jaw. "I've wanted you since the first time I heard you speak in Patchwork, Bobbie Jean. That's never been the problem. The problem is—" he remembered Warner's assessment of Roberta's brains and swallowed hard "—where do we go from here?"

She kissed his chest, but did not answer.

"In the summer, we both spend a lot of time on the road, Roberta," he persevered. "By sheer luck we're likely to end up in a lot of the same places. But I'm not much on summer flings and I reckon neither are you. Come September we'll have some hard choices to make if we're still together. And I might as well warn you right now—" he met her eyes gravely "—that I'll be in no hurry to let you go." His tender expression caressed her for a long moment before he asked, "What are your thoughts on the subject?"

Roberta did not answer right away. She studied Clay thoughtfully before she rolled up on her elbows and stared down at him, slinging one leg possessively over his own. "Let me put it like this, Clay," she whispered, a fresh smile brimming from her love-swollen lips. "It may be too late to talk me out of falling in love with you."

Clay felt a rush of shock-tinged joy jolt his entire system, but he wasn't sure what to say. He kissed her quickly, to cover his surprise, then pulled back to study her wide hazel eyes. He could see her love for him glowing there, see her passion shining through. "I could tell you I feel the same way, Roberta, and it would probably be true," he admitted softly. "But I don't think that would solve our problems."

Roberta glanced away. She tugged uneasily at the edge of her pillowcase. "Do you really want to solve our problems, Clay? Do you want to find a way for us to have something more than a summer fling?"

To his surprise, his own voice was husky when he answered, "Very much, Bobbie Jean."

Her eyes flashed back up to his, and he saw fresh fire and determination there. She cradled his head with both strong hands and kissed him once again before she vowed, "Then I have no doubt we'll find a way."

When Clay thought only of Roberta, he had no doubt of that, either. But when he remembered that his mother had once made the same promise to his dad, he cherished no hope for September.

CHAPTER TEN

ROBERTA ALL BUT SKIPPED through the history department halls on Monday morning. She felt schoolgirlishly giddy. In fact, she felt so terrific that she wasn't sure she'd ever feel bad about anything again.

She still had no voice—at least no more than a whisper—but that didn't bother her. Thinking ahead, she'd assigned some chautauqua presentations to several students this week and put Marla in charge of leading the ensuing discussions.

She reached her office an hour before class as she always did, allowing for plenty of time to get everything together and deal with unforeseen disasters. In the past, it had also given her plenty of opportunity to run into Charles.

At the moment, she wasn't sure she wanted to see the department head. She didn't have a date set up with him for the coming weekend, fortunately, but she did have a . . . well, an incipient tepid romance sort of lingering on hold. And after this astonishing weekend with Clay, she knew that for her own peace of mind, regardless of the outcome of their romance, she had to make her position clear to Charles. She belonged to Clay Gann. It was unthinkable that she should give the slightest bit of encouragement to some other man.

The moment of truth, however, came much sooner than she had anticipated. She'd barely had time to read her phone messages and morning mail before Charles himself appeared on the other side of her desk.

"Good morning, Dr. Wheeler," he greeted her grandly. "How was your weekend on the road?"

She read his face for some sign of wariness, but there was nothing there but that controlled, mildly friendly look he usually wore. He looked terribly blond and pale in the harsh desert light fighting its way in through the window. A sudden vision of Clay's dark, masculine features took her off guard, and she found herself gripping her desk tightly for balance.

"It was...nice. Very nice," she answered cautiously, her voice still a croak.

"Oh?" Surprise shadowed his even tone. "Was your voice this bad then? You were healthy as a horse the last time I saw you."

In that instant Roberta remembered that Charles was, first and foremost, her supervisor, and his arrival at this fortuitous moment probably had more to do with his concern about the success of her summer program than his interest in her as a woman.

"Uh...as it turns out, I wasn't able to give my speech," she had to admit, "but it wasn't a problem because I found a capable substitute."

He looked surprised. "You got one of your colleagues to do Susan B. for you?"

She shook her head. "No. It was a friend who happened to be in Kresky for the weekend."

"Your friend who runs the ghost town?"

Roberta shook her head, grateful for Charles's mention of Tess: it inadvertently gave Clay some legitimacy. "No. But she introduced me to this man."

"A man? I guess he took a different role."

"Of course."

"William Jennings Bryan? Stephen Douglas? Henry Clay?"

Roberta shook her head after each suggestion, then revealed the truth when Charles lifted his hands in an impatient gesture.

"Beale."

"Who?"

"Lieutenant Edward Beale."

Now Charles was staring at her with what could almost have been suspicion. He was a nationally known historian, and though his specialty was nineteenth-century European affairs, it was still rare that somebody presented him with a famous historical character that he'd never even heard of.

"Give me a hint." He looked a bit impatient.

"Beale was in charge of transporting the U.S. Cavalry Camel Corps from Texas to California in 1860."

A light glowed in Charles's eyes. "Ah, the Camel Corps supported by Jefferson Davis and scuttled in the wake of the Civil War."

Roberta nodded. The reasons for the Camel Corps failure were far more complex than that, of course, but Jefferson Davis's role as a southern sponsor had certainly been a major factor.

"Where does this fellow teach?" Charles asked. "I take it he shares your area of expertise?"

Roberta floundered. She felt a curious mixture of embarrassment and shame. She didn't want Charles to know that she'd asked a nonacademic to fill in for her, but her reluctance made her feel disloyal to Clay.

"Well, he's certainly an expert on western history and particularly well versed on the Camel Corps," she hedged. "I happened to hear him give an impromptu lecture on the subject before so I knew he had a chautauqua ready. I also knew he often travels with a cavalry uniform."

Charles looked surprised. Then his eyes narrowed, and he looked downright suspicious. "It sounds as though you know this fellow rather well."

The noose tightened. A whole host of feelings battled inside her. Her love for Clay was strong, but so was her respect for Charles. She felt that she'd betrayed her boss in more ways than one. As a professor, she'd bent the rules of their chautauqua agreement just a tad; as a woman, she'd gone straight from his tacit romantic invitation into the bed of another man. If she'd never expected to see him again, a tactful evasion might have been appropriate. Under the circumstances, she didn't have much choice except to tell him the truth and let the chips fall where they might.

Slowly she met Charles's eyes. Gently she said, "Yes, I know him very well. Much better now than I did before this past weekend."

He got it at once. His eyes widened for just a moment, as though he were surprised, or even a tiny bit hurt. Then his face rearranged itself into vintage Charles. Not a twinge of regret clouded his quiet voice as he said, "How fortunate that everything worked out so well."

Roberta swallowed hard. "Yes. I was lucky that he was willing to help me out of a pickle."

"Very lucky," Charles agreed suavely. For just a moment she read true pain in his eyes, read his wordless confession: *I would have been willing, too.* But the moment passed in an instant as he straightened and said, "Well, then, if that's all, Roberta, have a good day."

"You, too, Charles." But she knew that she'd already ruined his whole week. She was certain that nothing between them would ever be quite the same.

"HI, OZZIE! Howdy, Clay."

Ira looked genuinely glad to see the pair of them, though Clay suspected it was Ozzie who drew Ira's true attention. Although Ira functioned as a man in terms of the work he did on the Double T, it took no genius to guess that he might be hungry for the company of kids his own age. Every time Clay brought his camels through this end of Colorado on his way back from a race, he spent the night in Patchwork so the camels could bed down in a proper stable. And every time, Ozzie disappeared with Ira and came back talking about college and girls.

"Hi, Ira," Clay's sidekick declared, his eyes happy as he greeted his friend. "How's everything going?"

Clay noticed with pleasure that Ozzie had just made it through five consecutive words without stuttering, something that rarely happened when other people were around. As he watched the two boys instantly engage in conversation—if one could use that term to describe the monosyllabic mutterings of this month's teenage slang—he realized that Ozzie was stuttering less and less these days when he wasn't under tension.

He also realized that he, too, was starved for the companionship of people his own age. He was so hesitant to talk to strangers, especially teenagers, that Clay rarely gave much thought to the boy's social needs beyond the obvious one—protecting him from ridicule. But Ira wasn't a stranger, and clearly the two were becoming buddies. With an ache for Ozzie's pain, Clay realized how much Ozzie was missing by hiding his head in the sand in Fort Collins. There was so much more to the world.

As he left the two boys to their animated discussion—about the pros and cons of a current country recording star—he gave thought to his own world, which had expanded by leaps and bounds lately. A week ago he'd been perfectly content to give trail rides in the spring and fall and make the camel race circuit every summer; in the winter he got caught up on his repairs and reading. It wasn't a wildly stimulating life, at least not intellectually, but he called his own shots and made a decent living. It had always been enough.

But that was before Roberta.

He still wasn't quite sure what had happened last weekend. Oh, he knew that he'd shared his bed with an extraordinary woman who cared for him a great deal. And he knew that he very much wanted to do it again. But he also knew that, in terms of the big picture, absolutely nothing had changed since the day they'd first met. A tiny part of his world intersected with hers. It was a big enough part to pretend that the feelings he had for Roberta were returned, big enough to believe that they would last. But Clay was a rational man, and logic told him that it wasn't nearly big enough to build a loving relationship strong enough to survive the tussles of life.

"Penny for your thoughts," said Brady from his side. Brady's blue eyes were thoughtful, almost concerned. "Is this a private melancholia, or can anybody try to cheer you up?"

Clay smiled. "Oh, I don't think melancholia is the right word for how I'm feeling, Brady. Just... thoughtful." He wasn't sure how to explain it. After all, when he was *with* Roberta, he felt absolutely marvelous. And part of that delirious sense of pleasure—of coming home—remained with him still. But he was nothing if not practical, and he knew that there was nothing practical about falling in love with a history professor who lived in Arizona. It would have been impractical even if she'd been teaching college right next door.

"Is this something you want to talk about?" Brady wasn't one to push, and Clay was grateful for his friend's restraint. Part of him wanted very much to bounce his conflicting feelings off a sympathetic ear, but discretion kept him from sharing them with Brady. Roberta was virtually a sister to Tess, and it wasn't appropriate for Clay to reveal the recent change in their relationship to either Trent until—unless—Roberta herself wanted to do so.

It occurred to him, with some uneasiness, that once Roberta returned to her ivy halls, she might come back to her senses and realize the awkwardness of his lowly academic position in the scheme of things. She might be reluctant to let anybody know she was slumming it with a cowboy. She might even be ashamed to make love to him again when their paths crossed next weekend in Great Gulch, Wyoming.

"I wish I could talk to you about it, Brady, but . . . right now I don't think I can." He met Brady's eyes for just a moment, long enough to assure his friend that he wasn't giving him the brush off, just answering a higher law. Then he asked more casually, "So how are things at the Double T?"

Brady grinned. "About how you'd expect, with one small addition."

"Oh? What's that?"

His grinned widened. "Tess is pregnant again."

"All right!" rejoined Clay, slapping Brady on the back. He knew how much Tess and Brady enjoyed J.J. and how eager they were for more children. After all the dark years Brady had spent living alone, it made Clay very happy to see his friend so richly blessed. "When is this splendid event?"

"Next May or June. We planned it that way. No Double T babies scheduled during the winter, you know. Joey promises me the Slow Joe will always be fit and sassy, but it's hard to guarantee when the rails will be covered with snow. There's no other way into town in the winter."

Clay nodded. "I sure hope they're not covered with snow the weekend of the sesquicentennial. How are your plans coming along?"

"Everything's rolling. Oscar Reynolds, the Historical Preservation Committee chair in town, is coordinating the parade, so don't be surprised if you hear from him. We're going to want a set of camels, if that's okay."

"As long as I can pick the riders. I don't want greenhorns messing with my stock in a parade. Especially Luscious Laura. She's so clumsy that a tenderfoot can fall off even when she's on her best behavior."

Brady's eyes narrowed. "Are your camels unpredictable in that much chaos? Are they safe to ride?"

Clay hesitated before he said. "I've got six camels that are probably as steady in a parade as most horses. But as you know, parades are notorious for bringing out unexpected streaks of panic in the best of mounts. If I can't persuade enough of my own men or some of the other camel jockeys I know to come down here for the weekend, Ozzie and Ira can lead some of them covered with old packs. That ought to please the fans."

Brady nodded his agreement, then gestured with his hat across the corral toward the two boys, who were involved in an animated discussion that kept both of them in stitches.

"I'm not sure just what Ira's going to be doing this fall. Joe and Mandy are still pressing him to go to school, and he still says he wants to stay here."

Clay wasn't sure what to say. He liked Ira and wanted whatever was best for the boy. But he also believed that at his age, anything his parents forced him to do was likely to be counterproductive. He'd make better decisions if they made gentle suggestions or stayed out of the way.

"I imagine it's up to Ira whether he wants to go on with school."

"Sure it is. But I know that I can make him stay here with a few moans and groans about how much I need him. And I do need him, but I think it's in his best interests to go to college. It's not really the same situation that you have with Ozzie."

Clay eyed him warily and readjusted his lucky hat. "What do you mean? You think I don't have Ozzie's best interests at heart?"

Brady glanced away uncomfortably. "I'm sure you think you do."

"What the hell does that mean?"

Brady met his eyes. "It means that sometimes I think you get mixed up between what *you* needed when you were Ozzie's age and what Ozzie needs now. It's great that you took him in, Clay, and wonderful how he's blossomed under your care. But has it ever occurred to you that maybe at this point you're doing him more harm than good by continuing to coddle him?"

"Coddle him? I work the daylights out of that kid! I've got no featherbedders on my ranch."

Brady shook his head. "I'm not talking about work. I'm talking about stuttering. He's convinced that as long as he stays with you, he's safe from his problem. He'll never have to lick it. He considers himself handicapped because you shield him as though he were crippled."

Clay felt as though he'd just been punched. He wasn't at all sure what to say. "Stuttering doesn't make him a social cripple. His fear does that. I've told him three million times to kick that panic in the teeth and get on with his life. Someday he will. I think it would be even harder for him to handle if it weren't for me."

"That may be true, Clay, but I think you should just step back a moment and looked at the big picture here. Look at those two kids." He waited until Clay turned sober gray eyes on Ira and Ozzie. "They're practically the same age. They're both working on a ranch this summer. But Ira's eagerly planning his whole life—whether he goes to college this fall or not—and poor Ozzie's just holed up in his den, letting life pass him by. If something doesn't shake him up, he'll still be single and taking care of your camels until he's sixty-five."

Clay couldn't deny Brady's astute observation, but he didn't see what he could do about it, either. Rather lamely he turned the tables on his friend. "He reminds me of you before you met Tess, Brady. Hiding out on the Rocking T, licking your wounds while Joey Henderson ran interference for you with the rest of the world."

That stumped Brady. He stared at Clay without offering a word in his own defense.

"I'm not blaming you for that, Brady. You were wounded. You needed time to heal. You were lucky that somebody cared enough about you to give you the time. Do you honestly think you'd have been better off if Joey had kicked you out on your own while you were still bleeding?"

Brady glanced away, then slowly shook his head. "No, I guess not. I might have bled to death. But there came a time when Joey made me face up to the hermit I'd become." He stared at Clay. "He did it for my own good. I was angry for a while, but now I'm grateful."

Clay's glance didn't waver. "I'm all Ozzie's got right now, Brady."

"Joe was all I had."

"You were thirty-five. Ozzie is just nineteen."

For a moment Brady didn't answer, and Clay thought he'd finally gotten the last word. Then Brady said clearly, "He's like a man living in a foreign country. It'll get harder for him to come home with each passing year."

Clay was certain he'd think of an answer to that, but as much as he tried, no comeback came.

IT WAS LATE AFTERNOON before the two boys mounted up and took a ride toward the red buttes that cradled the cloud-dotted sky. Enjoying the silent camaraderie known to horsemen everywhere, Ozzie reflected that these moments were all too rare. Ira was the only person in his life who was under twenty.

"I promised my dad and Mandy that I'd go down to Tucson and talk to Roberta next week, Oz," Ira confided after they'd been riding along for sometime.

"Tess and J.J. are going to come with me and spend the night."

Ozzie wasn't quite sure what to say. "You don't sound very h-h-happy about it, Ira."

The other boy shrugged. "Well, it's just that I don't know if I'm ready to go to college. I've been in school so long, and not all of it's been great. I just think I need a year off to rest up and help Brady get Patchwork on the map. Then I think I'll be ready. But my stepmom's afraid that if I drop out now, I'll never go back."

Ozzie blushed. Hadn't he used the same arguments with his own parents when he'd gone to work for Clay. *I just need some time, Mom. Let me breathe a while, Dad. Then I'll go back to school.*

But a year had now gone by and he was no closer to going back than he'd been when Clay had first found him; he hadn't found a lick of the courage that had failed him then. If anything, his fears had only multiplied.

But Ira wasn't afraid of anything.

"What do you think I should do, Ozzie?" he asked. "You took some time off and you're going back, aren't you?"

Ozzie swallowed hard. "S-s-someday," he hedged. "It's different for you."

"How is it different? You mean because Brady really needs me and Clay's business was doing fine when you signed on?"

Ozzie's blush grew deeper. "No!" Was Ira stupid? He'd never teased him about his stuttering, but surely he understood why Ozzie was allergic to school! "I d-d-don't want to talk," he stammered out.

"Well, hell, Ozzie, I didn't mean to push. It's just that I figured if you were going back this year or next, maybe we could go together. Even room together, maybe." His blue eyes were sparkling. "What do you think?"

For a moment, a fresh new hope surged inside of Ozzie, a hope for something he'd thought could never be. With quiet courage he said softly, "Wouldn't you b-b-be embarrassed to have a roommate who st-st-stuttered?"

He waited for a long, tense moment before Ira turned surprised eyes his way and said, "Nope. It wouldn't bother me."

Ozzie wanted to hug his friend, but that, of course, he could never do. Instead he ended the conversation abruptly by kneeing his horse and calling out, "Race you to the ridge!"

Ira took on his challenge at once, beating him by half a length. After that they laughed and chatted for half an hour before heading back to the Double T, but the subject never came up again.

ROBERTA WELCOMED Ira, Tess and little J.J. with open arms when they arrived in Tucson. Her apartment was small but homey, reflecting her own tastes; every piece of furniture was practical and straightforward; every picture on the wall was an authentic painting of women in the west. The desk in her study-cum-guest room was piled high with student reports and personal letters; a postcard of the main street of Patchwork sat propped up by the green banker's lamp.

Tess, and J.J. in a portable playpen, spent the night in the guest room, and Ira sacked out on the couch. During the evening they chowed down on Roberta's homemade chili and talked about Brady, the Hendersons and the Double T; nobody mentioned college. It wasn't until the next morning that Roberta, still half-asleep in her robe, cornered Ira in the living room.

"I sense that this trip to visit me wasn't your idea," she observed straightforwardly once he'd blinked once or twice to indicate that he was awake.

Ira blushed. He'd known Roberta a long time and she was sure that he wasn't surprised by her bluntness, but she also suspected that he still had a healthy respect for grownups. "It's...nothing personal, Roberta," he apologized. "I mean, I'm always glad to see you, and it's real nice of you to put us up. It's just that... everybody seems to be pushing me into coming here. Or somewhere. And I'm just not sure that I ought to be going to school this fall."

Roberta looked him straight in the eye. "I'm not going to push you, Ira. I'm just going to let you see the campus and ask whatever questions you want to ask. You know that if you come to T.S.U. I'll be here if you need me, but I won't be dropping in to see you every day. I won't step on your toes."

He glanced at his feet. "Thanks, Roberta."

"Now, I just want to tell you one thing. Taking a year off of school isn't always a bad idea. In fact, it's good for some people. But everybody I ever knew who did it always said it was a lot harder to come back."

"Why?"

"Because you're always a year behind everybody else, struggling to catch up. While you're meeting general ed requirements, your friends are happily plunging into exciting classes in their majors. When your friends are doing their senior intern year, you're just starting your major. And when they're working on a masters' or staring to work in their chosen profession, you'll still be trudging along with that last year all by yourself."

He grimaced. "You paint a pretty bleak picture."

"I'm telling you the truth. Without an education, you cut your chances of success in half. By starting a year after everybody else, you're just that much further behind. It doesn't mean you can't make something of yourself anyway, but you're choosing to swim uphill. A lot of kids don't have any choice in the matter. You're lucky. Your parents have the money to send you to school and the willingness to back you up. Frankly I think you'd be a damn fool to throw it all away."

As she said the words, she remembered that Clay had once thrown away the same option. And he had carved out a successful career in spite of it. But the wasted potential made her heart ache. He had the mind of a lawyer, a diplomat, a research biologist! And he was doing a job that took only rudimentary business skills, a love of animals, and a streak of exhibitionism. It was a decent living, but it was a waste.

As it turned out, Ira was in little danger of making the same mistake because Roberta had loaded the dice. After an hour of showing him all the finest features of the school, she dropped by her office and presented Ira with her secret weapon: Marla. By this time she'd gotten to know her assistant quite well—they often had lunch together after class—and Roberta knew that she'd miss the young woman when she went back to Lubbock in August. Pretty, bubbly, friendly to any woman or man, Marla had Ira eating out of her hand in less than five minutes. By the time she offered to show him the library and the student union, he was all but drooling.

Roberta was wise enough to say nothing, but she and Tess exchanged several furtive grins. Once Ira was out of sight, they strolled off to eat lunch in a student snack bar that served Mexican, Pima and Pagago food. Over dessert, Tess pulled out some pictures of the Patchwork Opera House, which was nearly finished.

"Well, what do you think?" asked Tess, pride lilting through her voice.

"It's wonderful, Tess. You did a terrific job," Roberta assured her honestly.

The collection of pictures revealed that the walls had been painted a light lemony color; the heavy drapes were a burgundy shade. While the few remaining original chairs had been unusual, Tess had managed to find some similar, wide-seated wooden ones, which lined the cavernous audience area facing the stage.

"We're going to launch it on the sesquicentennial weekend," Tess informed Roberta, visibly sparkling with pride. "I want some fiery orations by Susan B. Anthony and Lieutenant Edward Beale—assuming I can convince Clay."

"I wouldn't count on it," Roberta countered gently, memories of his hyperventilation clearly etched in her mind. "Have you asked him yet?"

"Yes, last weekend. He didn't promise to hop up onstage, but he didn't give me a flat no, either. He said he'd think on it."

Roberta silently processed that information, proud of Clay for his willingness to even consider battling his phobia yet again. But she couldn't stifle her sense of foreboding at the thought that Clay had been at Patchwork and hadn't even mentioned their newfound love. If he had, surely Tess would have mentioned it three seconds after she'd said hello. The only reason Roberta had stilled her tongue this long was that she was waiting for a private moment to share her monumental news with her friend. But now she was beginning to wonder if the magic was all in her imagination.

Oh, she had no doubt that Clay had enjoyed their time together. And no doubt that she had, miraculously, pleased him well enough in bed, considering her limited experience in such endeavors. But to her their night together had been . . . well, nothing short of spectacular. Not because it had been wonderful physically—though it had been—but because it had signaled a major turning point in Roberta's life.

It had been the moment when she'd stopped trotting down life's path alone and started walking hand in hand with Clay.

Or so she'd thought. But two weeks had passed and she hadn't heard a word from him since then. Neither had he bothered to mention the joyful news to their mutual friends. The facts did not inspire her with confidence.

Now, a bit uneasily, she said, "I'd be delighted to perform with Clay. I just thought he wasn't much on public speaking." Not for the world would she have revealed his terror to anyone, not even Tess. But she'd heard Clay express his general feelings on the subject on several occasions, so his dislike of public speaking was hardly a secret.

"Oh, Clay underrates himself, Roberta. Especially when it comes to anything . . . well, academic or sophisticated. In fact, with him, being cowboy is almost a badge of honor. I think it has something to do with a bad experience a long time ago, but Brady's never shared the details and I haven't pressed. It's none of my business unless Clay wants to share it."

Roberta met her friend's eyes. *He shared it with me,* she longed to say. But out loud she asked, "And Clay didn't...seem to want to share anything... unusual...when he stopped at your place last weekend?"

It took a minute, but Tess got it. Her eyes widened—in surprise, disbelief, then downright joy. "Roberta, are you telling me...are you and Clay—"

Roberta grinned, shrugged and gulped at the same time. "Oh, Tess, it's just crazy, but I think I'm in love!"

"Roberta!" Tess gave her a fierce hug. "That's wonderful! When did all this come about?"

"Bit by bit as we kept bumping into each other on the road. The last time we were together, I thought...well, I thought we were done with the preliminary waltzing. But if Clay never even mentioned it when he was there, maybe I...put too much stock in what happened."

Tess didn't press her for details. Instead she pointed out, "Don't let that worry you too much, Roberta. Go with your instincts. If you think Clay felt something special for you or committed himself or whatever, then I'm sure he did. He's never been one to share his feelings freely. Besides, he may have felt it would be...well, indiscreet or something. Or he may not feel certain of your feelings, either."

"I don't know how he could doubt them," Roberta replied, recalling all too vividly the intensity of the time they'd spent in his bed. "I've been pretty blunt right from the start. The first weekend we met in Patchwork I let him know I was interested. But until a couple of weekends ago, he kept giving me some song and dance about why it would never work even though he was attracted to me, too. Now I'm wondering if he's having second thoughts."

Tess studied her quietly. "Are *you*?"

Remembering her last conversation with Charles, Roberta swallowed uneasily as she shook her head. "No. I have some... well, some concerns about the differences in our backgrounds, but certainly no regrets. I was—" she bit her lip "—very much looking forward to seeing him again."

Tess gave her friend another quick hug. "Roberta, I think there's a good chance that Clay is apprehensive, too. He may be afraid that a woman of your education would think he couldn't measure up to her expectations."

Roberta couldn't meet her eyes. "I know he's afraid of that. He's told me outright once or twice."

"So," said Tess, "perhaps you need to take some action to disabuse him of that notion."

"I was hoping," she countered softly, "that he'd make the first move." But she wondered if there was some move she should be considering. Something that would draw them closer together—something that had to do with a horse. "Truth to tell, Tess, I thought he'd call me by now. Or at least drop me a card."

Tess lifted her shoulders expansively. "Maybe he's waiting for you."

She shook her head. "I can't call him, Tess. I just can't. And it's too late to mail anything. He'll be leaving for Great Gulch, Wyoming, in two days."

"Well, maybe you'll have to think of something else. When you run into him in Great Gulch, you'll just have to make it clear that you're extremely eager to see him."

"I don't know if I'll even see him up there," Roberta admitted. "Apparently everybody makes reservations a year in advance for the Fourth of July celebration. By the time I called, all I could get was a room in Cody, and it's nearly an hour away. I'll be lucky to even bump into Clay when I drive out there for my two speeches unless I track him down at the arena."

Tess studied her dear friend, then shook her head. Her long ponytail waved back and forth freely. "Roberta, my girl, there's more than one way to skin a cat," she suggested devilishly.

"Meaning?"

"Meaning, won't Clay be staying in his own trailer?"

"I imagine so."

"And if you tell him you have nowhere to stay, don't you think he can find some room in his bed for you?"

Roberta flushed. Ripe memories of Clay's bed suffused her. "But I have a place to stay."

Tess rolled her eyes. "Not if you cancel your reservation."

"Cancel?" Roberta repeated. "You mean *pretend* I'm inefficient and helpless so he'll have to take me in?" Surely Tess knew better than that! She couldn't feign incompetence for any man.

But Tess was sighing with exaggerated impatience. "Honestly, Roberta, I guess I haven't taught you right. I'm not suggesting that you *pretend* anything. I'm suggesting that you *admit* the truth to Clay."

"The truth?" she squawked.

"The truth."

"Which is?"

"That you'd rather spend the weekend in his arms—tiny trailer or not—than in some lonely, swanky hotel fifty miles away."

It was the truth; of that there was no doubt. The only question in Roberta's mind was whether or not she could take the risk of admitting it to a man who may have viewed their last weekend together as no more than a casual romp.

Or might already have forgotten it altogether.

CHAPTER ELEVEN

IT WAS THE SUITCASE that caught his eye.

It was leather, a fine burgundy shade. Not brand-new but not very worn. An I.D. tag flopped carelessly to the right. He turned it over and read, "Dr. R. J. Wheeler, 4298 Saguaro Canyon Road, #6, Tucson, AZ 85722." He'd never thought about Roberta living in an apartment; he'd never thought of her in a house. When he thought of her—which was often—he thought of her on the road, in costume. Except for the weekend he'd seen her with nothing on, he'd only seen her in pioneer clothes. The thought of her in another world—as *Dr.* Wheeler, no less—was a bit of a jolt.

So was the suitcase. He had not expected Roberta to be so assertive, so sure of his feelings or of hers. He had, in fact, feared that he'd have to woo her all over again. If, indeed, she were willing to be wooed.

He'd given a lot of thought to wooing Roberta, to risking the ultimate disaster down the road, and he'd made a decision of sorts. For now he'd let their relationship run its course. If she wanted him, he'd enjoy her while he could. He wouldn't worry about the fall because the fall would take care of itself. When she went back to the hallowed halls of Tucson State University in September, she'd forget him soon enough—or realize that he just didn't fit in. In the meantime, he'd do his best to remember that it would end up like that, and try to keep his growing feelings for her in check. He'd never fallen in love with a woman one hundred percent; some part of him had always kept a safe distance. Surely this time he could do it, too. The only difference was that this time he wasn't trying to force himself to fall in love. He was trying desperately to hold his feelings back.

He watched the suitcase furtively most of the afternoon. Between getting the camels ready and the races themselves, he didn't have time to look for Roberta. Besides, the symbolic declaration of her luggage on his front step made him certain that she'd come to him soon enough.

It was after dinner, in fact, when he heard the firm knock on the door. "It's open," he called, recalling the last trip when Roberta's bold knock had turned his world upside down.

The door opened briskly. She stepped in and looked almost guiltily at the suitcase, which no longer sat on Clay's front step but now leaned against the trailer's small kitchen table. She didn't greet him; she just started talking.

"It was a mistake. I'm sorry. I had a reservation in Cody but I canceled it because I wanted to be with you and I wanted you to know that I really wanted to be with you but now I feel stupid and I've put you in an awkward situation," she babbled in a gush of panicky words. "For all I know you've changed your mind and even if you haven't I know I'm rushing things and—"

"Ro*ber*ta!"

She stopped. She glanced at his face, then dropped her gaze.

Deadpan, Clay said sternly, "Didn't you learn anything the last weekend we were together? For a smart college professor, you are slow." Deliberately he put down the book he was reading as he rose. "How many times do I have to tell you that the first thing you've got to do when you walk in that door is to *kiss me hello*?"

Her eyes swept up to his. "Clay," she started hesitantly, "you don't have to—"

She would have finished, but suddenly Clay was cradling her head, claiming her lips as though they'd been apart for six years. It was a thorough, aching kiss, vigorous but tender, a kiss that promised and pleaded and clearly intended to warm her through and through.

When he was done—when he released her face and stepped back, surveying her flushed cheeks and unfocused eyes—he said softly, "You see how it's done? Now you try it."

For a long instant she just stared at him. Then, very slowly, she smiled.

"I guess I could give it a try, Mr. Gann. I'm always open to new experiences."

He grinned. He'd known their first time together again would be a bit awkward, but he hadn't expected such contradictions in this compelling female. So strong, so assertive...and yet, at times, almost shy. "I'll be glad to give you some pointers as we go along in case you forget any of the major steps."

"I remember one."

"Which one is that?"

She turned and locked the door. "Yes?"

A low sultry chuckle broke from his throat. "Oh, yes."

He waited then, waited with a throbbing awareness of the quiet space in the tiny trailer, felt a curious itching on the palms of his hands. He watched Roberta untie her bonnet and toss it on the bed, watched her sashay in his direction, provocatively leaning toward him until her breasts skimmed his chest and her thighs pressed against his own.

"As I recall," she said teasingly, "the next step is to put my hands like so—" she slid her warm fingers over his ears and around his sensitive neck "—and my lips like this."

She brushed her mouth enticingly against his own; then her tongue grazed the bottom of his upper lip. A moment later it plunged inside, aggressively demanding what a woman of strength could be expected to ask for, and Clay found his own hands sliding quickly around her waist as he pulled her firm, female body hungrily against his own.

"Bobbie Jean," he whispered urgently against her mouth.

Sounds of joy filled the trailer after that, but for the next hour Clay said nothing else.

Neither did Roberta.

"YOU SAW HIM AGAIN, didn't you?" asked Marla, her eyes bright with intrigue.

"Him?" repeated Roberta. In any conversation, the graduate student's comment would have been a non sequitur, but in lieu of a greeting first thing Monday morning, it was downright bizarre.

"I know it's none of my business, Dr. Wheeler," the young woman continued with a grin, "but I've only seen you look like that once before, and it was on a Monday morning, too. Boy, I always figured that if any woman was immune to all that stuff, it'd be you. But you've got it bad for some fellow, don't you?"

Roberta considered telling Marla that any pleasure she might have read on her face reflected satisfaction of a job well done. After all, she'd just returned from another successful chautauqua weekend. She also consid ered telling her that a professor's private life was none of her business. But Marla had shared so many of her personal feelings during the lunches and casual office chats they'd shared that such a reply would have been rude. Besides, the young woman wasn't asking for intimate details.

Besides, I'd be a fool to think I could hide the way Clay makes me feel, Roberta realized. *Even my walk is different after a weekend in his arms.*

"Marla," she began with some semblance of sophistication, "I think it would be more accurate to say—" she hesitated, then gave up the effort "—that I'm head over heels in love with him."

"I knew it! I *knew* it!" Marla grinned as she shut the door. "Tell me *every*thing!"

That was enough to sober Roberta. "I'm not in the habit of sharing my personal life with my students, Marla, or with anybody else, for that matter," she declared a bit archly. "Suffice it to say that there is a special man in my life, and last weekend I was fortunate enough to spend some time with him."

Marla's expression grew more serious. "Are you thinking of getting married?" she asked bluntly. Before Roberta could answer, she tacked on, "I don't mean to be nosy, but since he doesn't live around here, if you marry him you might have to move away. I'd just hate to see you leave T.S.U."

Roberta had no desire to leave T.S.U, either, and she would refuse to do so if Clay ever demanded it of her. If, on the other hand, the time came when they both wanted to marry—and that time was a long way off—and he considered *his* relocation an equally viable possibility, then she might be willing to make the move if it truly seemed like the best choice for both of them. It was a fine distinction, which Marla might not be able to discern, and she had no intention of discussing her professional future with a grad student before she discussed it with Charles...let alone with Clay. Instead she asked more prosaically, "How do you know he doesn't live around here?"

"Because you only glow like this after a chautauqua weekend. Either you're meeting him somewhere after you speak or he's following you from town to town."

Roberta chuckled. "You're too romantic to make a good sleuth, Marla. Has it occurred to you that he may simply be involved in the small-town summer fair circuit himself? Our encounters may be purely coincidental."

Marla looked disappointed. "That doesn't sound nearly so exciting."

A smile of sensual memory lit up Roberta's face. It was all she could do to keep from purring. "Exciting enough."

This time it was Marla's turn to laugh. "Does he give chautauquas, too?"

"He filled in for me once."

"Where does he teach?"

"He doesn't," she hedged. "His interest lies in research." Before Marla could press her for details, Roberta pointedly glanced at her watch. "Speaking of research, were you able to pick up that book at the library for me? My paper for the historical review is almost done, but I've got to double-check a few points first."

While Marla explained her difficulties in tracking down the book in question, Roberta assured herself that the conversational shift had been a natural one. After all, she was excited about her chautauqua paper and grateful to Charles for arranging its publication.

It was only later in the week, when she came home to find a three-page letter in her mailbox from Fort Collins, that she realized she had deliberately sidestepped Marla's question about Clay's career because she didn't want to admit that she was dating a man who only had a high-school education.

On the heels of that discovery came the aching acknowledgement that she had, in some small way, betrayed Clay.

ROBERTA JOINED CLAY at his trailer every weekend in July and wrote to him faithfully in between chautauqua stops. When the waiting got too hard he'd call her, or sometimes she'd call him, and they'd talk about mundane things—weather, work, the price of tomatoes or hay—to keep from lamenting how very much they missed each other. The nights they spent together were more special because of the days they spent apart, and as they grew more relaxed and trusting of each other, their quiet times grew as rewarding as the hours they spent in bed.

Often, at sundown, they'd hold hands and walk beyond the fairground barns toward whatever stretch of land was the least hemmed in, sharing dreams and memories, old hurts and current joys. Whether they were strolling in the high desert, pine-studded forests or alkali flats, the magic of their time together heightened. Bit by bit Clay told Roberta about his mother, his browbeaten father, his adolescent terrors and mounting hatred of everything his mother had ever planned for him.

"Sometimes I wonder if I'm still too hostile to be healthy," he once confessed. "Every time I think it's out of my system, something happens to let me know that nothing's really changed in all these years."

Roberta had stroked his palm with her strong fingers. "Have you ever considered therapy, Clay?" she asked gently.

His answer was pointed and maybe a bit cruel. "Have you?"

Roberta had released his hand and slipped it into the pocket of her long gingham gown. "Riding has no effect on my life one way or another," she rationalized, pushing away the knowledge that she longed to go riding with Clay on their quiet nights together, longed to sit beside him in his frequent parades. "Your refusal to get an education is crippling your life."

"I'm hardly crippled," he snapped. Still seething, he pressed on, "Despite your rigid rules for successful academic endeavors, Roberta, I am a self-educated man and I have a thriving business that does better every year. Nobody ever snickers at me because I don't have fancy diplomas hanging on my wall." He glared at her. "Except, I guess, for you."

"Clay!" Instantly she regretted her sharp tone. She stopped and laid one soft hand against his cheek, waiting until he covered it with his own, apologetically tugging it to his mouth to kiss her palm.

"Roberta," he said more softly, "my life is full. I'm not rich, but I've got no financial problems. I've got good investments, a retirement plan, and I pay my own way. Whatever makes me happy, I enjoy." He kissed her tenderly, almost as though she were a child. "You, on the other hand, are crying inside all the time because you can't celebrate one of the great joys in life. Some people don't care about riding, or don't even like it, though that's hard for me to understand. If you were a city gal and were scared of horses, it wouldn't matter. It wouldn't merit a second thought. But when I see you talk to the camels, brush down my horses, sneak back to double-check Baby Bev's feet to make sure Ozzie's cleaned them right—" she blushed at this revelation that she'd been caught hovering over the young camel "—then I know that riding is still terribly important to you."

To his surprise, tears filled Roberta's proud eyes. It occurred to Clay that he'd seen her red-eyed, but he'd never seen her cry. He also knew that somebody would have to tear her heart out by its roots before that would happen. But it was obvious that the tears were close to falling.

Clay cradled her face with both warm hands and waited until she met his loving gaze. "Sweetheart," he urged gently, "please let me help you. I've got horses—and camels, too—used to handling every kind of greenhorn rider. We can go somewhere quiet, where we won't be watched or disturbed, and I can—"

With vigor, she shook her head. "No, Clay! I just can't. My whole spine stiffens even when you talk about it! I was on my back for *months*, Clay! I just can't risk it again."

"Honey, you take more risk getting in your car to drive to work. I'm not asking you to enter a rodeo or race or even jump a log. All you need to do is sit on a horse that's ambling along in its sleep. In Fort Collins I've got an Appaloosa mare who's the world's sweetest old gal and never bucked in her whole life. I'd be right beside you and—"

"No!" Anguish ripped through Roberta's tone and tore at his heart. She wanted to do it—her eyes begged him to understand—but it was still too much for her.

"Okay, sweetheart," he relented, taking her tenderly in his arms. "I'll let it drop for now. But you think about it, okay?"

She didn't reply, but took his hand and quickly started walking. When she spoke again—a good ten minutes later—it was on another subject entirely.

"Have you talked to Ira since he came down to see me?" she asked.

Clay shook his head. "Nope. We've been going either north or east so we haven't been near the Double T." He hadn't been back to Patchwork since Brady had given him a lecture on coddling Ozzie, in fact, but he'd already shared that conversation with Roberta. To his surprise, she'd agreed with Brady, giving him a lot of food for thought. "But I got a letter from Tess that mentioned some gal at Tucson who made quite an impression on Ira."

Roberta chuckled. "That was Marla, my teaching assistant this summer. She's too old for Ira, but I figured a bouncy, well-shaped flesh-and-blood female was the best advertisement I could give T.S.U."

"I guess it worked. She was the highlight of his trip."

"She's a nice kid and a hard worker. Actually I have a lot of respect for that girl. From what I gather, her parents seem to feel that a college education is a waste of time for a woman. They think she should be trying to snag a good husband, not mastering U.S. history."

Clay tightened his grip on her hand and said softly, "Are the two mutually exclusive? An advanced degree in history and a good marriage?"

"That's hardly the point, Clay. Poor Marla's got Neanderthal parents who—"

"I'm not talking about Marla." He waited until her eyes met his. "My question remains, are history and marriage incompatible?"

Her eyes were clear, open, unguarded as she weighed the question, soaked in the impact of what he hadn't yet said. Clay waited tensely, suddenly aware that her reply was terribly important to him.

"No, Clay," she finally answered in a calm, steady tone. "I think I could make room in my life for both, if the need should ever arise."

He pulled her a little closer and caressed her fingers with his own. "I'll remember that, Bobbie Jean. It could become important later on."

ROBERTA PLAYED CLAY'S WORDS about marriage over and over again in her mind in the next week while they were apart. While she couldn't say he'd delved into the subject in detail, he had brought it up—rather deliberately—and she wondered if he'd been trying to pave the way.

She was not the sort of woman who believed that a woman's job in the matrimonial game was to wait for a man to beg her on bended knee. But on the other hand, she couldn't see herself taking the lead in marital planning without some hint that Clay was thinking along similar lines. After all, they hadn't really known each other all that long, and though their relationship seemed so special, so unique that she couldn't imagine it leading anywhere but to the altar, the whole experience was so new to her that she couldn't be sure of much of anything.

There were a few things that made her hesitate. While she was alone with Clay, she was always blissfully happy. But back in Tucson, she found herself making excuses for not sharing her joy with her friends and colleagues—many of whom commented on the obvious change in her mellower personality—and she had to ask herself whether she would have been so "discreet" if she'd been dating a state senator or the dean of a neighboring college. Worse yet was the way she felt with Clay's friends, if that term could be used to describe the unlettered cowboys who worked for him.

Ozzie, of course, was always the soul of courtesy, and he idolized Clay rather than befriended him. But Warner, George and Roscoe always seemed to be around, feeding the stock or checking equipment, and their conversation often ruffled her feathers.

They joked about women, they joked about sex, and they never discussed anything of social significance for more than three sentences back-to-back. While there was never anything flagrantly crude about their comments, their conversations were so lightweight and chauvinistic that Roberta was irritated. Every now and then she found herself fighting back.

"Is it incomprehensible to you that a woman as pretty as Rita Rollins might have an intelligent perspective on world affairs?" she once demanded when they were joking about the cup size of a well-known actress who was raising money for starving children in Africa. "Have you ever considered the possibility that you might do something with your spare time to help the world?"

Warner, the oldest and most arrogant of the group, had snapped back, "Clay makes one of us give free rides to the poor kids in Fort Collins in the city park once a month, and me 'n' him do our routine for charity stuff all the time. It ain't Africker, Roberter, but it seems to me that it oughter count as doin' our bit for th' world."

That put her back on her heels a bit. She was impressed that Clay donated his time and livestock to a worthy cause, though it didn't do much to raise her esteem of his reluctant men. She wanted to ask about his other friends—surely he had some with more education!—but she wasn't sure how to bring up the subject gracefully. Then she reminded herself that Brady was his friend, and Brady had a ranch and a good education, proving that the two could go hand in hand. Just because her own rural background had been filled with cowboys who spit upon the world of academia didn't mean everybody in the ranching world felt that way.

She'd almost convinced herself that she could adjust to Clay's companions on the day that she reached the barn ahead of Clay and overheard a conversation that made the blood stand still in her veins.

"Nah, he ain't gonna marry her. Clay'd never do that to us!" It was Warner's voice.

"What makes you so sure?" answered Roscoe. "Ah've known Clay for seventeen years and Ah've never seen him hung up on a filly like he is on this one."

"Well, I give ya that. But Clay's a feller allus got his feet on the ground. He's smitten, all right, but it won't last. Can you see that hoity-toity nose in the air professor fittin' into a camel ranch? Why, hell, she's been ridin' Clay for two months and she still hasn't mounted up one of his camels—or even a baby-proof horse!"

"You hush now!" Roscoe warned. "If Clay hears you talk like that you'll be out on yer ear. Don't you remember what he did when that boy from Montana started pokin' fun at Ozzie?"

"That was different," said George. "Poor old Oz has a problem. This college gal just doesn't like to get her hands dirty."

"She helps bring the camels out when they're racin'," insisted Roscoe, winning great favor in Roberta's heart. "She knows her way around the back end of a horse."

"Don't make no never mind, Roscoe," countered Warner. "She's just slummin' it like one of them rodeo Annies that wear a hat and skintight breeches that would split wide open if they tried to mount anything on four legs. There ain't no place for a woman like that on a ranch, even one that caters to dudes like Clay's. I know he likes his books and all, but can you see him hitchin' up with a filly who won't even ride a kid's pony?"

It was George who answered, "I sure cain't."

Neither could Roberta.

"SO WHAT'S old Ira have to say?" Clay asked when Ozzie finished reading the letter from his friend one hot August day at the Fort Collins spread. It was a rambling set of trails and stables covering some sixty acres, half-hilly, half-flat, and all Clay's. He'd grown attached to it over the years, but it was only a place to him. It was the total composite of his life—the trailer, the camels, the crowds—that he thought of as his home.

Ozzie didn't get many letters, and Clay always asked about each one. Usually Ozzie was glad to share the information, but this time he felt unaccountably sad.

"He's decided to go to school in Tucson. Joe said he could go that far because Roberta's there and he wouldn't be all alone."

Clay nodded. He looked pleased. "Is he going to live with her?"

Ozzie shook his head. "No. He's g-g-going to stay in a dorm. But I guess she said he was welcome to come over for a home-cooked d-d-dinner whenever he wants to."

"Sounds great, Ozzie. It might be something you'd like to do someday."

Ozzie glanced at Clay with more than a little concern. Lately Clay had been making lots of "You ought to consider going back to school" sounds, which were making him uneasy. In fact, if Clay hadn't been acting just as friendly as ever the rest of the time, he'd wonder if his boss was trying to get rid of him.

He was about to ask if Clay was hoping he'd move on when he realized that Clay was no longer talking to him. He was intently reading a letter of his own from Tucson. He never shared the contents of his mail with Ozzie, but Ozzie picked up the mail often enough to know that Roberta wrote to Clay every two or three days. And he took the mail into town often enough to know that at least once a week, Clay wrote back.

"Any news?" he asked as the two of them strolled back toward Clay's old-fashioned house. "I mean, anything you w-w-want to tell me?"

Clay grinned. "You think Roberta writes hot letters not fit for your young ears?"

Ozzie blushed. "I d-d-don't know what she writes. I n-n-never look."

Clay picked up the letter and read out loud as he walked. "'I'm busy finishing up my manuscript for the historical review on the effects of the chautauqua movement on rural turn-of-the-century America. One of the perks of my job is that I have a graduate student as a gofer to collect and return library material to the old prof.' "

"Who's the 'old prof'?" asked Ozzie.

"Roberta."

"Roberta's not old. She's younger than you."

Clay grimaced and smoothed the sprinkling of gray hairs at his temples. "Thanks a lot, Oz. I hope you're in as good a shape as I am when you get to be my age." Playfully he slapped Ozzie's shoulder with the letter, then said, "If you went to T.S.U., you might get to meet this gal. Her name's Marla. From what I hear, she made quite an impression on Ira."

Ozzie blushed again. "If she's a g-g-graduate student, she wouldn't b-b-bother with somebody like me."

"Why?" said Clay, suddenly stopping in his tracks. He peered at Ozzie intently as he asked, "What on earth is wrong with a fine young man like yourself?"

"I st-st-stutter!" he burst out, hating the cursed word that he'd never in his life uttered clearly. "And a girl that smart would think I was st-st-stupid if I never went to sc-sc-school!"

"Then stop stuttering and go to school!" Clay yelled at him.

For the first time since he'd come to work for Clay, Ozzie felt the shame of tears in his eyes. Clay might as well have hit him in the face. "I c-c-can't," he whimpered. "You know I c-c-can't."

"Dammit, Ozzie, I *know* you *can*!"

Ozzie covered his eyes and hoped desperately that nobody but Clay could see he was crying. He knew there was no way to hide it from Clay. Miserably he spilled out the feelings he'd been bottling up for weeks. "If you d-d-don't want me here anymore, Clay, just s-s-say so. D-d-don't keep telling me to g-g-go to school. If you're s-s-sick of me, I can just g-g-go away."

There was a moment of long, tense silence before he felt Clay's warm arm embrace his shoulder. The older man pulled him close. "Is that what you think, Ozzie? That I don't want you here anymore?"

Suddenly Ozzie started to sob. He couldn't answer at all.

Mercifully Clay steered him toward the house. He didn't move his arm or say a word until they were safely inside. Then he put both arms around Ozzie and hugged him as though he were a small boy.

"Ozzie, this is your home. You are welcome to live with me until the day you die. I don't ever want you to waste a moment worrying about that again. Do you hear me?"

Ozzie couldn't stop crying—but now he was crying in relief. Clay clung to him for a moment, then let him go as he struggled to regain his composure.

"Now listen to me, Oz. What I've been doing the last few weeks may not have been smart, but I did it for your own good. Some people that I respect have told me that I was doing you a great disservice by letting you hide out from the world here forever. It's even been suggested that I didn't really want you to go to college because then I'd have to face the fact that I never did." He was quiet for a moment before he added, "You know I don't think school is the way for everybody, Ozzie, and I'm not certain it's the way for you. But I feel the tension in you every time the subject comes up. I see the longing in your face. I had lots of reasons for wanting to avoid college. You only have one. If you didn't stutter, nothing could keep you out of school—part-time right here in Fort Collins or full-time anywhere else."

Ozzie met his eyes bleakly.

"Isn't that true?"

Ozzie didn't have to think about it for a second. "Yes." He desperately wanted to spend his time with other people his own age. He desperately wanted to learn every subject on the face of the earth. He wanted to become a veterinarian. Above all, he wanted to feel normal. He wanted to belong.

"Now I've been telling you for months that you can stutter and go to college at the same time. In fact, I'm pretty damn certain that you'll never *stop* stuttering until you find the guts to go to school in spite of it. There are techniques you can learn, things you can do to help control the stammering, Oz, but none of them will do any good until you convince yourself that you can stutter till the cows come home and still be a full-fledged man."

Ozzie lowered his eyes. "I know." He did know. He'd known it for sometime. "But I don't think I'll ever f-f-feel like a man until I l-l-lick the stutter."

"Then maybe you need to carry on even though you don't feel like a man yet, Ozzie. You know, most of the people in college are still boys and girls."

His eyes flashed up. It was a thought he hadn't yet considered. "Ira's been working l-l-like a man for years."

"So have you," said Clay. "And in many ways, Ira *is* a man. But I bet he still gets his dad's advice when he wants to buy a car and I'll wager that his stepmom packs his lunch in the morning. Nobody grows up over night, Ozzie, and nobody's completely ready to try something new until he's done it." There was a long, pensive silence before he said, "I may have done you a disservice by promising you that you could overcome your stutter with enough guts. Some people do learn to stop stuttering. Some never do. The issue isn't how much or how little you stammer, Oz, it's what you do with your life. Do you rule the stutter, or do you let it rule you?"

It was a sunny Saturday morning when Roberta reached the Southside Stables for her first private riding lesson. She knew, in the deepest reaches of her heart, that she was nowhere near ready for this awesome step. But Clay had not been ready to give his chautauqua, either, and he'd survived. She knew she was going to have to cure her riding terror if she ever expected to make a life with him.

Or make peace with herself.

The instructor was a friendly middle-aged woman with a good reputation for handling children and beginners. Roberta had told her very little on the phone: "I rode a little, years and years ago, but I think I should start over from scratch." It was the truth, more or less. She told herself that she'd withheld the details because anonymity would make it easier to force herself to act like a normal rider. But Roberta also knew that she couldn't bring herself to admit to an experienced horsewoman that she was terrified to mount the tamest of beginner horses.

Pauline Mercer took Roberta at her word. She explained the use of various bridles and showed Roberta how to slip the bit into the training horse's mouth. She showed her how to put on a saddle. Roberta followed her directions with wordless precision, trying her best not to think about the nearby arena—where two teenage girls were jumping fences—or even the stolid palomino who didn't seem to notice that her hands were ice-cold. She put her brain in neutral; she didn't even think about Clay.

And she did all right—at least she went through the motions—until Pauline said, "Now put your left foot in the saddle and grab hold of the saddle horn."

Roberta put her foot in the saddle. She grabbed the saddle horn.

"Now swing on up. I'll give you a push."

She tried. She tried desperately. But nothing happened. Her body was as still as death.

"Roberta?" Pauline asked gently. "Would it help if I demonstrated first?"

Roberta stared at the saddle horn and tried to answer. Nothing came out of her mouth.

The next few minutes were a bit of a muddle, but when she started to focus on Pauline again, she discovered that they were back in the barn, away from the palomino, sitting side by side on a bale of hay. Incredibly Roberta seemed to be telling Pauline her whole sad story. Even the part about Clay.

"I admire your courage in coming out here," Pauline told her kindly. "But I'm not sure you're going about this in the right way."

Roberta sighed. "There is no right way," she bleakly confessed. "I just can't do this. That's all."

Pauline shook her head. "I'm sure you can. I just think you need some time to get used to the idea. And maybe a little help from a friend."

"You mean Clay?" A thousand times Roberta had considered his offer to help her, and each time she'd realized that it had to be something she did on her own. Their relationship was already too complicated.

"I meant the four-footed kind. Follow me."

Pauline led Roberta toward a corner stall where an elderly white mare dozed on her feet, one hip leaning against the wall. At the sound of the women, she blinked once or twice, then sauntered over. She had the saddest eyes Roberta had ever seen.

"This is Snowy," said Pauline, scratching the friendly mare's chin. "One of my students bought her during her girlhood horse phase when she was ten. Now the girl is off at college, and almost never comes out here anymore. But she won't let her parents sell the horse because of some misplaced loyalty to days gone by. We feed Snowy, of course, and try to give her some exercise, but she's too old to use for lessons, even though she's as gentle as a lamb."

Pauline stepped back as Roberta took over the chin-scratching, her eyes caressing the lonely mare's. "What she needs is somebody to talk to. To walk beside on a lead." She grabbed a halter from the wall behind her and handed it to Roberta. "You already paid me for an hour. You might as well do something useful before you go."

FOR SEVERAL DAYS after Clay's argument with Ozzie, he felt uneasy, but he wasn't sure why. Maybe it was because he'd failed to do what Brady and Roberta had suggested; maybe it was because he'd gone against his own instincts to try it at all. Maybe, he considered reluctantly, it was because he felt like a phony. He was counseling Ozzie to do something he'd never had the guts to manage himself.

Oh, he'd licked the stutter. And maybe, by giving that damn chautauqua, he'd proven he could face the fear. But he was a forty-two-year-old man who read obsessively and cherished learning, and he'd never so much as enrolled in a weekend seminar or a community class on some aspect of local history. And even though his mother had been dead for years, he knew—in the deepest reaches of his heart—that he'd never gone back to school because to do so would be to let her win.

It wasn't just school. It was a whole host of things that reflected her privileged upbringing. The list, in fact, was endless: wearing a tux, buying a new car, writing for publication, engaging in politics, attending a charity ball, rubbing elbows with the rich and famous... These were the trappings of wealth, of society, of his mother's value system that he'd eschewed in his youth. To commit any of those acts would be to admit failure, somehow. He knew it was irrational, but it was there, a living, grinding force in his gut, all the same.

The irony was, he had changed since Ozzie's age, and now, in hindsight, there were some things he wished he'd done differently. He enjoyed camels and he enjoyed being his own boss, but he did not know—would never know—what opportunities he'd passed up by boycotting college. And there were times when he knew that he longed to do some of the things on his mother's list—things he still refused to do out of boneheaded resistance and sheer masculine pride. His last automotive purchase, for instance, had been an old truck. He'd found a new one at the dealer's with a spectacular end-of-the-year closeout price that was well within his means. He'd researched his options thoroughly and knew it was an excellent purchase in every respect. It was built well enough to last for years and he'd dearly loved the way it handled. But in the end, he'd bought a used truck, which he didn't like nearly as well, because he knew the choice would have appalled his mother.

And then there was his love of books. He had always wanted to write a book, or an article, at least, on the story of camels in the southwest. There wasn't much information on the subject—he'd found every chapter and footnote in the archives of three different university libraries and his own extensive western book collection—and he knew that his own insights would be especially meaningful to a subject so dear to his heart. But getting published would have dearly pleased his mother. She'd have jumped through hoops, in fact, just to know that he was dating a woman who had published half a dozen professional papers and sported a Ph.D.

And she'd have been ecstatic if she'd known that he was, even now, vaguely toying with the notion of going back to school.

There were a dozen reasons why he knew he'd never do it. He was too old, too set in his ways, too busy. He was embarrassed; he was stubborn; he was proud. He owned a thriving business and saw no good reason to make a career shift in midstream. And his reasons for considering college made no sense to begin with. Did he want to learn more? Of course. But he could do that in other ways. Did he want to be a good example for Ozzie? Naturally. Did he want to lessen the incredible gulf between Roberta's education and his own? Yes, yes, yes! And no.

He wanted the chasm to close, but he didn't want to be the one to make the heroic leap. He wanted her to accept him exactly as he was; no woman was worth the kind of pressure his mother had placed on his poor father. And though he couldn't exactly accuse Roberta of browbeating him, there was a silent, insistent quality of pressure in their dealings, which troubled him. He always had the feeling that she wanted him to prove himself, to measure up. *To go back to school.* Once she'd even mentioned therapy to help him decide to do it! He wondered, sometimes, if she kept a mental list of his grammatical errors and cultural faux pas. And he was keenly aware that so far, they'd only spent time together in the artificial environment of historical fun and games. Except for the Trents and Hendersons, who were practically family, he'd never had to pass muster with her university colleagues or friends.

He'd never met a single one of them, and he was beginning to wonder if Roberta was going out of her way to make certain that he never did. If she was, then he had to rethink their relationship from square one. If Roberta was ashamed to be known as Clay Gann's woman, it was for damn sure that he'd never want her to be known as Clay Gann's wife.

CHAPTER TWELVE

ROBERTA SENSED THE TENSION in Clay's voice the minute she picked up the phone.

"This is going to be a long month, Bobbie Jean," he pointed out after half a dozen sentences. "We're not going to get together until the middle of August if we wait till our trails accidentally cross. I was thinking that this weekend might be a good time for us to get together on purpose. I'd like to show you my place."

Roberta longed to say yes, but the reality of her summer classload forced her to be prudent. "Oh, Clay, you don't know how much I wish I could come to Fort Collins. But I've been gone so many weekends already this term, and summer sessions are so intense that if you even blink you lose a grip on things. I need to spend the weekends I'm not giving chautauquas catching up."

He was quiet for a moment before he said, "I thought you had an assistant to lighten the load."

She chuckled. "Oh, Clay, she lightens the load but not the responsibility. The students are still mine. She's just helping around the edges. And I have other professional obligations that are really too complicated to explain." *And personal ones, like taking walks with Snowy.*

"I'm not retarded, Roberta, just short of formal schooling. Give it a try. I might surprise you."

That was when she knew that he hadn't just called to tell her he missed her. There was something else on his mind. Quickly she explained, "I didn't mean you couldn't understand it. I mean you'd be bored to tears if I went into the details. You're really too sensitive, Clay."

"Maybe," he conceded. Then his voice changed again, and he became the rollicking camel man she loved. "But I'm a lovesick boy a long way from my sweetie. Have mercy on me, Bobbie Jean. If you can't break away, invite me down there for the weekend. I could see the sights while you're grading papers. We can call it a busman's holiday."

She gave it a long moment's thought; she tried to lie to herself and failed. "Oh, Clay, I'd love it, but it just wouldn't work. I'd never get anything done. You're just too distracting."

"I do my best." The words were right, but his tone was strained. After a pointed pause, he quietly observed, "You do realize, Roberta, that you've never invited me to Tucson? Never even suggested that you'd like for me to see your place or meet your friends?"

She had no quick comeback for that inescapably accurate observation. Truthfully she said, "Well, Clay, we haven't been seeing each other very long and we've been meeting pretty regularly on the road. I'd love to have you come here as soon as the summer session grades are in and I can come up for air. I'll have the last few days of August free. You can come down here then or I can come up there."

It was the right answer; she could hear the quiet relief in his tone. "That sounds . . . reasonable, Roberta. I haven't been out of school so long that I've forgotten what deadlines are like."

It occurred to her, quite belatedly, that Clay's own business surely had its ups and downs, its periods of leisure and comparative stress. The simple truth was, she'd never asked him about running a camel ranch. Although she saw it as a way to earn a decent living, she didn't see it as a career at all.

"I'm sure you have peak periods in your operation, too, Clay," she suggested, deciding that showing some interest in his work—no matter how belated—was better than showing none at all.

There was a pause, as though her casual comment merited some special thought on Clay's part. She was sure of it when he replied, "Do you know, Roberta, that that's the first time you've ever acknowledged that I do anything with my time when I'm not at a fair on the weekend? Do you ever think about the rest of my life at all?"

Suddenly the conversation felt very quicksandy. Carefully Roberta said, "Clay, I think about you all the time. If I don't think much about your world in Fort Collins, it's because in my mind's eye I can't see you there. When I fantasize about you, I envision you in your trailer. As far as I'm concerned, that's our mutual home."

This time his silence went on so long that Roberta was afraid she'd really blown it. Why hadn't she ever learned how to talk to men?

But when Clay spoke again, his voice was warm and husky, and she knew that the small rift between them was on the mend.

"Do you fantasize about me, Bobbie Jean?" He was clearly delighted and amused.

"Well, yes, I do, if you must know."

"Oh, I *must*," he teased her. "I want to know every detail of these fantasies. What am I wearing? The uniform or my jeans?"

"Neither," she blurted honestly. "You're usually wearing half a sheet or nothing at all."

Clay laughed, and Roberta joined him. A moment later he confided, "Are you having one of your fantasies right now, Bobbie Jean?"

A sudden vision of Clay, very nude and very close to her own naked body, suddenly made it difficult to speak. She felt trembly when she answered hoarsely, "You know I am."

"Bobbie Jean—" his voice caressed her with such sensual luster that she could all but feel his skin slide along her own "—I'm having a fantasy, too."

For a long moment neither one of them spoke, but their communication was so rich that words would only have gotten in the way.

BY THE TIME they met in Three Teeth, Texas, on the third weekend in August, Clay was climbing the walls. Although he'd hated the long separation from Roberta, he'd learned something crucial from it. Even though she'd never been to Fort Collins, she was starting to fill up the cracks of his life there. He was beginning to see her in every female between the ages of eighteen and sixty, and he went to bed aching for her every night. He knew that her scheduled two-week vacation in Fort Collins—which would start a few days after this rendezvous—would be a crucial one, a time to start making long-term plans. It would be a wonderful opportunity to let their relationship develop more naturally. And despite all his very logical concerns about their future, he was starting to hope that they would find a way to stay together. Permanently.

He caught the last part of Roberta's act as Elizabeth Cady Stanton right about noon. He had not yet had a chance to greet her, though he was certain she'd spotted him in the crowd. She was at her thunderous best today, hurling accusations at menfolk everywhere. In the front row, he noticed, was a young woman in costume who kept cheering her on, tossing out energetic comments that sounded like quotes from Susan B. Anthony. He was not surprised to see the brunette rush up to Roberta's side when the speech was finished. She even beat Clay, and he was taking his longest strides.

"Oh, Dr. Wheeler, you were just sensational!" the woman declared. "You're always good when you do this in class, but here on the stage—with everybody all dressed up—oh, I've never seen you better!"

"Thank you, Marla. It's really sweet of you to say so," said Roberta, her eyes nervously sweeping the crowd.

"Oh, but I mean it! I'm going to tell Dr. Trumbull how great it is. I think it's going to make a wonderful graduate seminar next summer."

Clay grimaced at the mention of Dr. Trumbull. He still remembered how Roberta had oozed admiration when she'd first mentioned the man's name, and it burned him no end that she'd dated Charles briefly just before she and Clay had gotten together. But Charles did, ultimately, have to grant his approval of Roberta's brilliantly conceived program before it could progress, so Clay hoped she could remain on relatively close terms with him . . . the operative word being *relatively*.

Fighting an instinctive need to pull Roberta very close and greet her with a lead-me-to-the-bedroom kiss, he edged through the nearby bodies to her side and lightly slipped one arm around her waist in what could have passed for a platonic gesture. She did not glance up at him at once, which struck him as odd. Surely she recognized his casual touch, but after nearly three endless weeks apart, she was making no effort to greet him with her usual spontaneous joy.

A quiet claw of alarm tightened inside him, but he did not drop his arm. Before he could speak, Marla spotted him and cheerfully deduced, "Oh, Dr. Wheeler, is this your boyfriend? I can see why you come in smiling on Monday mornings after a long weekend on the road!"

The young woman smiled so radiantly that Clay couldn't help but return her winsome grin. "I go home smiling, too, young lady," he assured her warmly with what he hoped was just the right tone. Offering his hand he said, "I'm Clay Gann. Dr. Wheeler has spoken highly of you, Marla."

He'd never called Roberta "Dr. Wheeler" before, and the words stuck to the roof of his mouth like cotton candy. But it seemed to him that such formality was appropriate since that's what Marla called her, and he wanted to make sure that he handled this first contact with Roberta's professional world exactly right. Not a trace of Edward Beale or the Camel Man influenced his impeccable speech. Granted, he was dressed like a cowpoke—lucky hat and all—but so was everybody else at the fair, so that only meant he fit right in.

"Oh, Dr. Wheeler's just the greatest, Professor Gann," Marla assured him. "Meeting her is the most wonderful thing that's ever happened to me."

"It's pretty high on my list, too, Marla," he concurred, fighting a new sensation that he wasn't at all sure he liked. The girl had called him Professor. *I could have been one. I would have majored in history,* a quiet voice protested. But another voice, one more in tune with the present day, was asking, *Is this just an honest mistake on Marla's part, or did Roberta tell her I was a professor because she's ashamed of me?* "How do you happen to be here this weekend?"

"Oh, my folks live in Lubbock," she explained, "and I went home after summer session. I got to see Dr. Wheeler do her acts in class, of course, but I never got a chance to see her do a chautauqua on the road." She smiled happily at Roberta; clearly she felt the long ride from Lubbock had been worthwhile. "Besides, I really miss her. We used to get together every day."

"It was really nice of you to come hear me speak, Marla," Roberta cut in a bit bluntly, "but I haven't eaten since nine and I'm dying for lunch."

"I haven't eaten, either," said Marla, apparently failing to realize that she was being given a polite brush-off. "I saw a hot dog stand near the entrance when I came in."

"I think I'll need something a bit more substantial than that. Clay—" for the first time she acknowledged him "—have you had time to get your bearings?"

She didn't really look at him, and that made him uneasy. But the notion that this young woman had driven a hundred and eleven miles just to hear Roberta speak—invited or not—and was about to return without so much as a shared meal troubled him even more greatly. It was the sort of stunt his mother would have pulled. Roberta's insensitivity to the girl's obvious hero worship both worried and irritated him.

"Ozzie mentioned a buffalo grill down on the main fairway," he said truthfully. Then, in a moment of inspiration, he added, "I'm sure he'd be happy to join us to make it a foursome. Ozzie's my chief assistant," he told Marla. "He's about your age."

Like any young woman presented with such information, Marla's answering grin was both embarrassed and anticipatory. Clay suspected that Ozzie would feel the same way. But it would be good for Ozzie to be in a social situation, it would be good for Marla to feel that somebody appreciated her company, and it would be good for Ozzie to distract the girl long enough for Clay to find out why Roberta was acting as though she wished both of them would go away.

OZZIE WAS STUNNED when he spotted Clay near the barn with Roberta and an incredibly good-looking girl in her early twenties; he was flabbergasted when Clay beckoned for him to join them.

"Oz, this is Marla, one of Roberta's students," Clay announced casually, as though he introduced good-looking girls to Ozzie every day. "We're going out to lunch. Let's make it a foursome."

Ozzie just stared at him. Lunch with Clay was one thing. Even lunch with Clay and Roberta he could handle. But lunch with a girl who looked like that? Desperately he tried to think of something to say, but he was too surprised to even stutter.

Mercifully the pretty girl picked up the slack. "It's nice to meet you, Ozzie," she said without a trace of hesitation. "Professor Gann says you're his right-hand man."

Ozzie had heard Clay refer to him in this flattering way before and generally beamed at such praise. But at the moment, another one of the girl's comments drew his immediate attention. Was he imagining things, or had she referred to Clay as *Professor* Gann?

"I try to h-help out," he told her, hoping that his half-swallowed second *h* hadn't been too apparent.

Since it was obvious that he couldn't very well dodge the summons—and one look at this girl's face was enough reason not to—he fell into step with Marla and tooled along at Clay's heels. He was beginning to understand why Ira had had second thoughts about waiting out a year after his trip to Tucson. If *this* was what a guy could expect in college, why would he want to spend his time anywhere else?

As Marla bragged about Roberta's morning performance, Ozzie studied Clay's woman's back. He'd seen Roberta in lots of moods, but he'd never seen her march along as stiffly as she was doing so now. The funny thing was, Clay was moving just as awkwardly, and he was clinging to Roberta's elbow so hard that his knuckles were turning white.

Ozzie had only seen Clay look that angry once before. It was the time that cowboy from Montana had imitated Ozzie's stutter in front of him, and Clay had ordered him to clear off the place in twenty minutes or he'd feed him to the hogs. He didn't think Clay was likely to feed Roberta to the hogs, but he knew that the instant he and Marla got their hot dogs, he was going to volunteer to show her the camel barns and anywhere else he could to get out of the line of fire. Of course it meant he'd have to talk to her for an hour or so—maybe even longer—and that could be mighty awkward if he started to stammer.

And then he remembered that Clay had told him that *he* was the ruler of his stutter. and he told himself, *The stutter be damned.*

"YOU'RE OVERREACTING, Clay," Roberta insisted as Clay slammed the trailer door shut behind her. Ever since they'd left the two young folks at the midway, he'd dropped his superficial good cheer and stomped along beside her as pleasantly as a grizzly just unearthed from his winter's nap. Now that they were alone, she was certain that Clay was about to explode.

She knew she'd made a mistake in not telling Marla that Clay wasn't a professor, but it wasn't as though she'd lied outright to the girl. And she certainly hadn't invited her to drive all this way just to hear her speak. She'd seen Marla five days a week all though July and half of August and she hadn't seen Clay for weeks. "I just didn't want a student to share my private time with you."

"The hell you didn't. You didn't want her to know I wasn't a professor. You didn't want her to know I run a camel ranch. You didn't want her to detect any of the multitudinous shortcomings in my appearance, my speech, or my background that could embarrass you if it got back to Charles or the rest of your stuffed-shirt colleagues!"

"Clay, that's not true!"

"You're ashamed of me. I always knew you were."

"That's not true, either!" At least she didn't think it was true. Oh, there might be a few tiny things she'd change about him...a few details of his background she wouldn't be thrilled for everyone to know. But ashamed of this man she had learned to love? Oh, no. Never that.

He faced her furiously, his eyes full of hurt. "Why did you tell her I was a professor?"

"I didn't," she insisted. "She just assumed it. We've never talked about you much."

"She knew I was based in Fort Collins. She knew that you were seeing me every weekend you gave a chautauqua. That hardly strikes me as a cloak of secrecy."

"Clay," she reached out to touch his arm. "That's really all she knows. I don't make a habit of discussing my personal life with my students. She just happened to note a change of mood one day and made a comment. I admitted I was involved with someone special. That's really all there was to our discussion."

He didn't look the least bit mollified. "That may be, but that hardly explains why you treated me like Typhoid Mary when I showed up today. You didn't even look at me, Roberta, and it's been over three weeks! Normally you can't keep your hands off me when I kiss you hello. There must be some reason for the glacial treatment. I didn't even have time to stick my foot in my mouth before you started ignoring me."

"I wasn't ignoring you! I was just trying to get out of introducing you so we could slip off together sooner. I didn't want to get stuck eating lunch with her."

"Why not? She's a nice enough kid. Besides, she drove all the way from Lubbock just to see you."

"That's not the point. I'll see her all the time when school starts again next month. I don't get to see you very often."

"Neither does anybody else at your school, do they, Roberta? Nobody ever has a chance to know the real me. Nobody can take back embarrassing tales about your cowboy lover."

Roberta made no effort to hide her fear as she faced him. It was only the quiet shame—the tiniest suspicion that he might be partly right—that she tried to keep to herself. "I don't know why you keep harping on this point, Clay. You sound as insecure as Ozzie, as though you're ashamed of yourself. I've never done anything to make you believe that you embarrass me."

He studied her for a moment, then asked bluntly, "Have you ever told anybody in Tucson the truth about me?"

"Of course. I told Charles the first moment I saw him after we finally got together in Little Horn. By now most everybody on the staff knows."

Apparently that news wasn't enough for him. "But what do they know about me? Do they all think I'm a professor with a Ph.D. in history?"

She shook her head. "How would I know? I've never told anybody that you were."

"Have you ever contradicted anybody who jumped to that erroneous conclusion?"

Abruptly she glanced away. Honesty forbade her from making a flat denial. "Well, it hasn't really come up very often."

"How often?"

"Just once."

He waited.

Reluctantly she admitted, "Charles made the same assumption that Marla did."

"And of course you proudly corrected him?"

Roberta's eyes flashed up to Clay's, and the anger she saw there left her shaken. He looked more than furious, more than hurt. He looked positively beyond appeal or reason. A great rope of fear tightened around her middle. "I don't...remember exactly what I said," she hedged.

"The hell you don't!" He edged closer, his expression positively lethal now. "Did you tell him I did trick riding for a living?"

Roberta had to glance away. "No."

"Did you tell him I ran a camel ranch?"

She shook her head. Nausea knotted her stomach.

Clay stepped closer yet and took a firm hold on her arm. He did not hurt her, but he did not release her while he waited for her to meet his eyes. When she finally did, he demanded in a low, harsh tone, "Did you tell him you were with a man who only had a high-school education?"

"Clay—" she begged.

"Did you?"

Roberta covered her face. Tears filled her hazel eyes but—at great cost—did not spill over. "It just didn't come up, Clay!" she insisted. "He was worried about where *he* fit into the picture, not you. I told him that you'd won and he'd lost, as gently as I could. That was really all the situation called for."

Clay dropped her arm and stepped back. He walked to the sink, braced his back against it and crossed his arms over his chest as he glared at her. "I have one more question, and I want you to look me in the eye when you answer it." Again he waited for Roberta to meet his thunderous gaze. "Would it bother you, now or at anytime, to admit to your friends and colleagues that the man you were with hasn't taken a class of any kind since he was eighteen and probably never will?"

She wanted to tell him what he needed to hear. But she couldn't do it while she looked him in the eye, couldn't find the words while she was struggling so hard to triumph over the threatening tears.

Before she could find an answer, Clay walked over to the door and opened it with a tense, jerky motion. "I'm going to see if I can find you a room for the night, Roberta. If I can, I'll carry your things over there this afternoon. If I can't, you can spend the night here, but I'll bunk with the men."

Wild, serpentine panic wrapped itself around Roberta's ribs, pressing inward, cutting off her air. He couldn't be ready to give up on her, not so quickly, not for such a slim reason! "Clay, please!" she begged without thinking. "I know you're upset—you've got a right to be upset!—but we can talk this through!"

He studied her morosely, then took a step back to her side. For a long time he studied her face, as though to memorize each subtle contour. He did not touch her; no warmth lit his beautiful gray eyes. He faced her with dignity, and his voice was low as he insisted, "We can talk for a lifetime and it won't make any difference, Bobbie Jean. Being in love should never make a soul feel ashamed."

"Clay, I'm not ashamed of you!" Her voice spiraled in desperation. "Just because I—"

"Roberta," he interrupted coldly before he marched out the door, "I think you've got it backwards. I don't give a damn what you think of me anymore. The point is, prima donna, that *I'm* ashamed of *you*."

CHAPTER THIRTEEN

IF OZZIE HAD KNOWN ahead of time that he was going to be having lunch with a girl, he would have gotten tongue-tied just thinking about it. But the situation had occurred so spontaneously, he'd hardly had time to panic. Also, within the first five minutes of conversation he'd determined that Clay and Roberta were having a fight. He'd actually spent most of the afternoon trying to keep that fact from Marla, and it wasn't until much later, after he'd helped her into her car and said goodbye, that he realized he hadn't thought about his stutter for at least two hours. He knew he'd stammered a few times, but not too terribly, and certainly not enough to significantly block his communication with a very attractive if somewhat older girl.

He'd picked up two letters from Tucson since then, both very lightweight, and each had exacerbated the terrible mood Clay had been in since they'd left Texas. He had refused to talk about what had transpired with Roberta, but the details didn't really matter. Ozzie knew his boss well enough to know that Roberta meant the world to him, and even though he starchly maintained that their affair was over, any fool could see that the woman was still rattling around in his head.

The whole situation left Ozzie in a bit of a quandary. If Clay and Roberta had really broken up, could she—would she—still want to help him get into Tucson State?

Would it be disloyal to allow her to do so if she and Clay were hardly speaking? Well, they were speaking—on their last day in Texas he'd seen Clay stiffly tell her goodbye and good luck, but he hadn't kissed her goodbye. Besides, he'd run into Clay prowling around the camel barn in the wee hours of the morning, and it was perfectly obvious to any man, even one of Ozzie's inexperience with the other sex, that he didn't have a warm and willing woman waiting for him in the trailer.

Today's mail contained a letter from Colorado State University in Fort Collins and two college catalogs. One was from T.S.U., which Ozzie himself had ordered. The other was from a correspondence school based in New York, which he had not.

"Any mail for me?" Clay said grumpily when he got close enough to ask without shouting.

"Not from Arizona," Ozzie answered gently. "But there's a college catalog in your name."

For a moment Clay was silent. He stared at Ozzie, then at the correspondence course catalog, before he said dismally, "It's for you. You might decide to stay here and take classes by mail or something."

It was an option Ozzie had considered, but he'd never gotten around to doing anything about it because it seemed like the coward's way out. And now, after realizing that college was full of girls like Marla, Ozzie wasn't at all interested in remaining a coward.

"It wouldn't really be g-g-going to school, would it?" he asked.

Clay snatched the catalog off the pile and tossed it roughly in the trash. "Forget it. Forget the whole damn thing."

"Clay—"

He felt awful as Clay stomped off, and it didn't help much to realize that it was Roberta who was making Clay feel so lousy and not Ozzie himself. Nor did that knowledge help him explain the fact that—upon closer inspection—he didn't find his own name on the letter from Colorado State University in Fort Collins. Before Ozzie realized that it wasn't a form letter, he'd read two small paragraphs—which thanked the writer for his interest in the university—and started on a third. It started off with the incredible words:

> "In response to your request for specific information about students in their forties returning to complete an education, let me assure you, Mr. Gann, that most mature students do very well in our classes and many are better able to take advantage of the many educational opportunities we offer than young people right out of high school with no experience in the workaday world. Many courses may be challenged for credit in the student's area of expertise...."

Ozzie read the whole letter three times before it occurred to him that he was invading Clay's privacy. He was too stunned by the realization that Clay had—incredibly—been considering going back to school.

IT WAS A HORRIBLE, dismal month, and Roberta thought she would crumble to nothingness before it was over. She had received only a brief reply to her two letters of apology to Clay—a camel postcard, which said only that he wished her well. Desperately she sought comfort from the fact that at least he hadn't cut off all contact with her. She forced herself to believe that when she saw him again in Devil's Gold, California, she could find a way to patch things up again.

It didn't help anything that summer school was over and she'd made no plans for August because she'd expected to spend two weeks with Clay in Colorado. While he hadn't explicitly told her to cancel her plans, it was perfectly obvious that at the moment she wasn't welcome at his ranch, even as a tourist.

Over and over again she tried to make sense of what had happened in Texas. She knew that she was largely to blame. She *had* avoided telling her friends and colleagues the whole truth about Clay. But only because she was embarrassed about his background: she had never been ashamed of *him*. It was a subtle distinction... clearly too subtle for a man of Clay's sensitivity to tolerate. His lack of education was his Achilles' heel, and loving a woman with a Ph.D. had only complicated the situation. Her own discomfort with his academic status had only made things worse. Still, Roberta tried to believe that if she just gave him some time to cool off, Clay's love for her would be great enough to transcend the hard words that had passed between them.

She wasn't too proud to beg.

What frightened her the most was the possibility that Clay had used their fight as a smoke screen for some other truly insolvable problem. Was it possible that he'd been growing tired of her and this was just the last straw—one he had gratefully clutched to avoid explaining that he just didn't want her anymore?

Roberta wasn't sure which possibility was more terrible. The only thing she was sure of was that she *had* to find a way to get him back. Three months ago she'd believed that she would go to her grave a single woman, and she'd been able to live with that. She'd been complete, successful, happy in her work.

But from the first moment Clay had touched her face, she'd belonged to him completely. And she would not be a whole person again until she was once more wrapped in his love.

She explained the whole thing to Snowy, who listened patiently as Roberta shared her anguish every day. The mare had come to expect Roberta's nightly visits and actually hurried over to the stall door at the sound of her voice each time she arrived at the barn. She didn't seem to question why her halter was the only tack Roberta ever used.

One dismal evening a few weeks after Roberta had last seen Clay, she arrived at the stable in a desperate, reckless mood. She thought she would go crazy if she waited much longer for Clay to forgive her. In the beginning, she'd been almost certain that he'd calm down in time. Now she was almost certain that he never would.

"I've got to do something to shake him up, Snowy," she told the sweet mare with sudden determination. "If I could bring myself to ride with him at Devil's Gold, he'd have to realize how much he means with me."

Snowy showed no particular interest when Roberta traded the halter for a bridle and slipped a saddle on her back, nor did she protest when Roberta led her away from the stables on their regular route, then stopped and stood motionlessly by her head as soon as they were out of sight of the barn.

"We're friends, Snowy," she reminded the tired mare. "I know you'd never throw me. I know I can trust you as much as I trusted Flame."

But Flame went down through no fault of his own, memory flailed her. *He nearly crushed me before he died.*

Desperately Roberta pushed away the vision; desperately she battled the panic. She would do it! Clay had always told her he admired her fire, her spirit. She would prove to him that she could conquer fear.

But it took ten white-knuckled minutes before she found the courage, and it left her in a fraction of that time. In the end she only managed to swing up on Snowy's back, tuck her right foot in the stirrup and tug it right back out before the old mare even knew she'd been mounted.

A moment later she was following Roberta back to the barn.

"SHE CAME BY to see you," Ozzie declared when Clay returned to the camel barn from the fairgrounds near Devil's Gold on the last Saturday in August. "She showed up the minute we pulled in."

"Who?" said Clay, although there wasn't the slightest bit of doubt in his mind.

Ozzie flushed. "R-R-Roberta. She looked...funny."

"What do you mean, she looked funny? She always dresses in something weird, depending on her character." It occurred to him, with a jolt, that he'd never once seen Roberta in regular clothes. He didn't have the slightest idea how she looked in everyday life. Once he would have been intrigued by the notion. Now it made him unutterably sad.

"I mean, she looked s-s-sick."

Clay rolled his eyes. "She didn't come here hoping I'd give another damn chautauqua, did she?"

Ozzie shook his head. "Not s-s-sick like that. Not sick like before. S-s-sick like—" he seemed to struggle for the words "—like she just felt awful. Her face was w-w-white and she didn't smile even when she said hello." Ozzie's eyes were sad. "R-R-Roberta always used to smile at me, Clay."

You're not the only one, he longed to confess. But at the moment he wasn't too concerned about Ozzie. It was the notion of Roberta with a pasty-white face that haunted him. *If she feels like hell, she deserves it,* part of him maintained. But another part, the part that loved the woman and always would, countered softly, *You're the one who slung the most mud, Clay Gann. You're the one who has to make it right.*

"What did she say?" he asked. "I want to know exactly."

Ozzie shrugged. "She asked when you'd be back. I said I didn't know. She said she'd try to f-f-find you again or you could go to her hotel."

"She invited me to her hotel? She's got a lot of gall."

"T-t-to t-t-talk," Ozzie clarified, his increasing stutter revealing the depth of his tension to Clay's practiced ear. "I p-p-promised her you'd g-g-go over there or c-c-call when you c-c-could."

"You had no right to do that," Clay snapped, unbearably irritated by the boy's stammering. He had thought it was lessening; its intensity now revealed how disturbed Ozzie'd been by Clay's breakup with Roberta. Or maybe with how obnoxious Clay had been since then. "For all you know, I may not want to see her."

"You c-c-can be r-r-rude if you want to, Clay," the boy replied with surprising moxy, "b-b-but I was raised to b-b-be nice to my friends."

"Oh, hell! The last thing I need is a lecture on manners from *you*!"

Ozzie cowered. He visibly lowered his head.

Clay felt as though he'd just kicked a puppy, and if he had, he would have stooped down to pick up the little thing and scratch its ears. Because it was Ozzie he'd hollered at, all he could do was apologize.

"Forgive me, Oz. That was out of line. I'm just... I'm just not feeling any too great myself."

Ozzie didn't meet his eyes. But still, he maintained stoutly, "You m-m-might as well g-g-get it over with, Clay. You're not g-g-going to feel any better until you two m-m-make up."

He wanted to refute that piece of savvy advice, but he knew it was hopeless. The boy was dead-on, and there was no way he could avoid it. The best he could do was point out churlishly, "I don't have time to go over there until tonight. I'm riding this afternoon."

"And you'll do a l-l-lousy job of it if you d-d-don't fix things with R-R-Roberta first."

"Dammit, Oz!" His voice held no anger now. "It's not like we had a fight that we can forget with a quick apology. We came to a parting of the ways! It was inevitable. It just happened a little sooner and a little more roughly than I'd expected."

Ozzie shook his head. "You c-c-could still b-b-be friends," he pointed out. "You c-c-could just g-g-go say hello."

This time Clay didn't argue. He turned abruptly and mounted the nearest camel— Luscious Laura, whose gait was so awkward that even at a walk he wobbled from side to side—and promptly trotted up the street to the old hotel.

It looked a lot like the hotel in Patchwork where he'd picked up Roberta the first night he'd played Lieutenant Beale with her. And the damned thing was, he didn't feel much different now. Even then, he'd realized that she was something very, very special. Even then, he'd realized that it would never, ever work.

Nothing had really changed.

He pounded on the door with unhidden anger, waited impatiently while she opened the chain-latched door a crack. "It's Clay, Roberta," he barked. "Ozzie said you wanted to see me. I'm here and I don't have all day so let me in."

The door opened quickly, but Clay couldn't see much inside the room. The afternoon sun was hidden by the heavy overhang in front of the side windows, and no light at all drifted in from the hall. He could see the silhouette of a woman, nothing more. And suddenly it became imperative to see Roberta's face.

The face that had haunted his dreams all summer.

When she said, "Come in," he quickly did so.

As she shut the door, Clay turned to face her, surprised by what he saw.

Her hair was not bonnet-bound like Susan B. Anthony's; nor was it sprawled helter-skelter the way he was used to seeing it when his Bobbie Jean shared his bed. It was trim, curly, freshly combed. Roberta wore a clean blue T-shirt with no logo or picture of any kind and well-worn jeans that bagged a little on her hips. She sported no shoes, no makeup, and no smile. Ozzie's assessment had been absolutely correct. She looked as though there had just been a death in her family. She looked broken. Vulnerable. Defeated. Three words he would have sworn that nobody could ever have used to describe Roberta Wheeler, Ph.D.

He felt ashamed. He'd done this to her. He'd brushed away her worries and lied away her fears, promising solutions to problems that he'd known from the start would overrule their love in the end. Desperately he wished there was some way to take away her pain.

Desperately he wished he could ease his own as well.

A bit more gently he told her, "I'm riding at three."

Roberta glanced at her watch. He couldn't see the digits, but knew what they revealed: it was two-fifteen or thereabouts. Quickly she said, "I won't take much of your time. I just have three things to say."

He met her eyes with all the strength he possessed. He would be polite; he would treat her like a friend. But nothing she had to say could move him from the truth. *It was never meant to be.*

"Number one?" he asked.

He saw her shiver as she answered, "I'm sorry. My behavior with Marla was inexcusable, and you had every right to be mad at me."

Her reply knocked him back on his heels. It was far more than he'd expected; maybe a little more than he deserved. He resisted the urge to make his own apologies, at least until he heard her out.

"Number two?" he prodded.

She shrugged her shoulders helplessly. "I love you. Desperately." Her eyes filled with tears.

He battled the great claw that had seized his entrails, tried to remember why he knew it could never work out. She had never come right out and told him she loved him before, but he'd always seen it in her eyes . . . those beautiful eyes that were now filled to the brim with tears.

His voice had dropped to a whisper when he murmured, "Number three?"

She took a step closer and touched his hand. Her hands were Arctic-cold. Incredibly two brave tears spilled over as she whispered, "Please, Clay. I'm begging you. Please give us another chance."

It was the first time he'd ever seen Roberta cry.

It was the first time he'd ever seen her beg.

His arms closed around her in an instant, his grip so tight he was afraid she'd yelp in pain. As she sagged against him, sobbing now, Clay felt stupid and helpless and desperately relieved. He knew, with sudden neon-bright hindsight, that although he would not have begged her for forgiveness, he had been desperately hoping that she would make it possible for him to take her in his arms and make things right. He'd never even dreamed that she'd make it impossible for him to do anything else.

As she smothered her sobs against his neck, Clay tenderly kissed her forehead. Even when he hugged her fiercely, he could not ease the pain in his chest.

He buckled. He cracked. "Bobbie Jean," he murmured, throwing every resolution to the wind as his trembling fingers cradled her beloved face, "you're still my very best friend."

She pulled back then, tear-swollen eyes meeting his. There was fresh panic there, and he realized that she'd misinterpreted his high praise. She wasn't sure if he was taking her back or making sure they parted as friends.

Suddenly he knew that words would be useless, and he couldn't seem to get any out anyway. He longed to kiss her, but he was afraid to get started, afraid she'd think it was only his physical longing that kept him from pushing her away. Abruptly he reached up, snatched his beloved lucky hat off of his head and gently set it on her own. Her eyes opened wide as she recognized the meaning of the impromptu gift.

It was all he had left of his father.

"I'm sorry you wasted your money paying for this room," he whispered, one warm hand cupping her still-damp cheek. "You're not going to sleep here tonight, Bobbie Jean."

"No?" Her voice was tremulous.

He shook his head. "There's only one place for the woman who owns Clay Gann's hat." He waited a moment, then added truthfully, "Not to mention his heart."

Roberta closed her eyes and struggled to stop another torrent of tears while Clay took her back in his arms. She clenched him fiercely as he kissed her ear, her cheek, the pulse below her jaw; her grip grew tighter as he found her lips and claimed them with the fire of his soul.

They were both quivering by the time he let her go.

ROBERTA SPENT the next two weekends in Clay's trailer, but it was never quite the same. She knew he was capable of leaving her, knew how close she'd come to losing him for good. And she also knew that the wedge that had driven them apart before had only been set aside, not removed from their relationship. It hovered just beyond the fringes of their loving, ever ready to split the bonds between them.

At home, she weighed every word she said about Clay. It was imperative, she knew, to share Clay's precise background with all of her friends in the event that he ever met any of them; she was not one to repeat her mistakes. But at the same time she was leery of talking about Clay too much because she had less confidence than ever that their relationship would survive. The last thing she wanted was pity from her staff when their revived affair fell apart at some point down the road.

At least, that was what she told herself. But she had to admit that she squirmed inside when Charles chuckled over the news that she was in love with a trick rider and camelback roper. The fact that she'd led him to believe Clay was a professor only made things worse.

"Decided to air your secrets, did you, Roberta?" he teased her.

While Roberta sputtered a defense of Clay, she caught the dark look in Charles's eyes and realized that he was only half kidding. She wondered how much she had hurt him—or hurt his pride—and how much his feelings might still be affecting their working relationship.

Except for telling Clay that she'd rectified her earlier error, after they'd patched things up she tried not to talk to him much about her work or his, which eliminated discussion of a lot of meaningful aspects of their lives. Their conversations were still lively, peppered with debates on historical events and issues of the day, but there was a cloak on their zest that shrouded the majesty of their togetherness. Clay never asked Roberta about her writing or research, and she never told him about her unsuccessful efforts to ride Snowy. Neither one of them mentioned Roberta's aborted trip to Fort Collins, and she didn't dare suggest that Clay come down to Tucson now for fear he'd refuse.

It was with growing apprehension that she met him in Virginia City, Nevada, on the second weekend in September. Though Clay would continue to race his camels in a few more spots during the fall, this would be Roberta's last scheduled chautauqua of the season, and once the weekend ended, she would have no casual way to see Clay again.

She pulled into town on Saturday morning during the noisy parade in time to see Clay, Ozzie and three of his cowboys riding the camels in a dramatic display. Baby Bev was skitterish, and rough-gaited Luscious Laura was also clearly nervous. Roberta had ridden Flame in countless parades as a teenager and knew only too well how a good horse—let alone a camel—could panic in a crowd. Clay had encouraged her to join his group in this parade—on horseback or on foot, leading Baby Bev—but she'd declined the offer. She'd proudly marched in far too many parades on Flame's back to reveal her cowardice by walking with a baby camel, and she knew she lacked the courage to mount a horse in a small corral, let alone in this kind of public chaos.

After the parade, a series of precision riding troops made their debut in the arena specially built for the camel races, followed by a number of absurdly funny comedy acts. Roberta could hardly believe the popularity of the performers known as the Whistling Midgets—dancing men with their arms and heads buried in enormous corny hats, and faces painted on their bare chests, giving the illusion of whistling lips around each hairy belly button. To her amazement, the group returned to four curtain calls, and Clay's clowny roping routine on Violet seemed almost prosaic in comparison.

When the events were over for the day, Roberta met Clay by the camel barn. He looked as warm as ever; he even gave her a sound kiss in front of his staff and half a dozen strangers. And that night, when he joined her in the trailer, he was especially enthusiastic underneath the covers.

She dreaded bringing up the subject of their future, but she couldn't just ride off into the sunset tomorrow night without some plan to help her battle the empty weeks ahead. A month ago, this would have been the logical time to discuss more than their next weekend; with two glorious weeks at his place in Fort Collins fresh in both of their memories, they might have been planning a wedding instead. Instead they were still smarting from their month apart, and were not yet fully at ease with each other, even in bed.

"Clay?" Roberta murmured after a particularly playful hour of lovemaking, while the night was still all around them. "Are you still awake?"

"No," he muttered, rolling over to snuggle her more closely against him. They fit together like spoons in the small bed, his knees brushing the back of her thighs as his long arm snaked around her waist. "Why?"

"Oh . . . we can discuss it later."

He was silent a moment, but his arm seemed to go a little slack. "Let's discuss it now. I'm not likely to get much sleep wondering what's got you hot and bothered."

"I'm not hot and bothered, Clay." She took his hand and rubbed it once over her breast. "At least not anymore."

He chuckled and opened his hand, wrapping his warm fingers around her nipple.

"But you want to discuss something serious. I heard serious in your voice." He tugged lightly on the sensitive flesh and pressed his body more intimately against her backside.

"It's nothing that can't wait until morning."

His free hand, the one that had been curled beneath his head, swooped from under her shoulder to titillate her other breast. "I'm not sure I can wait until morning," he teased, looping one long leg over her knees.

She could feel his masculinity press against her thighs. The artistry of his fingers on her breasts was making her womanly needs come alive. She knew that they had to discuss the future, but at the moment she couldn't bring herself to dull the brilliant colors of their togetherness. Not while Clay was so warm, so willing, so near.

"You sure know how to get the last word in a conversation," she countered, her voice growing husky now.

"You want me to stop talking?" he asked, his fingers ceasing to move on her breasts.

A sudden wave of urgency gripped her, and Roberta knew that it was more than sheer desire. It was a sense of panic, a moment of wondering if this might be the last time they'd ever "talk" like this. The possibility that this might be the last time they ever shared a bed together filled her with despair.

"Don't stop, Clay," she begged in a haunted whisper. "Don't stop loving me."

If he realized that her words could have been taken two different ways, he gave no sign. He simply rolled her onto her back and gathered her up close against him. He kissed her deeply, then dropped his lips to her collarbone, inching his way down below. His massive hand insinuated itself between her willing thighs as he whispered, "I'm in no mood to stop, Bobbie Jean. Hell, sweet pea, I ain't barely got started yet."

She took comfort from the laughter in his voice until she caught sight of his expression, barely readable in the light of the street lamps cast on the trailer's inner shades. Although his hands gave her warmth and his teasing voice spoke of promise, his gray eyes held far less joy than sorrow.

OZZIE DID NOT notice the change in Clay right away. In fact, for most of September his boss seemed fairly normal. The only time he got snappy was when Ozzie would mention school or comment on the college catalogs that still kept arriving in Clay's name—for correspondence classes, school-of-experience colleges, and three different universities in Arizona. Clay picked each one up somewhat hesitantly, as if daring Ozzie to make a comment. Then, a day or two later, he'd casually hand the latest book or brochure to Ozzie and say, "This came the other day. Thought you might be interested."

Ozzie *was* interested. He was also confused. And above all, he was frustrated. Ira had made his decision; Ira had gone to school in September. And Ozzie had made a decision, too—to go to college just as soon as he could find the courage for more than twenty-four hours at a time. He told himself that he was waiting to see how things went for Ira before he committed himself to T.S.U., and he told himself that he would wait to see how things went with Clay and Roberta before he put his future in her hands. But he knew, in the deepest reaches of his heart, that his excuses all added up to shame.

Although he hadn't done too badly talking to Marla one-on-one, he was still scared to death that he'd humiliate himself by stuttering incoherently in front of a classroomful of strangers. He had nightmares about it at least once a week. If it had been a life or death choice, maybe he could have done it. But for the nebulous possibility of a veterinary career? He could stay right here and work with animals. And who was to say that he was smart enough to survive all those science classes anyway? Or that he'd have the money to set up his own practice? Sure, his parents would help all they could and so could Clay, but none of them had much excess money. And none of them could help his stutter go away.

The first few weeks in September, the letters from Roberta came to Clay pretty faithfully. And once she sent him a big manila envelope, which turned out to be a copy of her university's historical review, featuring a paper she'd written on the influence of the chautauqua on rural turn-of-the-century America. On Ozzie's birthday in October, when Clay invited the whole staff up to the house, Warner happened to spy it on the coffee table while Clay was in the kitchen cutting the cake.

"What the hell is this?" the old cowboy chortled, picking up the slick review. " 'The Intellectual Impact of the Chautauqua Movement on Rural Turn of the Century America,' by Roberta Jean Wheeler, Ph.D.' " He glanced up at old bald Roscoe and laughed out loud. "The boss never told us that his girlfriend had fancy letters after her name."

"Or that she wrote books for a living," said skinny George.

The half dozen other men chuckled; one or two commented proudly that they barely knew how to read.

"She doesn't write books," Ozzie defended her bravely. "She teaches history. Professors have to publish papers sometimes."

"An' I reckon we gotta read 'em to git smart." George gestured toward the magazine. "Warner, you go ahead and read us some of them fancy words Clay's girl has to say. Hell, I've allus wanted t' know what she did with her time when she wasn't ridin'."

That brought a hearty communal laugh from everybody but Ozzie; he didn't know what to say.

"'The mentality of the average rural American at the turn of the century reflected that of European peasant stock for centuries: about the land, his knowledge was *awwwwesome*," drawled Warner, sarcasm poisoning Roberta's thoughtful words. "About any subject that required enlightened, educated thought, he was woefully *naiiiive*.'"

"Come on, Warner, don't read it like that," protested Ozzie. "Roberta really knows her stuff, and—"

"You mean she's not 'naive'?"

"What the hell does that mean, anyhow?" asked one of the men.

"It means she's not stupid, like us." Warner stood and pranced around on tiptoe with his nose in the air. "It means she knows how to talk good and hold a teacup with her pinkie pointed straight out." He demonstrated. "It means she'd never dirty herself by climbin' on a horse, let alone muckin' out a stall."

Abruptly Ozzie rose, really angry now. He still remembered the look on Roberta's face when she'd watched Clay fall, and he knew how much time she spent with the camels. He was certain it was terror, not uppityness, which kept her earthbound. "That's enough, Warner," he heard himself proclaim. "If Clay were here—"

"Clay *is* here," Clay suddenly announced from the doorway. Three words that sounded like thunder. Three words that sounded like the end.

Clay's face was darker than Ozzie had ever seen it. His eyes were fierce as they pinned Warner to the wall. Slowly, with quiet fury in each footstep, he marched across the room and held out one hand.

For a long, mutinous moment, Warner stared at him, then finally lowered his eyes as he relinquished the journal. Clay snatched it almost possessively, pressing it closely to his side. Then, in a low, quiet growl, he said, "Get out."

Warner's eyes flashed open wide. "Ah, Clay, come on! We was just havin' fun. Ya don't have t' ruin Ozzie's party."

"I'm not talking about the party," Clay informed him coldly. "I'm talking about your job."

There was a shocked communal gasp as the men took in his words. For Ozzie, he'd fired a cowboy who'd only been around for a few months; for Roberta, he'd just fired one of the best riders in the business after six years as his performing partner. And Warner, in his own offbeat way, was a friend.

For an endless moment Warner stared at Clay, slack-jawed as though he was waiting for a reprieve.

But none was forthcoming. The eerie silence was not broken until Clay growled, "Go pack your gear while I figure out what I owe you. I'll have your check ready in half an hour."

Now the room was utterly still. For a long, stunned moment, nobody moved. Not even Warner, who had considered his fabulous skill on horseback invaluable to Clay Gann and had taken his tenure at the stable for granted.

Some of the men may have wondered if Clay would back down, but Ozzie never did. He knew that nothing on the face of the earth mattered more to Clay than Roberta, and the fact that she wasn't here to listen to Warner's insults made the sting of them no less venal.

Warner stared at his hands. He did not look at Clay; for once he had no wisecrack to make to the other men.

For a moment he glanced at George, as though waiting to see if his sidekick would also walk out, but George lowered his head and stayed in his chair.

Warner shook his head in disgust, then slowly walked toward the front door, his spurs jangling his retreat as he slammed it on the way out.

Nobody else so much as breathed.

A full minute passed before Clay turned to Ozzie and apologized softly, "Sorry to throw cold water on your party, Oz, but it had to be."

Ozzie didn't argue, but secretly he wondered how much good Clay had done. Out of loyalty to those he loved, he could muzzle his men, but he couldn't change what they were thinking. Secretly Ozzie was sure that they still thought he was an idiot because he stammered. And secretly, every man in this room would still think that Roberta had more brains than common sense, because none of them had ever seen her on horseback.

Firing Warner wouldn't open up a place on Clay's ranch for a woman who was earthbound.

BY THE BEGINNING of November, Roberta was beginning to wonder if her affair with Clay was nothing more than a summer romance that had withered in autumn's darker hue. She had received exactly two phone calls, one letter and a postcard since she'd seen him last, and the postcard, her last communication, had arrived almost three weeks ago. She had answered it with a friendly, noncommittal note and was still waiting for a reply.

Actually she was waiting desperately for a reply, but none seemed to be forthcoming. In retrospect, she was sorry she'd sent him the *Historical Review* with her latest publication. Had she sounded as though she were bragging? Had she reminded him of the difference in their occupations? Academic training? Would he think she was thumbing her nose at him again?

She longed to call him, to ask outright what was wrong. And before their snafu in August, it would have been the easiest thing in the world. But since then things had been so tense and uneasy between them that she didn't feel she could make any move without some encouragement from Clay—unless she had some amazing news to tell him.

I've conquered my fear of riding and I'll take Warner's place in the next parade, she envisioned herself declaring. *Give me a few weeks' training and I'll be doing double possum belly passes in a show with you.*

It was an impossible dream. She still went walking with Snowy, because the old mare had come to depend on her, but Roberta never bothered with the saddle anymore. She had given up trying to conquer her fear of riding.

But she couldn't give up on Clay. How long could she just twiddle her thumbs, dreading the moment when he asked her to give back his lucky hat? It went against her grain. Sooner or later, she'd have to take action. She couldn't just wait indefinitely. *If I haven't heard from him by the end of the month,* she vowed, *I'll have to take the bit between my teeth and call him anyway... and let the chips fall where they may.*

AS THE LEAVES STARTED FALLING and Clay awoke each morning wondering if he'd find snow on the ground, he grew increasingly restless, increasingly certain that something inside him was about to snap. It had been over two weeks since he'd last heard from Roberta, and that letter had been brief, general and all but meaningless. She'd signed it "Love, Roberta" but otherwise it could have been written to any friend.

He couldn't really blame her for that; his own correspondence had nearly dwindled to a halt. But it was hard to write when he felt the need to proofread every sentence, fearful that he might commit some linguistic faux pas that would leave her rolling her eyes or laughing with her friends.

He had not forgotten the night Warner had made fun of the *Review*. Just thinking about it still made him sizzle. But the incident had crystallized what he'd known from day one—there was no way that his current social world and hers could ever fit together. Even if he sold his ranch and moved the whole operation to Arizona—a possibility that had crossed his mind—he'd still have fellows like George and Roscoe chuckling over his choice of a female who couldn't sit on a horse, and Roberta would still be ashamed to tell her colleagues—or even her students!—that he'd never darkened a college classroom door.

Intellectually, he knew it was hopeless. Intellectually, he knew they were through. Logic dictated that he had two choices—tell her outright that it was over, or let their relationship dwindle to nothingness until it died of sheer neglect.

A letter would have done the trick. A phone call might have been better. But Roberta meant too much to him to shut her out of his life with such cowardice. Besides, he couldn't give her up without a struggle; he couldn't say goodbye if there was any other way.

And he sure as hell couldn't believe it was over until he held her in his arms once more.

IT WAS ALMOST TEN-FORTY-FIVE on Friday morning—a good hour after Roberta's final class of the week—when the History Department secretary put through a call.

"This is Dr. Wheeler," she answered briskly, eager to head home for the day. "How may I help you?"

There was a slight pause before she heard Clay's voice—low, husky, uncertain.

"Do I have to call you Dr. Wheeler when I call you at work?" he asked. It was a joke—at least she assumed it was—but there was nothing comical about his tense tone.

"You can call me anything you want," she admitted, nearly flattened by the great whoosh of relief in her heart. No matter how awkwardly the conversation started, he *had* finally called her, and that was a start. "This isn't a censored phone."

He chuckled then, just barely. The humor was clearly forced.

Roberta couldn't laugh at all. After another awkward moment, she asked, "How are you, Clay?"

"Fine." His tone was colorless. "How 'bout yourself?"

"I'm fine, too."

More silence.

"But I've missed you, Clay."

A heartbeat's quiet.

"I've missed you, too."

She tried to think of witty conversation. She tried to think of anything safe to say. Never, in all the time she'd known Clay, had such awkwardness come between them. She knew, as surely as she knew anything in life, that his dwindling correspondence and ultimate silence was not accidental. A great, gaping pit seemed to open in her stomach. She pressed her hand against the pain.

"Just tell me," she blurted. "Don't try to be kind. Just tell me straight out, Clay. Why did you call?"

"I called to see if you might be free this weekend," was his surprising rejoinder. "I know it's short notice and you probably have other plans, but I thought we needed to talk."

She closed her eyes. Hot tears pierced her eyelids. "It's a long trip for either of us," she pointed out with all the objectivity she could muster. "Wouldn't it be easier to just say goodbye and good luck on the phone?"

This time the silence was eerie. It was endless. It was punctuated only by one smothered gasp as Roberta strove valiantly not to cry.

"Is that what you...want to do, Roberta?" he finally answered, his voice low and uneven. "Tell me goodbye and good luck?"

"No!" she burst out, starting to lose control. "That's the last thing I want to do! I'm dying to see you, Clay. I've missed you like hell. But I'm not stupid. You've been drifting away ever since Virginia City...probably even before then, but I forced you into taking me back. I wanted this to work out between us, wanted it so much that maybe I lied to myself about what was really going on." She gulped and tried to catch her breath. "Now if there's a chance that you...that you really still want to be with me, I'll set everything aside and fly up there this weekend, even though I've got an important faculty shindig at Charles's place on Saturday night that I really shouldn't miss. But if you're trying to lead up to some way to let me down easily—" she smothered an incipient sob "—don't...don't play games with me, please.

If it's over, Clay, just tell me. I can't start getting over you until I know there's not a single shred of hope."

There was another silence, but this one didn't last too long. This time it was Clay who sighed... a heavy sigh wrung with relief.

"Bobbie Jean, I'm downstairs," he drawled softly. Fresh warmth colored his tone. "You want to hurry down or you want me to hurry up?"

Roberta blinked and tugged on the phone cord. Shock and joy pirouetted in tandem through her heart. "You're downstairs *where*?" she demanded.

"In the history building. *Your* history building. Right outside—" his voice seemed to move away from the phone "—Room 124. There's a handful of vending machines in a little nook here by the front door. Do you know the place I mean?"

Roberta didn't answer. She didn't even lock her office door. Oblivious to the stares of the students and colleagues who saw her gallop past them, she bypassed the ponderous elevator and bolted down all six flights of stairs.

She was sobbing in Clay's arms a moment later.

CHAPTER FOURTEEN

CLAY COULDN'T BELIEVE how good it felt to hold Roberta close. In the weeks they'd been apart he'd begun to wonder if he'd only imagined the love she felt for him.

It wasn't like Roberta to cry. In fact, in all the time he'd known her, he'd only seen her cry once—the day she'd begged him to take her back. But she was sobbing now, sobbing with joy and relief, and he was feeling a bit choked up himself.

Her soft dark curls brushed against his face as he kissed her cheek, then met her lips with hungry reassurance.

"Oh, Clay," she whispered when he finally let her go. "I was so afraid. I really thought you were trying to break it off. I didn't think I'd ever see you again."

He shook his head. With desperate tenderness he pulled her closer. "Not a chance, Bobbie Jean," he whispered huskily. "I never wanted it to end. Not for a minute. I just didn't know what to do to keep it going."

Roberta's grip on his shoulders tightened. "You didn't need to do anything. My love for you is a runaway train."

Deeply moved, Clay longed to tell her that his love for her was just as potent, but he couldn't seem to find the words. Trembling, he kissed her temple, then the top of her head, before he rested his chin there. "I didn't doubt your love for me," he told her softly. "I just wasn't sure that I could...well, fit into your world here. And I know you don't want to fit into mine."

Roberta pulled back then, met his eyes with care. "That's what's wrong? That's why I haven't heard from you?"

Slowly he nodded. "That's what's always been wrong. Right from the start." And then, in a rush, he told her what he'd been unable to put down in writing—how he'd fired Warner because of what he'd said about her. And how afraid he was that even if he could force the cowboys in his world to accept her, the intellectuals in Roberta's world would always look down on *him*.

While he talked, Roberta pressed a little closer, and when he finished, she lifted both slim hands to cup his face. "I think it's time to fix this problem, Clay. Once and for all. I love you, and I refuse to let anything get in our way."

She looked so intense, so deadly serious, that he wasn't sure how to answer at once. The only sensible thing to do was to kiss her again, so he did it.

It was a brief kiss, however, and this time it was Roberta who pulled away.

"I think we'd be better off talking about this somewhere...private," she suggested, an impish look now gleaming in her eye. "I wouldn't want either of us to be interrupted in the middle of a good...idea."

He grinned back. He felt a hazy, delirious warmth spread through his heart that had nothing to do with the legendary Tucson sun. "We're on your turf, Bobbie Jean. I'll follow wherever you lead."

In the end she lead him upstairs to her office, a small but tastefully furnished jumble of books and papers on the sixth floor. She didn't introduce him to anybody, but then again the only people they passed were a couple of students near an office with a plaque that said, Charles Trumbull, Ph.D., Chairman, Department of History. But the door was closed and no sound hinted that someone might be inside.

Clay was relieved. Someday he knew he'd have to meet the legendary Charles Trumbull, but he wanted to be fully prepared before that occasion. And he wanted to be on his own turf.

Roberta gathered up a pile of students' papers, jammed them into a briefcase and hurried Clay out the door. "I don't know how much time I'm going to get to correct anything this weekend, but I won't feel so guilty if I at least take them with me. I promised the class I'd return them by Monday."

Clay glanced at the briefcase, then at Roberta's flushed face. "You really like teaching, don't you?" he asked softly.

Busy with the lock, she didn't notice the tension on his face. "Oh, I love it. It's all I've ever wanted to do." She paused a moment as she dropped her keys into her purse. "Professionally, that is." She grinned at him, but the grin faded as she studied his own thoughtful visage.

"You really love teaching *here*," he amended. "Under Charles Trumbull."

Roberta met his eyes straightforwardly. She laid one strong hand on his face. "I love teaching here and I'm happy having Charles as my immediate supervisor. But that doesn't mean I couldn't be happy working somewhere else. I'm sure there are several fine institutions in Colorado that would be glad to hire a historian with my credentials."

He knew she was trying to tell him that she'd be willing to uproot herself to live with him, and he was grateful for her willingness to do so. But the terms of her sacrifice had only underlined the great vacuum between his lowly career and her lofty one. And therein lay the problem. She could teach in Colorado or he could run a camel trail herd right here in Tucson. He was open to either option and so was she. Either way they'd be together. But their worlds would still be light years apart.

ROBERTA LEFT HER CAR in the faculty lot so she could ride with Clay to her apartment. The joyful shock of his arrival had left her dizzy and winded, not to mention aroused. Despite her tour-guide chattiness as she pointed out each famous landmark and endearing relic of old Tucson—one of the first cities settled in the west—her jubilance almost left her incoherent.

By the time they reached her apartment, Roberta knew she was babbling, but she just couldn't seem to stop. As she led Clay up the stairs she realized she was starting to point out truly irrelevant features around them—her neighbor's potted cactus, the hammock on a distant balcony, a particularly appealing stray cat.

Clay said nothing, just favored her with a happy grin. But as soon as they were behind closed doors, his demeanor quickly changed.

"This is my place," she blurted out, tossing her briefcase on the nearest armchair. "I moved here in—"

She never finished the sentence, because suddenly Clay's lips had claimed her mouth. Under some other circumstances, she told herself, she'd fight such caveman tactics, but at the moment surrendering to Clay's arms seemed like the most natural thing in the world. She felt a jolt of desire clear down to her toes, and she didn't waste much time fighting it. Although her life had turned upside down in less than an hour, the facts were simple. Clay was here, the agony had ended, and the weekend had begun. This was one night poor Snowy would wait in vain for Roberta's visit. If everything went well, maybe she could tell Clay about the mare tomorrow and take him to see her.

She curled against him, releasing the tension of weeks of waiting—waiting to hear from him, waiting to feel his body close to hers, waiting to believe that his love for her was still intact—as she eagerly returned his urgent kiss. His bushy mustache erotically tickled her upper lip as she opened her mouth to admit his questing tongue.

It was a long, deep, utterly bonding kiss, and when it was over, Clay held her close as he whispered, "Are you done with all that noise now?"

Slowly she nodded.

"Do you want to talk about important things, or would you rather not talk at all?"

She met his eyes, shining with need, as she snuggled her body yet closer. "I'd like to finish giving you a tour of my apartment, Lieutenant. I don't believe you've seen the bedroom yet."

The last tension faded from Clay's beautiful gray eyes, and his lips curved into a smile that made her tremble. "I'd like to see where you sleep, Bobbie Jean. I'd like that very much."

Roberta meant to take his hand and lead him down the hall, but half an hour passed before either one of them mentioned the bedroom again.

By that time, they were undressed and fully intertwined on the living-room rug.

"SO HOW'S IT GOING, Ira?" Clay asked, his eyes on the sunny-haired boy who was busy devouring something the local college students called a Grossburger—an aptly named humungous slab of meat with all the trimmings spilling out over a gargantuan bun. "Are you glad Roberta talked you into coming down here after all?"

Ira grinned. "Yeah. I don't like having to study all the time, but I've got two classes I really like."

"Coed, no doubt," Clay teased.

Ira's grin grew almost bashful. "Well, I'm too busy taking notes in my history class to notice if there are many good-looking girls in there. But in algebra there's this—" he stopped, glanced shyly at Roberta, then turned back to Clay "—this attractive young lady who helps me with my homework."

Roberta laughed. "And here I thought it was the hallowed halls of learning that inspired you, Ira. Mandy was wasting her breath trying to get you to go to school. She could have just sent you a photo portfolio of the female student body."

Clay grinned, then reached out with one arm to pull her a little closer. It had been a perfectly glorious Arizona day. They had spent a lazy, delicious morning in each other's arms before she'd cooked him breakfast—straightforward scrambled eggs with lots of ham—while he'd teased her about giving up her career to become a hausfrau. Then she'd called Ira to set up lunch since Clay had promised Brady he'd visit the boy and bring him up-to-date on the parade plans when he came to Arizona. Roberta reported on Ira when she could, but she was trying not to hover; Clay's arrival gave the folks back home a good excuse to get a bit more reassurance that everything was fine.

"So how's old Ozzie doing?" Ira asked after they'd gone over Brady's latest plans for the parade. "Is he about ready to go back to school?"

Clay wasn't sure how to answer that. Ozzie had been thinking about it since the day he'd come to work for Clay, but he didn't really think he'd ever find the courage to face his peers again. "Not quite, but he's working on it."

Ira shook his head. "I tried to get him to start down here with me. I thought it might be easier for him if he, well, you know, if he had a friend."

Clay knew exactly what he meant, and he appreciated the kindly thought. But he told Ira honestly, "Ozzie's got to find the courage in himself. And he's got to understand that he's still got things backward."

Ira's eyebrows raised. "I'm not sure I follow you, Clay."

He trailed his fingers down the side of Roberta's neck—partly so she'd know he hadn't forgotten her, partly so he could feel her soft flesh—before he answered, "Ozzie thinks he has to stop stuttering before he can face the world. He still doesn't understand that he'll never stop stuttering until he can face the world as a stutterer and say 'I don't give a damn.' He's got to be ready and able to do whatever he wants to do in spite of his stutter. He'll never be able to lick it until then."

Ira hunched his shoulders. "It's really too bad. I mean, he's such a smart guy. I bet he'd do ten times better in school than I would."

"You're doing just fine, Ira," Roberta pointed out. "You've got a B average in your classes so far, and for your first semester away from home, that's quite impressive."

Clay was surprised. He'd assumed that Roberta's idea of doing well in school was straight A's. His mother had always considered anything less naked failure.

"I got mostly A's at home," Ira pointed out, looking a little embarrassed. Then he glanced at Clay and asked bluntly, "Did your grades drop a little when you first went away to school?"

It was the first time in years that Clay could recall feeling tongue-tied. He was downright embarrassed. He didn't think he would have been if Roberta hadn't been snuggled up beside him, but the simple truth was that he didn't know what to say.

"I...uh...I didn't go to college when I left home, Ira. I just...left. Took off on my own."

Ira nodded as though he understood, but his next question clearly proved that he'd missed Clay's point. "But later, I mean, when you went back, was it harder than high school?"

Clay removed his arm from Roberta's neck. "I didn't go to college, Ira," he said tensely. "I escaped high school with a diploma and never looked back."

Ira blinked. "Never?" He glanced at Roberta. "You told me that making it in life without a college education was like swimming upstream! You gave me this whole song and dance about how I'd always regret it if I didn't go to school. And here's Clay doing just fine with—"

"I told you that you'd be a thousand times more successful if you had more education, Ira. I told you you'd be sorry later if you dropped out now. And every word was true." Her tone was passionate. It was a teacher's voice, the voice of a woman committed to nurturing young minds, committed to the magic of education.

Ira turned back to Clay. "Do you think you'd be more successful if you had a college education?" he asked bluntly.

Clay's stomach did a somersault. He swallowed hard.

"Answer the question, Clay," Roberta ordered.

He couldn't look at her. Instead he looked at Ira. "I like what I do for a living, but I'd have had a lot more choices if I'd stayed in school."

"So you're sorry you quit?" Ira pressed.

Clay had to ponder that a moment.

"Tell him the truth, Clay."

Roberta's insistence irritated him. His own embarrassment irritated him more.

"I'm not sorry I quit when I did," he declared a bit too sharply. "I was going crazy. I had to get out. I would have lost a grip on myself if I'd done anything else."

"He felt like Ozzie," Roberta said. "Clay's situation was completely different from yours, Ira."

Clay heard the fear in her voice, understood what she was trying to do. She didn't really want to embarrass him in front of the boy; she just desperately wanted to keep him from saying anything that would encourage Ira to drop out of school. Still, her censure rankled, and his instinctive defensiveness made him angry with himself.

"But you said Ozzie had to face the world, Clay. You said he couldn't lick the stutter unless he went back to school."

"*I* licked the stutter without going back!" he snapped. "I licked it twenty years ago."

"Then why didn't you go back to school?" Ira asked.

Because I licked the stutter, but never the fear, he realized angrily. His recent bout with stage fright—despite his quasi-victory over it—had told him that. But even then he had not completely realized what was suddenly crystal clear to him now: it was the fear—not the lack of education—that crippled his future with Roberta... the absolute terror of putting himself in any academic situation where he might make a fool of himself. He'd bolted from that terror after graduation day and he'd never really stopped running.

"I was busy earning a living," he justified himself to Ira. It was partly true. In fact, it was entirely true. But it didn't account for the ambiguity of his life since then. It wasn't that he was too busy or too poor to go back to school. He read in all his spare time, completed the equivalent of years in college. And always he longed for more—more challenge, more success. But fear kept him from signing up for so much as a summer course, and he knew it.

But he wasn't about to confess it now.

ONCE ROBERTA JOINED CLAY in the truck, she didn't mention the awkward discussion they'd had with Ira. In the end, Clay had done his best to convince Ira to stay in school without admitting that he himself was sorry he'd dropped out. But he'd been perspiring heavily by the end of their visit, and she knew he was unhappy with the way things had turned out.

She hadn't meant to lacerate his ego or even remind him of the great chasm between his education and hers. She had convinced herself—more or less—that it didn't really matter. She couldn't love a man who lacked intelligence or learning, but Clay had both in abundance. He possessed more keen insight and was better educated in the ways of the world than most men who'd spent years in college. She loved him just the way he was.

She'd tried to assure him of this, of course, when they'd returned to the apartment, but Clay had insisted that the subject was closed. He'd also insisted that the one change of clothes he had with him—brushed cords and a long-sleeved western shirt—would be perfectly appropriate for her faculty shindig at Charles Trumbull's that night. He had no qualms about showing up in his best cowboy boots.

"People always dress rather formally at Charles's," she pointed out gently, certain that Clay would rather not go. "I don't have to go to this shindig. I can call and—"

"Are you afraid I'll embarrass you, Roberta?" he asked bluntly, apparently still a bit edgy from their discussion with Ira. "Afraid I'll leave a dangling participle in the middle of a sentence or use two negatives back-to-back?"

Roberta coolly met his eyes. "I'm not afraid of anything, Clay. I'd be proud to have you meet my friends."

He'd studied her for a long, tense moment, then dipped into the bathroom to shower and change. Roberta considered following him in—they had time to romp a bit under the shower's soothing spray—but something about his tense back arrested her impulse. She decided to spend the time getting dressed herself, deliberately picking out something simple that matched his attire—a gathered denim skirt, a bright turquoise blouse and silver Navajo earrings. And then—to make a statement she felt needed to be made—she added the squashed lucky hat he'd given her.

We look like we're on our way to a square dance, she decided glumly when they finally strode out to the truck at five o'clock. She thought about all the times she'd gone to other gatherings dressed outrageously and wondered why she felt so shy about her appearance today. She glanced at Clay—so handsome in his western attire—and reminded herself that western dress was common in Arizona at any gathering. Abruptly she realized that she wasn't afraid that Clay would look like a cowboy when he got to Charles's house. She was afraid he'd act like one.

AS THEY WALKED up the sweeping driveway of Roberta's mentor's dramatic Spanish mission-style home, Clay asked sarcastically, "I thought you said he lived alone?"

"He does."

He shrugged. "For one person, this strikes me as more house than is absolutely necessary."

Roberta rolled her eyes but made no comment. He knew she was upset with him, knew he was acting badly. But he was still steaming from the way she'd pushed him into giving pro-college speeches to Ira, still smarting from her obvious disappointment that she'd given herself to a man without a college education. Worse yet was his disappointment in himself. Until Ira had so bluntly compared his own cowardice to Ozzie's, Clay had never really seen it. For a year and a half he'd been pushing the poor young kid to do something that he'd never had the courage to do himself. It made him feel very small.

Trailing Roberta to a party full of card-carrying Ph.D.s made him feel smaller yet. He knew that if he'd been alone, he wouldn't have cared nearly as much about the impression he'd make on them. But he felt edgy squaring off with Charles Trumbull under Roberta's watchful eye.

His hostility rose as he watched Roberta press a bell, which signalled their arrival. The Pima Indian servant who answered clearly recognized her name—perhaps her voice as well—and opened the door in an obsequious manner, which made his hackles raise. "The lord of the manner still keeps slaves?" he asked sarcastically when he was out of the elderly woman's earshot.

"Hardly. Sarah has been with his family since Charles was a child."

"Of course. A Trumbull family retainer. How could I be so naive?"

Roberta glared at him. "He pays her well and he asks very little of her," she pointed out archly. "She's probably too old to get work anywhere else."

Under normal circumstances, Clay would have applauded the other man's kindness. Because it was Charles, he struggled to think of some other reason to dislike him.

He didn't have to worry about it for long, because a moment later the man himself appeared in the garden.

Roberta didn't have to point him out to Clay. Although there were at least eighteen people on the patio—half of them men—he knew in an instant which one ruled this roost.

And he knew the moment the delicate blond features lit up at the sight of Roberta that Charles Trumbull still wanted to rule her, too.

WHEN ROBERTA INTRODUCED the two men, she felt like a referee explaining the rules in a boxing ring. They shook hands, but both sets of fingers looked stiff, and both handsome visages were set in fierce lines.

As an opening gambit, Charles said, "Roberta tells me you ride camels for a living."

"I can ride anything," Clay answered the challenge.

"I'm not so bad in the saddle myself."

When Clay made a sound that could have been a grunt, Roberta didn't wait for the conversation to get any murkier. Quickly she said, "I'd like to introduce Clay around, Charles. Maybe later you two can talk horses."

Charles chortled. "Why, Roberta, I'm surprised at you. I doubt that Mr. Gann's interest in livestock would coincide with mine."

She watched Clay tense his jaw as he countered, "I've got some superbly trained quarter horses and a roping camel I'd pit against any horse you own. I'll wager none of your animals would tolerate what she endures with a whistling rope spinning around her head."

Charles laughed again. "I'm tempted to tack you up on that bet. I've got the finest roper that money can buy."

"Trained by an expert, no doubt."

"Of course. The very best."

"You paid top dollar for the training, of course."

"Certainly."

Clay sneered. "If you don't know enough about roping to train him yourself, that horse probably knows more than you do."

Roberta could tell that Charles hadn't seen that one coming. He seemed to reel a bit as Clay continued. "Anything on four legs can read its rider. No horse is ever better than the man on its back."

He stared hard at Charles, his eyes unwavering until Charles, who had to greet another guest, was the first to look away.

"Please come meet some of my other friends," Roberta whispered, already seething. Any thoughts of explaining her efforts with Snowy vanished for good.

"Are you sure that's a good idea?" Clay growled. "I might mix my metaphors if you let me say more than a sentence or two. Besides, I've got a few more things to say to Charles."

"Over my dead body," she snapped. "I don't give a damn about your grammar, but the chip on your shoulder is going to be hard for me to explain."

"Did I snarl at the king? I'm so sorry. You didn't tell me I should bow down and grovel. I'm just a country cowpoke, you know. I ain't never been in the presence of royalty before."

"Clay, *please*," she begged him. "Couldn't you just bottle up your insecurities for an hour or two? I work with these people. I'll have to face them long after you gallop off to Colorado."

"Which can't be too soon for you, I take it."

"That's not what I meant! Oh, honestly, Clay, must you be so irrational?"

"I was only being myself."

"Your worst self."

"Okay. I'll try another persona out today."

And he did. In that instant, without hesitation or debate, he turned into Clayton Gann the Camel Man, and the intelligent, rational fellow that Roberta loved just slipped away.

CLAY DIDN'T KNOW just what had triggered his shift into his alter ego. Maybe it was the way Charles had ridiculed Violet without ever seeing her inspired, if uneven, performances. Maybe it was Roberta's insistence that he stay out of the way. Maybe it was the way one of her woman friends had asked Clay what "subject he taught" and another had jokingly replied, "Seminar on Rodeo Tricks and Camel Riding 1A."

All he knew was that from the moment he became the Camel Man, he had his audience in the palm of his hand, and he was sure they were laughing with him, not *at* him. And if they did find him silly or outrageous and simply out of step, it wouldn't be Clay Gann who'd have to feel embarrassed. It was that other man, the rodeo clown.

He knew, without daring to face Roberta's eyes, that he was embarrassing her. He knew he was doing everything wrong. He hadn't come to this party intending to act anything but sociable, but the moment Charles had gone for the jugular, he'd sprung to his own defense with all the verbal karate he could command.

He only had one other weapon, and he'd use it if push came to shove. Charles might talk big about his prowess on horseback, but Clay was certain that no matter what horse was running between his legs, he could ride Charles Trumbull right into the ground.

BY THE TIME they'd been at the party for half an hour, Roberta was so angry that she'd deliberately disappeared into the kitchen, taking refuge there until Clay—hopefully—came to his senses. Surely he'd track her down, hat in hand, when he realized how terribly he was embarrassing her.

But hiding out in the house didn't do her much good. Clay never showed up, but at least three women wandered in to remark that Clay was a hunk and a marvelous ice breaker.

"Does he always come to parties dressed in costume, Roberta?" redheaded Stella asked. "When you said he worked at a stable, I got the impression that he supervised trail rides. You didn't tell me he does comedy routines for a living!"

Roberta hoped the red flush on her cheeks didn't show. "He doesn't work at a stable," she corrected Stella firmly, trying not to blush. "He owns one. A very special one in Colorado. He does excellent trick riding and comedy roping in between camel races, and I guess he just decided to liven up this party with one of his acts."

The women seemed to accept her story at face value, but later she overheard Stella say to one of the secretaries, "Isn't it the funniest thing? Roberta's always spouting about women's rights and then she picks up a genuine Neanderthal. I bet he's a kick between the sheets, but there's no way he'll ever hitch up with a professional woman. She's dreaming if she thinks this will last. Poor girl."

The next couple who came into the kitchen was chuckling over Clay's drawled quote: "Ain't no horse that can't be rode and ain't no rider can't be throwed." It was a common enough cowboy proverb— Roberta had heard it all her life—but she also knew that it was a key line in one of his acts, a signal for Roscoe to bring in Violet so he could start his roping routine. In the mood Clay was in, she didn't want him anywhere near a lariat: he was likely to start roping chairs and footstools on the patio.

Seething, Roberta decided that she'd heard enough. She stomped out of the kitchen, determined to haul

Clay Gann away before he did her reputation any irrevocable damage. Assuming it wasn't too late already.

But by the time she tracked down Clay, Roberta realized that she was far too late. She found him clear out in Charles's private arena, mounted on a magnificent, high-strung black Arab that was prancing and frothing at the mouth. Only Clay's skill as a horseman was keeping the gelding under control, and he wasn't even moving yet!

Charles—hovering inside the arena like an overly protective parent—kept giving Clay advice on how to handle his horse, while Clay ordered him tersely to get out of the way. Despite the animal's obvious jitters, Clay was circling a long rope around his arm. Not his usual trick rope with a honda to help hold the loop in place, but an ordinary stable rope from Charles's barn.

Roberta's anger sputtered and died as she rushed toward the arena with a mounting sense of forboding. She knew that Clay was a superb rider and excellent at his craft, but she also knew that he was riding a roping horse only partially trained for the procedures he was about to execute. Worse yet, Clay himself was not likely to be concentrating on his riding; his heart and soul, she was certain, were focused on showing off...and showing up Charles.

Charles was grinning when Clay released the horse and started cantering around the ring. Twenty years off horseback had done nothing to weaken Roberta's memory. She knew what he was doing; getting the kinks out, establishing that he was the boss, checking to find out exactly what the gelding did and did not know how to do. Her fear abated just slightly as she realized that Clay was still in command. But then, five minutes later, he started to snake out that long and clumsy barn rope, and her panic fluttered anew.

She held her breath while he started his regular routine. She'd seen it all before, done from the back of a clumsy camel, when he'd played the role of a galloping rodeo clown. But there was nothing funny about the way he rode now. And his routine, which normally looked so effortless, took on a new tension on the back of this fine animal. Even with a standard western saddle, he braved some of the tricks she'd seen him do with Warner. He wasn't just proving he could rope; he was doing handstands and Cossack Passes, and a few new tricks she'd never seen him do before.

Fear forced the last dregs of anger out of Roberta's heart, but Charles looked mad enough for both of them. The darkness in his eyes made it clear that he had no intention of providing a horseback demonstration of his own when Clay was finished; he knew he'd been outclassed. Nobody could put on a better show than Clay just had. Charles knew it, and the partygoers knew it, too.

But none of them knew what Roberta did: that Clay always finished his camelback roping demonstration by looping Ozzie...as though it were an accident. But Ozzie wasn't in the arena this evening. Charles was the only man inside the corral.

With a sudden sick sense of dread, Roberta tried to duck under the fence, waving Clay's lucky hat. She wanted to signal Clay to rope her instead; she wanted to warn Charles to hop the fence while he could still escape. But she couldn't bring herself to betray Clay to his rival. And it became all too clear—as Clay's rope whizzed past her an instant later—that she was already far too late.

As the loop found its target, Clay pulled the rope up tight. Charles looked shocked; he stared at the rope around his chest as though it were a boa constrictor. And then he looked at Clay, his eyes wide as the motion of his own favorite horse began to pull him forward. Roberta wanted to tell him that the worst was over; she'd seen Clay do this trick a dozen times on the back of the world's most uncooperative mount, and Ozzie had never so much as gotten dust on the hem of his jeans.

But despite Clay's legendary skill on horseback, the Arab kept loping across the arena until the rope pulled Charles down to his knees. To a casual observer, it might have looked as though the horse had failed to heed Clay's command to stop, but Roberta knew better. He hadn't given the horse any such order.

A moment later, while his entire staff looked on, Charles Trumbull III lost his balance altogether and sprawled facedown in the dirt.

CHAPTER FIFTEEN

ON SUNDAY AFTERNOON, Clay draped both arms over the edge of the Double T corral where he'd stopped on his way back home, stared at the ground and confessed, "Brady, last night I stuck both feet in my mouth and swallowed my boots."

Brady climbed up on the fence. One leg swinging, he said calmly, "That good, huh?"

Clay laughed with no hint of humor. "It was incredible. Here I was, meeting all of Roberta's highfalutin friends for the first time, and what do I do? I bend over backwards to make a fool of myself. She thinks I made a fool of *her*. Actually I think I was trying to make a fool of her boss. I wanted to hate him, you know. He's everything Roberta has ever wanted . . . everything my mother ever wanted me to be. And it did feel awfully good to see him covered with dirt after I roped him while I was doing tricks on the back of his high-stepping Arab."

Brady stared at him. "Aw, Clay, you didn't!"

"Aw, Brady, I did!"

They shared a chuckle, but it wasn't a hearty one. Then Clay admitted wanly, "The damn thing is, he was a good sport about it. In fact, he was such a good sport about it that I realized that I was the one who was acting like a jerk. Of course, Roberta was also quick to point that out to me."

"In four-part harmony and living color, no doubt."

"No doubt about it. She was steamed."

There was a moment of silence, broken only by the soft nicker of a horse and the soothing rush of wind from the southern canyon. Clay leaned against the fence, thinking, feeling, processing just what had happened in his mind. He was certain that he'd been in the wrong, just as he was certain that he hadn't really patched things up with Roberta. Oh, he'd apologized profusely—for hours and hours—and they'd made their peace, but the bottom line was that there was a glitch in their relationship that wasn't going to go away unless somebody made a fundamental change. She lived in a world of high academics and a fair degree of professional formality. He lived in a world of cowboys and camels. She could move to Fort Collins or he could move to Tucson, but that wouldn't change the basic problem. They were reaching out to each other over a chasm that just seemed too broad to jump. And it had nothing to do with geography.

"Sounds to me like it's time for some serious groveling on your part," Brady observed. "If I were you I'd start thinking of some major sacrifice." He waited a moment before he added, "Unless you're willing to give Roberta up once and for all."

Clay turned briskly to stare at his friend. His eyes were haunted, his voice strained. "Tell me, Brady," he asked softly, "do you really think I've still got a choice?"

"HI, TESS. It's Roberta." Roberta hoped her glum mood wasn't evident, but she doubted that she could fake Tess out even over the phone. Still, with Redpoint's grand celebration of its one hundred and fiftieth birthday looming on the horizon, she expected her friend's mind to be full of exciting plans and last-minute details.

"Roberta! How's it going? You're not calling to tell me there's a problem, I hope?"

"No, nothing like that. I'll still be there next month with bells on. I just wanted to find out if I'm supposed to march in the parade."

"No, you're not supposed to *march*. You're supposed to ride in one of our wagons."

"Do you need me to drive a team?"

"Brady says no. He's talked his dad into doing it. We know you're a better driver, but it's important that...well, that Jake feel he's part of Brady's life. You understand?"

Roberta understood only too well. For years Jake Trent—and everybody else—had taken second place to Brady's first ranch, the one he'd given up for Tess. Although Brady and his dad had come a long way in healing old wounds between them, there were times when memories of the Rocking T required some tactful handling of other situations.

Thinking about the Rocking T, and what it had cost Brady—emotionally—to sell it for Tess, Roberta wondered why Clay couldn't make the tiny sacrifice of wearing a suit and acting civilized for half an hour with her colleagues. Was it really so much she'd asked of him?

There was a silence on the line that Roberta noticed in hindsight when Tess said quietly, "Well?"

"Well, what?"

"Well, are you going to tell me why you're so down?"

Roberta managed a feeble chuckle. "Pretty transparent, huh?"

"Clear as glass."

She sighed and struggled for words. "Tess," she finally said sadly, "I think it may be over with Clay."

"No!" It was a sharp cry of denial. "It can't be!"

Roberta felt sick inside as she relayed the sorry tale of their last weekend together. Although Tess revealed that she'd heard Clay's version of it, she didn't make any judgments and listened lovingly.

"Oh, Tess, I just can't lie to myself any longer," Roberta lamented when she finished with all the grim details. "I could live with a man who didn't have an education. I really think I could. But Clay doesn't just *ignore* my academic priorities and professional contacts. He goes out of his way to kick my values in my face and humiliate my friends."

After a moment, Tess said, "You know, Roberta, I've known Clay a long time, and I've never seen him go out of his way to humiliate anybody. And he's a man who rarely makes judgments on other people's lifestyles."

"So what's your point? You think I'm making this whole thing up?"

"No, Roberta, I don't. But I think that there may be a reason why Clay's behaving so badly. A reason that has something to do with you."

"You mean I'm triggering his behavior? You're blaming me for what he did?"

There was a long silence, a silence that made Roberta squirm.

At last Tess said, "I'm not blaming anybody, Roberta. But I do think you may be missing the forest for the trees."

"What do you mean?"

"I mean, for ten minutes all you've talked about is this terrible thing Clay did to you. Has it occurred to you that there must have been some reason *why* he did it? He loves you, Roberta, so he didn't do it out of some twisted sense of revenge. I think he may have been trying to cover up his own embarrassment—his fear of not measuring up to your friends. Maybe he was subconsciously testing your loyalty, or maybe trying to prove that the qualities you value in a man like Charles really aren't so noteworthy after all."

"There's nothing wrong with Charles's values, Tess. He's a good man. I just didn't have the good sense to fall in love with him."

"I know that, Roberta. But does Clay?"

"Yes, I think he does. He's jealous of Charles, but not because he thinks I'm . . . well, tempted. It's more a matter of fear that he won't measure up to Charles in my eyes."

"Do you think Clay might have some basis for that fear, Roberta?" rejoined Tess. "Have you ever done anything to make Clay think you respect him less because he lacks your education?"

Roberta could not answer that. At least not out loud. The simple truth was that she'd badgered Clay about going back to school more than once. Always indirectly, and subtly, she'd thought. But Clay was a man of keen perceptions and deeply, quietly held beliefs. He'd fired Warner—his trick riding partner and his friend—because of the gulf between her professional world and his, and she'd still found no way to make it up to him. Instead, she'd rubbed in his lack of education a dozen times—the last time being the day they'd had lunch with Ira and she'd complained about his clothes.

Just hours before they'd gone to the faculty party.

"I think," Tess said, "that you're going to have to decide whether or not you want Clay enough to give up some of your dreams."

"What dreams?" Roberta asked.

"Dreams of finding a man who fits into your faculty lounge without a murmur. A man whose name is splashed on the cover of *Atlantic* or *Time*. Clay Gann is a brilliant person and self-educated to the 'nth' degree. But he's never going to have a college education, never going to earn kudos for academic expertise. He is who he is, Roberta. You either have to love him just the way he is—corny cowboy, camels and all—or let him go."

"Oh, Tess," Roberta whispered, suddenly feeling her life blood drain away. "That's the one thing I can never do."

BY THE TIME Clay returned from Tucson, Ozzie knew that something was terribly wrong with his boss. Things only got worse over the next week. Clay was not snarling at anybody, but his jaw was clenched tight and his skin looked a bit clammy. He fussed over the camels and kept pacing back and forth whenever his hands weren't busy. He almost looked as bad as he had on the day he'd given that Lieutenant Beale speech.

He was afraid of something. Ozzie knew it as surely as he knew his own name. And since Clay was not a man who feared physical danger or financial ruin, his agitation had to have something to do with the only two things that Ozzie had ever seen rattle him—public speaking and Roberta Wheeler. Ozzie knew that Roberta was scheduled to arrive in Redpoint for the sesquicentennial in two more weeks, and he knew that Clay had returned from Tucson quite depressed. Since then he hadn't made the slightest effort to find a replacement for Warner, or even work on his own routine.

Instead he'd spent hours of each day locked in his house and frequently appeared with a book in his hand, but each time Ozzie asked if he had to give another speech, he'd shaken his head.

One night, Ozzie decided he couldn't stand it anymore. He didn't want to press, but when a friend was hurting the way Clay clearly was, he felt he had to do *something*. Slowly he gathered his courage and went to knock on Clay's door.

"It's open," Clay barked from his desk in the front room.

Ozzie pushed the door open and poked his head inside.

"Are you busy?"

"I sure as hell am," Clay said grumpily. "What do you want?"

Ozzie took a deep breath. He refused to be swayed. "I need to talk to you."

Clay glared at him, then tugged a piece of paper out of his typewriter and rolled it into a ball. "Talk," he ordered him as he threw it across the room.

Ozzie felt a moment's anger. He hadn't come to bellyache; he'd come to offer his support. Still, he wasn't about to tongue-lash his boss. He took three bold steps toward the desk, then stopped and said firmly, "I came to see if I could help. You've been a mess ever since you came back from Tucson."

Clay closed his eyes. "You mean I've been obnoxious and you're sick of it?"

"I mean you look miserable and I'm worried about you."

"I feel miserable and I'm worried about me, too."

Ozzie took a step closer. "Can I help?"

Clay raised his hands in a helpless gesture. He studied Ozzie for a minute, then said, "Nope, you can't. But thanks for asking."

Ozzie stared at him, feeling helpless. "You've always bucked me up when I was feeling down, Clay. I wanted to do the same for you."

To his surprise, Clay smiled, albeit slightly. "You have, Oz."

He looked doubtful. "How?"

Now Clay's grin widened. "By reminding me that love for a friend is strong enough to conquer fear."

Ozzie was flattered, but still confused. "But I'm not afraid of anything right now. All I was thinking about was trying to do something for you."

"I know. And while you were worrying about me, Ozzie—" now the smile suffused his whole face "—you plumb forgot to stutter."

"YOU WANTED TO SEE ME, Charles?" Roberta asked as she poked her head into the chairman's office. She had a lot to do before she left for Redpoint that afternoon—the sesquicentennial was in the morning—but she'd found a brief note from Charles in her box that morning. She had not found a message from Clay.

In fact, she had not heard from Clay in almost three weeks. A few days after he'd left Tucson, he'd sent her a brief but contrite apology for his behavior at the party, coupled with an enigmatic promise to "try to sort things out before I see you again." She didn't know just what that meant but it certainly didn't sound promising. As eager as she was to see Clay in Redpoint tomorrow, she was afraid of what might happen when they got together again.

"Come in, Roberta. I've got something to show you. Something you're just not going to believe."

She tried to summon up some interest, but at the moment it was hard to concentrate on anything but Clay. Dutifully she asked, "What is it, Charles?"

He grinned. "A manuscript submitted for the *Review*. On camels."

"Camels?" she repeated, afraid, for one terrible moment, that he was making fun of Clay. "You wrote a paper on *camels*?"

"No, *I* didn't write it! And it's not on camels, *per se*. It's on the history of the U.S. Camel Corps, a fascinating twist for the review. Best of all, the writing is articulate, witty and colorful. It's a gem. I'm utterly delighted."

Roberta stared at him, not quite certain why he was going into such detail. After all, Charles knew that her only interest in camels was that Clay owned some, a fact that had filled him with amusement until the night of the party.

But now he did not seem amused. In fact, he was so serious—happy, but serious—that she was almost certain he wasn't pulling her leg.

"Have you read this?" he asked, waving a manuscript in her direction. "Silly question. You probably critiqued it already. In fact—" suddenly his eyes narrowed "—you might have ghostwritten it for all I know."

Roberta's eyebrows raised. "Charles, what are you talking about? I'm too proud of my achievements to put anybody else's name on my work. Besides, all I know about the Camel Corps is what Clay has told me. It's a fascinating story, but it would take a lot of research to flesh out a quality paper for the *Review*."

Charles nodded, apparently in agreement. "Well, I guess he took the time to do the research, Roberta, because every assertion he makes is well-documented. Frankly I'm surprised as well as impressed. I didn't think he had it in him."

Suddenly Roberta's hands felt clammy. It couldn't be! "Are you telling me that *Clay* wrote a paper for the *Review*?"

Charles stiffened. "Should I take your surprise to mean that you don't think he's capable of such scholarship on his own? That perhaps he had had some assis—"

"Oh, I know he's capable of the scholarship! I just never believed that he'd...*yield* to the academic world! Let alone humble himself to *you*!"

Now it was Charles who looked shamefaced. "Roberta, not only did he send me this submission, but he also sent me an apology as well. And the truth is, I'm the one who owes him one."

"*You* owe *him* an apology? After what he did to you?"

"The truth is...I was asking for it, Roberta." He gestured somewhat helplessly. "I'm not proud of it, but I baited your friend at the party cruelly after you went inside. I wanted him to act the cowboy, play the fool, to show you how he failed to fit in with your friends. I called his bluff on riding rodeo. I goaded the hell out of him." Sheepishly he shrugged. "In his shoes, I think any man worth his salt would have found a way to knock me down a peg."

Roberta swallowed hard. Not once, in all the hours of fighting and apologizing after that party, had Clay ever tried to lay the blame for that roping incident on Charles. He'd just admitted that he'd behaved like a Neanderthal and begged her to forgive him. He hadn't even pointed out that she owed him one. After all, he'd once taken her back when her heart was scraping the floor.

When Charles handed her the manuscript, Roberta could tell at a glance that it had been prepared with professional skill and concentration.

"It took a lot of courage for him to send me this," he observed.

More courage than you'll ever know, Roberta added silently. She thought about Clay's fear and courage on the day he'd given the Beale chautauqua and her recent realization that it wasn't public speaking that frightened him so much as academic failure in any regard. It was an irrational fear that haunted him as much as her own fear of riding still crippled her—despite her recent purchase of dear old Snowy. But he'd overcome the fright, thrown aside the excuses solely to reach across the great chasm that lurked between them. He'd given up waiting for her to cross to his side. He was making the big jump to risk a rocky landing on her side...in her world. The world he'd always hated and feared.

"The subject alone is a brave departure," Charles was saying, "and his lack of credentials would make me hesitate even if we had no... well, history between us."

Roberta gripped the cluster of papers. "But you're going to publish it?"

Slowly he nodded. "I have no choice. It needs some minor editing, but the work is just too excellent for me to justify turning down."

The words rang in her head as she rushed back to her office. She memorized them, determined to repeat them to Clay word for word. Then she read the article he'd so painstakingly written and realized that Charles was absolutely right. Clay was as much of a wordsmith on paper as he was in person.

An academic man in his own right.

She knew what had gone into that paper. Not the work—though that was evident—but the courage. And the love.

Not love for his beloved camels, but love for her.

For a long quiet moment, she thought about all the sacrifices Clay had made to try to make things work; she thought about how little she'd given up for him. Desperately she tried to think of a way to let him know—in one fell swoop—that she'd do anything to make their future a reality.

And suddenly she was suffused by a vision of his pasty-white face right after he'd given her chautauqua, battling his greatest terror *just because he loved her.* There was only one way she could think of to prove that she was willing to do the same for him.

BY SATURDAY MORNING, Clay was tense. He'd only heard from Roberta once since he'd left Tucson—a rather terse note formally accepting his apology but doing little to reassure him of her love—and he hadn't heard from her at all since he'd submitted that manuscript to Charles. He still wasn't sure if it had been an act of supreme courage or utmost folly. If the paper failed to measure up to Charles's high editorial standards, Roberta—as well as Clay himself—would be humiliated again. And he wasn't at all sure that she would sustain another embarrassing demonstration by her cowboy lover.

But if, by some miracle, Charles was impressed with Clay's scholarship, Clay had a fighting chance of being redeemed in Roberta's eyes. And he'd left Tucson sure of one thing: if he couldn't find a way to fit into Roberta's world, she would never marry him. And though few things frightened him more than risking humiliation at the hands of academic intellectuals, losing Roberta frightened him even more.

Now, as he and Violet joined Brady's four Conestogas lining up to head the parade between pairs of mounted Ute warriors, he waved to Harry Painted Hat, then eagerly scanned the familiar faces on the wagons for the one he cherished most. On the first wagon he found Joe and Mandy Henderson along with Joe's three kids and Mandy's sister, Ruth, and Ruth's daughter, Karen. On the second he found Brady and round-tummied Tess and little J.J.; on the third sat old Ragweed Willie with a pair of brothers who were Brady's hired hands. The fourth wagon was driven by Brady's dad, Jake Trent, and his smiling wife, Arleen.

There was no sign of Roberta.

"Tess?" he called out above the roar of the jubilant spectators. "Isn't Roberta riding with you?"

Tess waved at him, but gave no sign she'd heard the question, which was not surprising in the noisy preparade hubbub. He started to repeat the question, but just then he caught sight of Ozzie, Roscoe and George bringing up his camels. He was sorry that Warner wouldn't be there to handle spooky Luscious Laura, but he had no time for regrets. Even if he ended up losing Roberta, he was glad he'd stood up for her with his men. They'd agreed that Ozzie would lead Laura and

George would lead Baby Bev; they'd look like a pack train of miners. Still, Laura was easier for a good rider to control in the saddle than on a lead, and he hoped she wouldn't give Ozzie any trouble on the potholed blacktop parade route past the historic old buildings of this gold rush town.

As he and Violet cleared out the stray tourists from the section of road he'd reserved for the camels, Clay proudly watched his troops approach. At a distance, he could not identify each adult camel, or even each rider that perched precariously between neck and hump. But he *could* see the flounce of skirts that flowed around the face of the camel flanked by Baby Bev. And he could see two pantaloon-draped legs on the left side of that camel—surely Luscious Laura—a certain sign that some incredibly brave horsewoman was riding sidesaddle on the world's most awkward stead.

She was wearing his dad's lucky hat.

Clay gulped a deep breath. He knew, even before he could read the fine lines of her beloved face, that the courageous soul before him was Roberta. And he also knew, by the rigid set of her arms and the paralytic hardness of her jaw, that she was absolutely terrified.

A wash of love and understanding greater than anything he had ever felt for another human being washed through Clay, purging him of all the dregs of fear and pain from his past. Suddenly he didn't care about his mother, or his speech coach, or even Charles Trumbull III. The departmental dean could laugh at his camel paper till the cows came home; it didn't matter.

Nothing mattered but Roberta.

She was riding—my God, she was *riding*!—to prove to him that she could fit into his world, that her courage was as great as his own. He'd pressed her to ride, but he'd always imagined the most gentle of relearning experiences on a baby-sitter horse in a quiet corral, not an obstreperous camel in the middle of a chaotic city-street parade. Sidesaddle, no less!

But she had done it. White-lipped, wide-eyed, she'd managed to get this far on sheer chutzpah, sheer determination . . . and sheer love. So far, she'd come by herself. That was one thing he could change this instant.

With quiet knees he urged Violet forward, swinging quickly into place beside the woman that he was now certain would share his life. Softly, without calling attention to her terror, he lay one hand over her trembling fingers, swaddling Roberta with the warmth of his love.

She did not look at him at once. She merely gripped his hand with fierce relief. For a moment, the parade seemed to stop for Clay. The chaos around them—people, animals, creaking wagons and stagecoaches that had brightened old Redpoint for a hundred and fifty years—seemed to disappear. By the time her eyes met his, there was nobody for a thousand miles but Clay Gann and Roberta Wheeler, side by side and heading somewhere—anywhere—together.

Her trembling stilled. Her lips found a smile.

Clay swallowed hard, then squeezed her hand once more before he let her go.

And then, before his eyes, he watched her straighten, watched her fingers grip the reins like a woman who had ridden from the cradle, watched her take control of her mount, her conquered terrors and her life.

"Since I'm taking over Warner's job, husband," she told him bluntly, "you better tell me which way the parade route goes."

Clay was not surprised by her unorthodox proposal, and he no longer doubted that the two of them would find a compromise that embodied everything that mattered deeply in both their lives. The powerful woman he'd chosen for his wife was the epitome of truth and courage. He would never give her any less.

"Don't reckon it makes no difference, Bobbie Jean," he vowed in the rollicking voice that belonged to Clayton Gann, the Camel Man. As her radiant grin swelled to match his own, he promised her, "North, east, south or west, sweet pea, from here on in, we're headin' there together."

The Slow Joe whistle blew just once—a long, hearty blast—before the camels lumbered forward.

"Wagons Ho!" Brady shouted, and the Conestogas started rolling.

* * * * *

PASSPORT TO ROMANCE SWEEPSTAKES RULES

1. **HOW TO ENTER:** To enter, you must be the age of majority and complete the official entry form, or print your name, address, telephone number and age on a plain piece of paper and mail to: Passport to Romance, P.O. Box 9056, Buffalo, NY 14269-9056. No mechanically reproduced entries accepted.
2. All entries must be received by the CONTEST CLOSING DATE, DECEMBER 31, 1990 TO BE ELIGIBLE.
3. **THE PRIZES:** There will be ten (10) Grand Prizes awarded, each consisting of a choice of a trip for two people from the following list:
   i) London, England (approximate retail value $5,050 U.S.)
   ii) England, Wales and Scotland (approximate retail value $6,400 U.S.)
   iii) Carribean Cruise (approximate retail value $7,300 U.S.)
   iv) Hawaii (approximate retail value $9,550 U.S.)
   v) Greek Island Cruise in the Mediterranean (approximate retail value $12,250 U.S.)
   vi) France (approximate retail value $7,300 U.S.)
4. Any winner may choose to receive any trip or a cash alternative prize of $5,000.00 U.S. in lieu of the trip.
5. **GENERAL RULES:** Odds of winning depend on number of entries received.
6. A random draw will be made by Nielsen Promotion Services, an independent judging organization, on January 29, 1991, in Buffalo, NY, at 11:30 a.m. from all eligible entries received on or before the Contest Closing Date.
7 Any Canadian entrants who are selected must correctly answer a time-limited, mathematical skill-testing question in order to win.
8. Full contest rules may be obtained by sending a stamped, self-addressed envelope to: "Passport to Romance Rules Request", P.O Box 9998, Saint John, New Brunswick, Canada E2L 4N4.
9 Quebec residents may submit any litigation respecting the conduct and awarding of a prize in this contest to the Régie des loteries et courses du Québec.
10. Payment of taxes other than air and hotel taxes is the sole responsibility of the winner.
11 Void where prohibited by law.

COUPON BOOKLET OFFER TERMS

To receive your Free travel-savings coupon booklets, complete the mail-in Offer Certificate on the preceeding page, including the necessary number of proofs-of-purchase, and mail to: Passport to Romance, P.O. Box 9057, Buffalo, NY 14269-9057 The coupon booklets include savings on travel-related products such as car rentals, hotels, cruises, flowers and restaurants. Some restrictions apply. The offer is available in the United States and Canada. Requests must be postmarked by January 25, 1991. Only proofs-of-purchase from specially marked "Passport to Romance" Harlequin® or Silhouette® books will be accepted. The offer certificate must accompany your request and may not be reproduced in any manner. Offer void where prohibited or restricted by law. LIMIT FOUR COUPON BOOKLETS PER NAME, FAMILY, GROUP, ORGANIZATION OR ADDRESS. Please allow up to 8 weeks after receipt of order for shipment Enter quickly as quantities are limited. Unfulfilled mail-in offer requests will receive free Harlequin® or Silhouette® books (not previously available in retail stores), in quantities equal to the number of proofs-of-purchase required for Levels One to Four, as applicable.

PR-SWPS

OFFICIAL SWEEPSTAKES ENTRY FORM

Complete and return this Entry Form immediately—the more Entry Forms you submit, the better your chances of winning!

- Entry Forms must be received by **December 31, 1990**
- A random draw will take place on **January 29, 1991**
- Trip must be taken by **December 31, 1991**

3-HS-3-SW

YES, I want to win a PASSPORT TO ROMANCE vacation for two! I understand the prize includes round-trip air fare, accommodation and a daily spending allowance.

Name____________________________________

Address__________________________________

City____________ State__________ Zip____________

Telephone Number__________ Age_____

Return entries to: **PASSPORT TO ROMANCE**, P.O. Box 9056, Buffalo, NY 14269-9056

COUPON BOOKLET/OFFER CERTIFICATE

Item	LEVEL ONE Booklet 1	LEVEL TWO Booklet 1 & 2	LEVEL THREE Booklet 1, 2 & 3	LEVEL FOUR Booklet 1, 2, 3 & 4
Booklet 1 = $100+	$100+	$100+	$100+	$100+
Booklet 2 = $200+		$200+	$200+	$200+
Booklet 3 = $300+			$300+	$300+
Booklet 4 = $400+	____	____	____	$400+
Approximate Total Value of Savings	$100+	$300+	$600+	$1,000+
# of Proofs of Purchase Required	4	6	12	18
Check One	____	____	____	____

Name____________________________________

Address__________________________________

City____________ State__________ Zip____________

Return Offer Certificates to: **PASSPORT TO ROMANCE**, P.O. Box 9057, Buffalo, NY 14269-9057

Requests must be postmarked by **January 25, 1991**

ONE PROOF OF PURCHASE

3-HS-3

To collect your free coupon booklet you must include the necessary number of proofs-of-purchase with a properly completed Offer Certificate

See previous page for details